You in Five Acts

You in Five Acts

Una La Marche

RAZORBILL

An Imprint of Penguin Random House

RAZORBILL

An Imprint of Penguin Random House
Penguin.com

Copyright © 2016 Penguin Random House LLC
Janus Academy logo courtesy of Shutterstock.com.

ISBN: 9781101998939

Printed in the United States of America

1 3 5 7 9 10 8 6 4 2

For you.

Every song has a you
A you that the singer sings to
And you're it this time
Baby, you're it this time.
        —Ani DiFranco,
            from the song "Dilate"

Overture

Diego

IT'S ALWAYS BEEN YOU—you know that, right? You didn't have to be onstage for me to see you in a spotlight; when you were around, everything else faded to the background, like some cheap cardboard set. Looking back, it doesn't even seem real, what happened with us. I see you in flashes, a fouetté turn that won't end, my eyes focusing for a split second, grounding me in between spins: your smile, your laugh, the way you looked so mad when you got nervous. The curve of your waist in your leotard. Your silhouette on the train that night, looking out the window with the whole city stretched out behind you like some crazy constellation. The weight of you in my arms as we practiced our lift, and how our eyes locked, so full of trust.

I swore I'd never let you down. I didn't know then it was a lie.

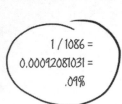

1 / 1086 =
0.00092081031 =
.09%

JANUS
ACADEMY
Founded 1978
Where Talent Meets Opportunity

−Pas de couru
−tombé
−manège of piqué pirouettes

Spring Semester Calendar:

January 4	First Day of Classes
January 8	∞ Senior Showcase Auditions ⟵ Aaaaaaahhhhh!!!
January 16	Martin Luther King Day (Campus closed)
February 20	Presidents' Day (Campus closed)
March 11–12	Admissions Auditions, Class of 2021
April 17–28	Spring Break (Campus closed)
May 1–5	Senior Tech Week (Opera, Theater)
May 8–11	Senior Tech Week (Music, Dance)
May 12	Senior Showcase Performances (Opera, Music)
May 13	THE DAY Senior Showcase Performances (Theater, Dance)
May 14	Senior Showcase Gallery Show Opening (Visual Arts)
May 15–19	Final Exams
May 22	Senior Awards Luncheon
May 26	Commencement Ceremony

Act One

Joy

Chapter One

January 6
127 days left

PAS DE COURU, tombé, manège of piqué pirouettes. I ran the steps in my head, over and over, one after another like subway cars hurtling through an endless tunnel. Every move, every turn, every line of each leg, each elbow, each vertebra every second had to be on point. En pointe. I had to be on my toes, literally, and light on feet that felt like bricks by the end of each rehearsal. The puns were endless, but, as we liked to joke back then, the struggle was real.

"She's not even paying attention." Liv flicked the back of my neck through my scarf with a thin, icy finger, and I heard you laugh.

"What?" I snapped back to life, or as close to life as I could get in the unforgiving January chill. My breath danced in front of me in a quick burst of cloudy vapor.

We were huddled at our usual spot at the Revson Fountain even though the marble was so frigid that sitting down meant sacrificing all feeling below the waist. Liv and Ethan always bitched about my love of the fountain because it wasn't the squares, or the steps, or the clock, or any of the other "normal" hangouts. You were the only one who understood why I wanted to go—*had* to go—where we could pull our sore legs up against our jackets and look out at Avery Fisher Hall, those big cement columns encasing the delicate glass interior like a ribcage, and behind that, deep inside, its beating heart: ballet.

"He's here," Liv sighed, turning my head manually with her hands. "Three days late, but who's counting, right?"

Of course Liv had seen him first. She'd always had a knack for knowing when a fellow Beautiful Person was in her orbit, almost like her brain came equipped with a thermal sensor for figurative hotness.

"Calm down, he's not even that famous!" Ethan scoffed, peering through his glasses across the square. "He was basically only in one movie, six years ago. I don't know why everybody's flipping their collective shit."

Despite its proximity to greatness in the heart of Lincoln Center, the Janus Conservatory had never had a celebrity before. I mean, there were plenty of famous alumni, and even a few teachers who used to be big deals. But all of the students, regardless of talent, were decidedly wannabes. Until Dave Roth.

Ethan was upset because Dave's sudden second-semester senior year transfer was all anyone could talk about, which meant that everyone had *stopped* talking about the original play Ethan was producing for Senior Showcase. It was no secret that he liked to think of himself as the star of the drama majors, even though he'd switched from acting to directing sophomore year.

"Yeah, he's just a normal dude," you said matter-of-factly. You'd been perched next to me on the icy marble, bouncing restlessly on the toes of your well-worn Converse high-tops, but then you leapt down in front of me, holding out a French fry like a long-stemmed rose. "C'mon, you have to eat," you grinned, your eyes twinkling out from your messy mop of dark curls.

"I *am* eating," I said, inspecting my locker-smushed turkey-and-spinach wrap with trepidation. I wasn't sure I'd be able to get much down with the wave of nausea I'd been riding all day. You, on the other hand, could pound junk 24/7 and still dance circles around everyone else—including me. It was completely infuriating. You shrugged and popped the fry into your mouth.

"A 'normal dude' who played Angelina Jolie's son," Liv said. "I mean, didn't he win a Golden Globe?"

Pas de couru, tombé, manège of piqué pirouettes. My Showcase audition—the single performance that would likely determine my entire future—would begin in three hours.

"No!" Ethan practically screamed. "He was *nominated* for a Golden Globe. Which means nothing, by the way. It's a drunken circus."

"You guys need a hobby," you laughed, crumpling up your greasy paper lunch bag. "And *you*," you said, putting your hands on my knees, "Need to chill. You got this."

I forced a tight smile. Senior Showcase would be attended by industry VIPs and recruiters from elite companies all over the country. If I didn't do well at the audition, I wouldn't get a featured role. And if I wasn't featured, I would barely be seen, which would mean that I could probably kiss a professional dance career goodbye, effectively rendering the previous ten years of my life a complete waste.

"Shit, remember that hospital monologue?" Liv asked, ignoring you. She reached out and caressed Ethan's face, sending a blush racing up his already winter-pink cheeks. "I'll always . . . be . . . with . . . you," she whispered, her face contorting into a mask of tragedy. Then she burst out laughing.

"You'll always be crazy," Ethan said, but his eyes on her were soft and reverent.

I took a tasteless bite of my wrap and looked across the plaza to where Dave and Ms. Hagen, the drama head, were standing near the entrance to the Metropolitan Opera House. He was cringing against the cold, wearing only a knit skullcap and a pretty flimsy-looking green hoodie. *L.A. Boy's going to have to get himself a proper coat*, I thought, feeling a little flutter in my chest that, for once, wasn't born of pure dread.

I don't know if it's fair to say I had a crush on Dave Roth; it was more like a *curiosity* . . . made slightly more interesting by the fact that he looked like some kind of lush-lipped boy bander crossed with a Greek statue. And in a graduating class of 125 that was 70 percent female, any new Y chromosome was bound to make waves. Besides, Janus *never* took transfer students. It had been founded in the 70s by a crazy-rich art lover named Roberta Zeagler who had, according to the quote carved into a block of marble in the lobby, wanted to "democratize the path to cultural greatness." That meant it was a free ride—tuition, supplies, even pointe shoes, which were $80 a pair and lasted one or two days—and, presumably, that talent was the only factor considered in the application. But each class only had room for twenty-five students per major, and there was a single audition period every spring, no exceptions. No one knew what Dave had done to get special treatment. "P.S.," Liv said, turning to me like she could read my mind. "I saw his medical records in the nurse's office this morning, and he's six-foot-one, one hundred and sixty pounds, and does *not* have any STDs." She plucked a baby carrot out of her ever-present Ziploc baggie and snapped it in half with her incisors. I knew Liv well enough to know that A) "saw his medical records" meant "opened the nurse's file cabinet when she left the room"; and B) she was gearing up to play matchmaker again. She did that every so often—made a big show of trying to set me up with someone, and then lording over me how I never followed through. You never liked that; you always told me I should stop letting her act like I was some kind of pet project. What you didn't understand was how far we went back, and how I helped her, too. Liv was just a lot louder about it. But then, she was the actress. Drama came with the territory.

"He seems more like your type," I said, trying to deflect attention.

"He's probably gay," Ethan said, unconvincingly. "Anyway, you basically live in the nurse's office, so that's not exactly Sherlock-level sleuthing." He smiled down at something on his phone. "And for the record, Wikipedia says he's only five-nine."

"I have adrenal fatigue, asshole," Liv snapped. (Another Liv translation: her "adrenal fatigue" was what the rest of the world called "a hangover.")

"Can we talk about something else?" you asked. You

climbed up onto the bench and leapt into a perfect tour en l'air, landing with a squeak on the soles of your ratty sneakers. I rolled my eyes. I loved cheesy Hollywood dance movies—that was an established fact—but doing ballet jumps in street clothes was a little too *Fame*-y even for me.

"Attention whore," Liv grinned, tucking her crudités lunch back into her enormous purse.

"Enjoy this, Ortega," Ethan said. "It's your official last day of being the Cute Guy."

"Aw, you think I'm cute, E?" you asked, plopping down next to Ethan and draping an arm across his shoulders.

"No one thinks that," I said with a smirk. That was a bald-faced lie, of course. Everyone loved you, and I wasn't blind. You were the world's biggest flirt *and* a straight-boy ballet dancer. Back on our very first day at Janus, I remember being instantly drawn to you, but not in the way other girls seemed to be. Standing there in Ballet 1 with the tags on my brand-new leotard still scratching that unreachable spot between my shoulders, I just got this déjà vu feeling of already knowing you. It had felt, somehow, that you had always been there, and I just hadn't noticed until that moment.

"It doesn't matter if you're cute if you're not famous," Liv said, pretending to check her texts while she took a zoomed-in photo of Dave with her phone.

"We're not unfamous, we're *pre*-famous," Ethan shot back. "Which is better than peaking at age eleven, if you ask me."

"Make sure to lead with that when you meet him." I laughed, trying to ignore my stomach's enthusiastic somersaults.

"I probably *should* go introduce myself," Ethan said, fondling the script sticking out of his messenger bag. "I could use a big name in my play."

"Oh, so now he's a big name," Liv teased. She wiggled her eyebrows at me. "You know what they say about guys with big names."

Even in the icy air, my cheeks lit up like burning coals. "Please," I groaned. "I have to focus." But I was secretly sort of grateful to her for taking my mind off of my audition.

"Aaaaand, that's my cue," Ethan said irritably, shoving his hands in his pockets as he stalked off toward Dave and Ms. Hagen.

"You guys are worse than us," you laughed, shaking your head.

"Don't be jealous," Liv chided. "You'll still have your dance groupies. But he's new, and hot." She reached over me to ruffle your hair. "It's just like Shakespeare wrote: 'Everyone has their entrance, everyone has their exit.'"

"Speaking of entrances," you said, nodding toward Ethan. We all watched him make contact. It was like some nature documentary, where two species at opposite ends of the food chain face off on the Great Plains. Ethan immediately started gesticulating wildly.

"Ten bucks says he's already name-dropped Arthur Miller," Liv said. She was the only one of us who'd been allowed to read Ethan's top-secret Showcase script, because Ethan had not so secretly written the leading role for her.

"Maybe he's showing off your *Godspell* photos," you said. Liv and Ethan had first become friends in ninth grade when they had played Jesus and Judas, respectively. In many ways, their relationship still mirrored that doomed Biblical pair.

"Maybe he's inviting him to your party," I said, my heart starting to race at the heady thought of Dave Roth, in a warm room, close enough to touch. Liv's parents had left that morning to visit her aunt in San Juan, so she was throwing what she called a "soirée" for "a select group of dope people." Knowing Liv, though, that could have easily meant the entire senior class.

"God, I hope not." Liv cringed. "I actually want him to *come*."

"You're not both seriously into this dude already, right?" you asked incredulously, looking back and forth between us. I met your eyes and made a face like, *You don't know my life*, and you looked legitimately taken aback. "I expected more from you," you sighed. Your lips stretched out over your teeth like a smile but your eyes were flat.

"Excuse me, what kind of patriarchal bullshit is that?" Liv asked, turning on you. "Joy can do whatever, or *whomever*, she pleases. And you don't get an opinion." We high-fived over your head, and you held up your palms in surrender.

"OK, OK, I'm sorry," you said. "I was just—"

"You can make it up to me," Liv interrupted. "Jasper's not invited, for obvious reasons, so I need your help making sure our good friend Mary Jane makes an appearance." Just before Christmas break, Liv had broken up with her boyfriend of almost two years, who also happened to be Janus's primary pot connection.

You raised your eyebrows. "C'mon, you know I don't smoke. Stop stereotyping my people."

"*Excuse me*, I'm Puerto Rican," Liv said.

"Puert-Jew-rican," you corrected with a smirk. "Olivia *Gerstein.*"

"Now who's being racist?" Liv snapped. "Plus, I know your cousin Dante deals. Jasper was always pissed about how he was moving in on the uptown schools."

Your smile disappeared. "I don't know anything about that," you said. "That's his business. Not mine."

"Fine, sorry. Forget I asked," Liv sighed. "Just bring a six-pack of something, then."

"What do you want?" you asked, turning to me, the tension of the previous seconds gone as if it had never happened.

I rolled my ankles, drawing circles on the stone with my toes. I'd been dancing all morning in class, and had made a point to stretch the hell out of my feet beforehand. "You're flat in the wrong places," Ms. Adair would often chide, looking me over like she wished she could telepathically force the curve of my hips down into my arches. But I could already feel my muscles tightening and shortening. It was torture to sit still.

"I want to speed up time," I said.

You rolled your eyes. "What do you want to drink tonight? We have to celebrate."

"Don't say that yet," I said, smacking you in the arm. "You'll jinx it."

"Damn, girl!" you cried, rubbing your triceps. "You're a ballerina, not a boxer." You'd known me for four years, but you never seemed to understand: To get where I wanted to be, I had to be both.

"I just don't know how you're not freaking right now." I did know, actually. Being a guy meant you were one of seven dancers competing for the male roles, not one of eighteen competing for the female ones. Boys were always needed in ballet, and boys who could dance like you . . . ? They were golden.

"I guess I just don't think there's anything I can do right now to change what's going to happen," you said with a shrug. Or maybe it was a shiver. It was freezing outside. Your words would come to haunt me later, but all I knew right then was that I was definitely an asshole.

"You could get drunk," Liv suggested.

"Fine," you said, "Aside from getting wasted or breaking a leg or something, there's nothing I can do between now and then to seriously change whatever I'm going to do in that room."

"Are you saying it's fated?" Liv asked, peering over at Ethan and Dave's tête-à-tête. "What the *fuck* are they still talking about?"

"Nah, I don't buy into fate," you said. "I just mean you can't prepare past a certain point.

"Are you kidding?" I looked at you incredulously. "I feel like I can't prepare *enough*." Ballet was all about drills and repetition. There was no room for whimsy.

"I just mean . . ." You squinted up into the bright winter sun. "Like, you have to learn the steps and then trust that they'll be there when the time comes."

"I wish I could switch brains with you," I sighed.

"You'd be downgrading." You grinned, showcasing two deep dimples. "But sure."

"Shut up, they're coming back," Liv stage-whispered, immediately pretending to be engrossed in her phone.

"*They?*" I glanced up to see Ethan practically running toward us, trailed by a reluctant-looking Dave. He looked straight at me and I lost my breath.

"Relax," you laughed. "He's just a pretty white boy. I hear they're very tame."

"Remember," Liv said under her breath, "We have to balance out Ethan's bullshit by being cool."

"Don't act like you don't love him," I said, relishing the opportunity to tease her back for once. Even though it was easy to make Ethan the scapegoat of the group, he was smart and funny and even kind of good-looking when he wasn't frowning like the world was about to end. And as much as Liv gave him shit, I knew she cared what he thought of her. Once, when she was drunk, she'd told me he was the only person she'd ever met who might be an actual genius.

"Whatever," Liv sighed as Ethan and Dave reached the bench.

Up close, Dave was taller than Wikipedia had given him credit for, and hotter than seemed fair to the rest of the gene pool. He gave us a tight smile when Ethan introduced him.

"Dave, this is Liv, Diego, and Joy," Ethan said. "Liv you might recognize from her appearance in *Law and Order: SVU* as Teen Girl Number Three, and Diego and Joy you probably saw on the landing page of JanusConservatory.com."

It was true, that was the only fame we could claim to date—the year before, a photographer had come to school for a week to "capture life on campus," according to the release form our parents had to sign, and a shot of you, me, and a few other dancers lined up at the barre during group class had made it onto the website. We were in profile, eyes focused, spines straight, left arms extended in tendu. Words floated above our heads: WHERE TALENT MEETS OPPORTUNITY. Based on the graphic design, you were talent, and I was opportunity.

Opportunity. The fact of the Showcase auditions, which I had blissfully forgotten about for approximately two minutes, settled back into its permanent spot at the forefront of my brain, and a fresh wave of nausea washed over me.

"Hey," I said to Dave, when it seemed like my turn. With game like that, it was downright shocking I was still a virgin.

"Dave has graciously agreed to audition for my play," Ethan told us, beaming.

"It didn't really feel like I had a choice," Dave said, shoving his hands in the pockets of his hoodie. His lips turned up in a little half-smile while he read our faces, trying to figure out if it was cool to rib on Ethan within the first ten seconds of meeting us.

It was.

"I'll be there, too," Liv said. Her mouth glistened with a fresh coat of gloss I hadn't even seen her apply. "So if you need someone to shield you from the drama-department drama, let me know."

"Thanks," Dave said. "I literally haven't met anyone yet." He looked around the square, shivering. "Is this, like, the lunch hangout?"

"For a select group of masochists," Ethan said through clenched teeth.

"It's only the most beautiful place in Manhattan," you said, nudging my shoulder. I looked up at Dave, trying to think of something witty to say, but his eyes were on Liv.

"I'm having a party tonight," she said, leaning into you casually—a physical checkmate. "You should come."

"Cool," Dave murmured noncommittally.

"OK, well, I for one am freezing my nuts off, so can we please move this lovefest indoors?" Ethan asked.

There were murmurs of agreement, the shuffling of books and bags, the metallic swish of zippers.

"Are you OK?" you asked. I looked up; the others were waiting impatiently.

I shook my head, tucking my knees up under my chin. Getting off the bench suddenly felt huge, like a step I wasn't ready for. I knew you were right—that there was nothing I could do to predict what was about to happen in the audition room. But it didn't make me feel calm; it just made me feel powerless. I wanted to fast-forward, skip ahead to when everything had already been decided. (If I could go back, I would stop time, just so you know. Freeze us forever when we were all together, when nothing had broken. I'd give it all up to go back to that day.) "I need a minute," I said.

"You know you're gonna own that audition," you whispered, crouching down next to me. "You're gonna blow the doors off that room."

"Yeah?" I smiled.

"Yeah. And someday—" you pointed to the banner stretched across the front of Avery Fisher Hall, advertising the New York City Ballet's production of *Sleeping Beauty* "—that's gonna be us."

"I'm holding you to that," I said.

"Hurry up!" Liv yelled. But I still wasn't ready.

It never got old: the theaters rising up out of the square like mid-century modern monoliths; the twinkling lights, like distant stars; the water that leapt tirelessly behind us even when temperatures dropped below freezing; the tourists crossing back and forth, arguing in foreign tongues, snapping pictures of *our* city; the dancers we could sometimes spot with their telltale duffle bags and muscular calves, walking quickly with spines so straight they could balance plates on their heads. It felt like the center of the universe, especially with those tiles that radiated out to the edges of the square, drawing paths to the door of each theater, fifty feet and a million dreams away. The future seemed tangible and invisible all at once back then, like a specter, like a promise. Like seeing your breath on a cold day.

There one second, and then—gone.

Chapter Two

January 6
127 days left

I LOCKED EYES with myself in the mirror, scanning my features for signs of tension. Another thing Ms. Adair was always telling me was that my face hardened when I danced. "Make it look *joy*ful, Joy," she would say with an audible smirk, and it was all I could do not to rise up en pointe and give her a *joy*ful double finger.

While the professional ballet track had its moments of rapture, it was anything but easy. As my parents liked to remind me, it was essentially a full-time job exempt from child-labor laws: four hours of intensive classes every morning, followed by afternoon academics, followed by another two hours of rehearsal and conditioning, followed by homework, followed by stretching, alternating applications of ice and heat, and then, finally sleep—which was the only part of the routine that was optional. Add to that sore muscles, bruises, tendonitis, bunions, blisters, rubbed-off skin, black toenails, aching feet covered in callouses, and you had a recipe for exhaustion, fierce drive and competition, and sometimes flat-out resentment.

But Ms. Adair was right: ballet was about appearances—people wanted to see the sleek swan floating on the lake, not the crazy paddling beneath the surface. The hard part wasn't supposed to show, and my expression gave me away every time. When left to their own devices, my eyebrows knit together, my lips thinned out, my nostrils flared. I looked like I was trying to move something with my mind, or solve an advanced calculus problem. But it seemed impossible *not* to tense up when the whole point of ballet was being in control—I never understood how anyone could expect the real estate above my neck to look all slaphappy when I was concentrating so intently on keeping everything below positioned perfectly. I shook out my muscles and did a few warm-up plié relevés, forcing a wide smile on every exhale. (Ms. Adair also liked to tell me that smiling, even when I didn't feel like it, could stimulate feelings of elation. So far, it wasn't working.)

"OK, you look insane."

I hadn't even noticed you walk over, but suddenly there you were in the mirror, leaning against the wall behind me in your warm-up sweats and JANUS FOOTBALL ringer T-shirt (which was ironic since our school had no organized sports unless you counted the tap elective). You broke into a grin that slowly morphed into a cartoonish grimace, like something you'd see on a deranged clown.

"That supposed to be me?" I spun around, my arms crossing

into *say-that-to-my-face* position. Somewhere nearby I heard girls giggling, but I couldn't tell if it was at me or for you. Either way, you didn't seem to notice.

"You just don't have to try so hard," you said. "Don't think about your face, I can tell it's psyching you out." I pursed my lips and looked around the room I had been intentionally turning my back on for the past ten minutes. It was warm and stuffy from so many bodies in motion. All around the barre, which spanned three walls, girls—and the few and far between boys—were stretching, practicing, whispering excitedly as they massaged their legs and stretched their feet and wrestled their pointe shoes into submission. None of them had to dye their ribbons and straps to match their skin tone. They didn't have to specialty-order mocha-colored tights online because none of the dance supply companies considered "brown" a variation on "nude." You were right; I didn't have to try so hard. I had to try *twice* as hard, every day, just to get half as far.

When I was ten, my mom had clipped an article from the *New York Times* that still clung to our refrigerator, held up by two novelty magnets from our family trip to the Grand Canyon. *Where are all the black swans?* the headline asked. I swallowed hard, looked back at you, and practiced my fake smile. Wherever they were, they weren't in the room with me. I was paddling all by myself.

The accompanist, Mr. Stratechuck, started warming up at the piano then, banging out an off-key version of the overture from *La Sylphide*, which drowned out the nervous chatter. Every single senior ballet major was gunning for the same coveted Showcase solos. Janus was the kind of place that only took students who were already the best in their classes. "Look left and look right," Ms. Adair had told us on the first day of orientation. "The days of being teacher's pet are over. Now you *really* have something to prove."

"Hey, zombie." Your voice swam up through the clang of piano keys and I realized that I'd forgotten you were there, for the second time in as many minutes.

"Sorry," I said, unconvincingly—because I wasn't. "I'm just trying to relax."

"You better." You leaned in and gripped my arms, the corners of your mouth curled in a teasing smile. " 'Cause if I end up with Lollipop in the pas de deux, I'll never forgive you."

I glanced quickly to my left, where Lolly Andersen was admiring her form en pointe, her sleek auburn hair swept back in a chignon so tight it threatened to drag her eyebrows right off her face. Lolly had what most people considered the ideal ballet body, as pale and fat-free as a diet vanilla yogurt. She thought she was hot shit because she'd understudied a Marzipan in *The Nutcracker* when she was twelve. She was a self-described "bunhead," which is why, I guess, she thought it was her place to tell me, in the locker room freshman year, that I had "more of a modern dancer's body," before trying to touch my hair without asking. I'd never forgiven her.

"If that happens, I really will look like this—*permanently*," I said, baring my teeth in a psychotic fake smile. You had to press your lips together to keep from laughing.

"Good," you said. "You and me, blowin' up like spotlights, right?" I can't remember when you'd started saying that, but it was an inside joke by then. You held up a closed fist and I bumped it, both of us sending our fingers splaying out backward like fireworks. It was never a question whether you'd get a lead in Showcase. I, on the other hand, was a long shot. I'd seen the performance every single year, so I knew the kinds of girls they picked to do dance solos: the willowy, flat-chested ones with the perfect form and delicate bones and all the stage presence of a feather. Not the ones with strong, curvy thighs or breasts that had to be squished into too-tight leotards so they wouldn't "be a distraction." *Being a distraction* meant that a part of your body was acting like a curve instead of a line—or that your skin didn't match your tights, or that your short, natural hair refused to transform into a gleaming, flat-ironed Barbie bun. I heard it a lot, and every time it made my blood boil. Nobody had ever told me outright, *You shouldn't be here*, but I'd gotten wise to their code words. I knew what they meant.

Still—"Just like spotlights," I said, holding my breath.

At 4:30 P.M. sharp the teachers filed in and we all sat down along the periphery of the room. I ended up between Lolly and Eunice Lee, but both of them immediately turned away from me to whisper to the person on their other side. Not about me—at least, I don't think so. It's hard to tell who rejected who first, me or them. All I know is I came in on the first day, kept my head down, clung to Liv in between classes like an oxygen tank, and then showed up on the second day to find everyone had found their people already, and that there was no room for me. Except with you.

I caught your eye across the room and, when I was sure

none of the instructors were looking, mimed a silent scream. You shook your head and then pointed at me, nodding. *You got this.*

"So," Ms. Adair said, letting the word hang in the air for a while, suspended on the tension. "Welcome to the last audition of your Janus career." There was some scattered murmuring and a few weak claps until you let out a jubilant howl that got the whole room laughing.

"Thank you, Diego," Ms. Adair said with a slightly annoyed smile. "This *is* a cause for celebration. You've all come incredibly far in your training, and now is your chance to show it off." She drew in a dramatic breath that seemed to pull an invisible string through her spine, raising her up a few inches. Her skin was almost translucent, the veins weaving like wires over the muscles in her arms and legs. When she wore all black, which was most of the time, it gave her the look of an extremely toned vampire.

Sofia Adair had been a principal dancer with New York City Ballet and had taken over the department hell-bent on making Janus competitive with her own alma mater, the company's feeder school. (The reason she didn't just teach there, according to gossip, was a stormy affair with a fellow principal dancer that had ended badly and led to a falling-out with ballet master Peter Martins.) She liked to constantly remind us that we were "dancing uphill" as far as professional recruitment was concerned.

"We're going to be brutal today," she said. "If we see something that needs work, we'll tell you, because our goal for May is across-the-board *flawlessness*." Ms. Adair glanced at me as she said that last word, drawing it out in a hiss like water on a hot pan, and I instinctively sucked in my stomach and drew back my shoulders. They were, I'd been repeatedly told, "problem areas" that I needed to "work on lengthening." In ballet-speak, that meant *thin out*. But I was built like my mom, a high school track star, tall and strong, all muscle except for the places my grandma awkwardly called my "womanly parts." Sometimes it felt like the only thing that could make me rise in my teachers' esteem was to reduce myself. That didn't seem right. It didn't seem fair.

I looked over at Mr. Dyshlenko, crammed onto a folding chair by the piano, and caught him subtly but unmistakably rolling his eyes. He was a former member of the Bolshoi Ballet who looked like an angry, aging Ken doll and who liked to yell at people for being too perfect. "Dance is about expressing the passion of the human spirit!" he had told us one time when we got paired for a sophomore recital. "You've got to have blood in your veins to move, so feel it pulsing! You should look like tortured lovers, not robots! If I want to look at robots I can watch the E! channel." But I hardly ever got to take class with him; he was mainly dedicated to training the boys or working on the Showcase pas de deux. Since Ms. Adair was my advisor *and* the teacher for Pointe as well as Ballet 7 and 8, the highest-level classes Janus offered, I mostly worked with her. I knew this was supposed to make me feel lucky, but I didn't feel lucky. Ms. Adair demanded surgical precision. She liked her dancing bloodless.

"We know what you're capable of by now," she went on, taking her sweet time walking in a slow circle around the room, her slippers landing soundlessly on the shiny hardwood floor. "We've all had a chance to teach you intimately, and we know your technical strengths and weaknesses. Today is about showing us what you *want* to do. That's the reasoning behind the free dance format of the audition. We want to see who you really are as a dancer so that we can place you in the best role to fit your talent."

If I'd had anyone to talk to, I would have whispered, *Bullshit.* But I didn't, and anyway, there wasn't time. Ms. Adair clapped her hands together and gestured to Mr. Stratechuck, who winked at us and started playing the theme from *Jaws* as she walked back to her seat. The teachers clicked their pens and rustled their notebooks, the nervous whispers faded to a dead silence, and then, just like that, it was happening. Something like fate, and I had a front-row seat.

Alphabetically, Juliet Allison went first, even though everybody knew her last name was really Zenkman (but stage names had just been covered in our senior career-management seminar, and besides, who could blame her?). She stepped into the center of the room and assumed fourth position, staring out calmly at a far-off focal point with her dark doe eyes.

I often wondered what the other girls thought about when they were getting ready to dance. Was it mundane stuff, like counting the music, or wondering if they'd properly hammered out the boxes of their pointe shoes enough to keep their toes from killing? Or did they picture some vague montage of success, a never-ending loop of tulle and satin and grand jetés and roses littering the stage? Whatever Juliet was thinking right then, I knew it wasn't *1 in 1,086*. That's the only thing that ran through my mind when I danced, because that's how many black ballerinas were principal dancers at an American company. One. And it wasn't just present-day. That's as many as there had ever been. In history. *One.*

I knew that statistic inside and out because I'd looked up a list freshman year, just sat down and googled a Wikipedia roster of every notable ballet company in the country (133, although a handful of them, like, for example the American Negro Ballet Company, were defunct). I'd gone to every single website, scrolling down the faces, counting, writing down numbers—although often there was nothing to write. At the end of my project, out of 1,086 female ballet dancers in the country, I'd seen only 39 black faces . . . and out of the 106 female principal dancers, *zero*. In 2015, when I marked down an X for Misty Copeland, I actually cried, even though I still had less than a fraction of a 1 percent shot at principal. *One in 1,086.*

My father, a cultural anthropology professor at Columbia, made it his business to know about human culture—especially the *specific* culture of *specific* humans his only daughter was looking to be a part of. Dad didn't see 1 out of 1,086 as inspirational, as the start of a revolution. He saw it as just plain racist. When we got into it over dinner—which we'd done almost every night during winter break, since College versus Company was the reigning Family Fight Topic—he would rail about systemic oppression and institutional elitism while I just shouted names into the spaces between words: Olivia Boisson. Francesca Hayward. Aesha Ash. Misty, Misty, Misty.

Mom, for her part, usually waited until things had quieted

down before launching into a stealthier attack—fitting for a psychologist. "Even if you *do* make it," she'd say, her tone reminding me that this dream was just shy of opening a water park on Mars in terms of probability (what would that be, 1 in 1,087?), "what's the long-term plan? Most dancers can't work past their late thirties, right?" This was dad's cue to jump in with a plug for school, any school. He and my mom couldn't understand why I wouldn't at least audition for Juilliard, if I insisted on continuing to dance. They didn't get that I would be wasting four of my best years. A conservatory program was for serious actors, singers, and musicians. Serious dancers didn't have time to waste. We had, as Ms. Adair was fond of saying, "the life cycle of a fruit fly." She was full of uninspirational zingers. I wondered if she practiced at home, spirit-breaking the way some people do jumping jacks.

My ballet life cycle had started when I was six. I'd seen a class practicing through an open door at the dance studio my mom went to every Monday for her old-school aerobics. One look at the tutus and the tights and I was all in, shattering my parents' dream that I would throw myself into team sports and science like everyone else in the family. They famously tried to bribe me to take piano instead, but I'd been adamant and unwavering— "stubborn," if you asked my dad. I informed them that I wanted to dance "in a bathing suit," meaning a leotard. So they'd lectured me about intersectionality and traditional gender roles and finally said yes to one class, which became another class. They told me I had to keep my room clean to keep taking ballet (I did). They told me I had to get straight As to keep taking ballet (no problem). They told me I had to start paying for my own classes, so I spent a whole summer selling lemonade to the runners on Riverside Drive. Finally, though, when I asked to audition for the School of American Ballet at age ten, they drew a hard line. I could dance, but my life wasn't going to revolve around dance, not while I was living under their roof. They'd only let me try out for Janus in the first place because it was A) free and B) they never thought I'd get in.

Oops. Sorry not sorry.

What they really wanted for me, though, was the dance history program at Barnard College, which would still fall under my dad's faculty tuition discount from Columbia. History—now, that was academic. That was social science. *That* was something my parents could get behind, something they could brag on the way they bragged on my twin brothers' twin MBAs. In the Rogers-Wilson family, a ballerina wasn't something a serious person aspired to. She was just a little plastic white girl who spun when you opened a music box.

Julia finished a fluttery bourrée and everyone started clapping. Her sixty seconds were over . . . which meant that mine were that much closer to starting. I pulled my knees up to my chest and pressed my thumb gently into the flesh of my right ankle. There was a dull ache—not unusual, but troublesome. I'd been dancing hard all through break, prepping for the audition, but I hadn't been resting enough and was starting to get the feeling that something was off with my foot, the way you can feel a cold coming on. It didn't seem like there was any time to stop, though; when I wasn't dancing I was studying, tutoring, writing papers, submitting essays to Barnard and Brown and Wesleyan so that I would have something to fall back on

if everyone else was right, and I wasn't good enough. I pointed
and flexed my feet, feeling the blood race up my legs toward
my thundering heart.

Lolly went next, and when Mr. Stratechuck announced her
selection, my head nearly exploded: she had chosen the same
music as me, the Kitri variation from *Don Quixote*. I had
picked it because Kitri is one of the few leading female roles
that's technically supposed to be nonwhite; she's a Spanish flamenco dancer type, which is frankly as close to black as anyone
can get in classical ballet unless they feel like playing an evil
Muslim or a character called "the Blackamoor," who prays to
a coconut. We were supposed to showcase our strengths, and I
had been planning on owning everything that supposedly made
me so different by embodying a character who was more peacock than swan. But now Lolly had gotten there first. And she'd
even brought a fan as a prop, which she popped open with a
flick of her dainty wrist as she launched into her routine.

I wished Liv had been there to give me one of her pep talks,
or even just to whisper something bitchy, like that Lolly was
about as Latina as Taylor Swift eating an empanada—which
is a real thing she said once after peeking in on our ballroom
class the day we learned merengue. But all I had was the back
of Eunice Lee's head, so instead I focused on deep breathing
as I watched Lolly triumphantly rise into a series of perfect
arabesques, flapping that fan like she was fighting off a bee.
She got more applause than Juliet, and I even saw Ms. Adair
clapping discreetly against her notebook. The instructors were
supposed to be neutral; that was not a good sign.

One by one the auditions came and went, as my nerves

soared, panic rising slowly but surely in my chest, each second unleashing new tangles of branches, like the big reveal of the *Nutcracker* Christmas tree. I distracted myself by counting how many times people did passés (eight), sauté arabesques (ten), entrechats (eleven; Ana Kulikov did four in hers alone), grand jetés (thirteen), and pirouettes (seventeen). And that was only *A* through *M*. It was kind of amazing, actually, how similar all of the dancing looked given that we had supposedly choreographed our steps in isolation. Then again, we'd all been trained to give the ballet masters what they wanted. So while Ms. Adair had asked us to show them who we were, it made sense that most people were showing them who they thought they should be instead.

But then it was your turn, and for the first time all day I stopped feeling nervous. You walked out like you were walking up to meet me at my locker—rounded shoulders, relaxed gait, big smile, shaggy brown hair hanging always a little bit in your eyes because for some reason you happily wore ballet slippers but drew the line at headbands. Watching you in the seconds before you danced made it easy to see how consciously you changed from Diego the boy from East Harlem, raised with two brothers by a single mom, who could only dance the salsa—and only then at family functions, and only then under duress—to Diego the prodigy, who'd been discovered by an after-school teacher hired to introduce fine arts to inner-city kids. You were twelve, too old by most standards to start training seriously, but you had such a natural gift they fast-tracked you; you got your acceptance letter from Janus eighteen months after you did your first plié.

You'd picked *Don Quixote*, too, the Basilio solo, and as soon as the piano started, you transformed, eyes sparkling, shoulders squared, posture like a matador. You launched immediately into a series of powerful cabrioles, getting so much height that if I hadn't known any better I'd have thought the floor was rubberized. Everyone was quiet; the air in the room seemed to change. You weren't flawless, but you were better than flawless—you were *alive*. It was like your body just knew what it needed to do. It didn't seem forced, or even choreographed. Sometimes, when Dad and I were arguing, he'd try to tell me that ballet wasn't about talent, that it was pay to play, and that no one without money could ever make it. I wanted to tell him that he just needed to see you dance to see that no overstuffed bank account could make anyone else even half as good as you. And you had more to gain—or lose—than anyone. If I didn't become a professional dancer, I'd go to a liberal arts college and pick some nice white-collar career. Cry me a river. If you didn't get a scholarship, or a place in a company, there was no money for school. You'd end up making minimum wage at some crappy job that didn't deserve you. But if any of that was on your mind, it wasn't showing. You were on fire. I had to contain my own howl as you *nailed* eight pirouettes at the end of your routine. Mr. Dyshlenko looked like he might weep.

"Oh my God, he's *so* cute," I heard Maple Rhodes whisper to Lolly as you jogged back to your place across the room. "When you dance the Showcase with him, can you please, *please* get on that and then tell me all about it?" Then, a few turns later, Maple got up and did a completely lackluster dance to—of all possible things—the Sugarplum Fairy solo. It made me feel much better. Until they called my name.

I'd been imagining the moment of my Showcase audition for four entire years, so actually living it was incredibly surreal, like a dream, or a nightmare—maybe both at once. I walked out to take my starting position, my brain reeling off a laundry list of reminders: *Pas de couru, tombé, manège of piqué pirouettes. Relax your face! Smile, but not too much! Keep your chest lifted! Tighten your core! Squeeze your glutes! Remember your turnout! Don't roll your ankle! Don't overthink it!* I shook out my legs, hoping the thoughts would go with them.

"You'll just have to give us a moment, Joy," Mr. Stratechuck said, peering under the piano lid. "One of the hammers has been giving me trouble." I nodded and smiled tightly, feeling like an idiot for standing in front of everyone for longer than I needed to. I was facing the teachers, which meant that Lolly and Maple and pretty much everyone had a nice front-row view of my butt. Much like my chest, my butt had not gotten the memo that it was not supposed to *be a distraction*. It was not a flat line, but then again, I didn't want my heart to flatline either, from eating nothing but rice cakes and Diet Coke. Having a healthy body was not something I was willing to sacrifice, for anyone or anything.

While Mr. Stratechuck fiddled with the piano guts, people relaxed and started talking. Suddenly my moment seemed a lot more like a pause.

"Should I sit back down?" I asked.

"No, no," Ms. Adair said. "You're fine where you are." Then she looked me up and down. It was no more than a blink, really, almost imperceptible. I felt it more than I saw it. But then she gave me a stern look. "You need to trim down before May."

My mouth nearly dropped open. Ms. Adair could be a bitch, but she almost never called anyone out publicly; she liked to whisper things, make a point of coming up during class and getting all cloak and dagger with her insults. Somewhere behind me came a burst of laughter, and Ms. Adair pursed her lips.

"It's not a joke," she said, addressing the whole class this time. "George Balanchine said that dancers are instruments, and it's true. You all should treat your bodies with the care that you would use to tune an instrument."

"Speaking of which, I'm ready when you are," Mr. Stratechuck said, banging out a few high Cs on the piano.

Nervous adrenaline flooded my system, and I felt the words coming before I could swallow them: "Balanchine also said ballerinas should have skin the color of a peeled apple," I said. "So if it's OK with you, I think I'll be selective with his advice."

Before the shock could register on Ms. Adair's face, I nodded at Mr. Stratechuck, who started to play. As soon as the first note rang out, I wasn't thinking anymore about my face, or my body, or my weak right ankle. All I was thinking was that I needed to show Ms. Adair—show everyone—what it was that I really wanted to do.

I wanted to become 1 in 1,086. But before I did that, I wanted to blow the doors off that room.

Chapter Three

January 6
127 days left

"*TONIGHT IS GOING TO BE CRAZY*," Liv said, stepping back to take another picture of the mantel. Before a party, Liv always took down anything breakable, stashing framed photos, vases, and various precious family knickknacks in a laundry bag at the back of her closet. But first, she took photos of everything so that she could put it all back perfectly before her parents got home from wherever they had gone off to. It was pretty impressive, but also kind of messed up given how many opportunities she'd had to perfect her system.

"Crazy like fun, or crazy like fire hazard?" I asked, taking a sip from the red Solo cup full of water I had already marked with my name even though we were the only people in the house. I didn't want to risk taking an accidental glug of Liv's drink, an amaretto and Coke mixture she'd gleefully dubbed "the Amaghetto."

"Well, some junior I've never met before invited me to my own party, so . . ." She raised her eyebrows excitedly and then turned to photograph the wall lined with her mom's collection of African masks. She was wearing a sleeveless, skintight sweater dress, which was such a Liv thing to buy: its form completely undermined its function. She also owned more than one pair of open-toed boots.

"Doesn't that make you nervous?" I asked.

Liv put down her phone and drained her cocktail. "No, it makes *you* nervous," she said. "Come on, you know it's always fine. Hector knows what's up—and he's basically legally blind—the apartment across the hall is being renovated, and the people with the baby next door are still on vacation in Miami." Hector was the building's near-sighted night doorman, whose loyalty Liv purchased with care packages of cookies and long conversations in Spanish about his sick grandmother. "Besides," she said, splashing some more amaretto into her cup, "If anyone needs to relax tonight it's you. You've been *so* uptight about the audition, and now it's over." She raised the drink in a "cheers" motion, fixing me with an expectant smile.

"It's definitely over." I crossed my arms and stared down at the Oriental rug, a dizzying blood-red pattern of interlocking vines. Liv and I had already gone over what had happened with Ms. Adair numerous times, and I knew she was desperate for me to move on and focus on the party. But I couldn't shake the ache of humiliated anger I felt, not only at being body-shamed in front of the entire ballet program, but also at being so quick to talk back. "They'll never give me a solo now," I said morosely. "I'll be lucky if I'm, like, a tree in the background."

"You are not a tree!" Liv said. "You are a total badass. Everyone will be talking about how you shut down that bitch."

"Yeah, well, that's not really what I wanted everyone to focus on." I sipped my water again, shifting uncomfortably in the fleece-lined boots I hadn't thought to change out of. Compared to Liv, I felt like a lumberjack in my hoodie and cords.

"Fuck them," Liv said dismissively, arranging stacks of cups on the dining table around the bottles she'd had her downstairs neighbor Kyle—a balding twenty-six-year-old who still lived with his parents—buy for her. "If they don't think you're perfect the way you are, they don't deserve you. And I bet you danced the shit out of *Don Coyote* or whatever."

That made me smile for the first time in hours. "I *did* dance the shit out of it," I said. The looks on some of the girls' faces had been priceless. It was like their features were confused, trying to figure out how to express *slay* but not having the cultural reference.

"See?" Liv smiled. "We're celebrating. Now please have a drink with me so I don't feel like an alchy."

"Oh, hey, how was your audition, by the way?" I asked, trying to stall. "All day I've just been complaining about mine." Aside from keeping myself Amaghetto-free for the time being, I really did want to know what had gone down at the Drama Showcase tryouts. I was sure Liv had sailed through—everyone knew Ethan had written the part for her—but there was someone else I was a little more curious about.

"It was fine," she said, rolling her eyes. "You know how Ethan is. He made us do it like five thousand different ways with different 'motivations.'"

I fanned out some cocktail napkins. "Which guy do you think will get it?"

Liv gave me a look. "Oh my God, you're so obvious," she said.

"What?"

"You're fishing." She wiggled her perfectly waxed eyebrows. "For a big, shiny Californian catch."

"Nope." I tried to swallow my smile, but it was pointless; my poker face didn't work on Liv, who was the emotional equivalent of a card counter.

"It's OK to like him." She looked at me for a few seconds, narrowing her eyes a little like she was trying to read something on my face. Then she nodded, took a sip of her drink, and set it down dramatically. "That's your party goal," she said. "It's decided."

"No thanks," I said. "I don't want a goal for the party. I just want to have a good time." (Look, would I have stopped him if he tried to kiss me? No. But I just thought he was beautiful and rare, like a hoodie-wearing peacock. Any feelings I thought I was catching weren't real. And the last thing I had time for with the Showcase looming was a boy to distract me. Or so I thought.)

"And what would be your definition of a good time?" Liv pressed, smirking. "I know you won't get drunk, or smoke, or even dance, which makes no sense."

"I dance all day!" I protested. "And if I want to grind up

against some wack people in a confined space I'll just take the subway."

Liv let out an exasperated sigh. "You know I love you, but you honestly make it so hard sometimes."

"You forgot the Guatemalan nipple bowl," I said, nodding at a piece of pottery covered in pink and brown concentric circles, which had been prominently displayed on the entry table since we were nine and had been making us laugh for just as long.

"You still haven't answered my question," Liv said, grabbing the bowl and stalking off down the hallway to her room.

"I have fun!" I yelled.

"Standing in a corner with the Tostitos!" she called back.

I opened my mouth and then shut it again. She had a point— I generally liked to hang back with the snacks and avoid the foolishness, but that didn't mean I couldn't enjoy myself.

Liv reemerged, reaching into her neckline to adjust her bra. "When was the last time you even hooked up with anyone?" she asked.

"I don't know," I said, like I couldn't remember, even though of course I knew, since there had only been one person in the entire past year, Caleb Cooper, who I'd dated for a hot second after the junior semiformal. And even then, all it amounted to was some kissing and awkward fondling in the orchestra pit that had abruptly ended when I sat on Caleb's clarinet. Not a euphemism.

"All I'm saying," Liv said, reaching up to unhook a mask, revealing a perfect circle of emptiness three shades lighter than the rest of the wall, "Is that you could get Dave if you wanted him."

"Yeah, looking a mess, like I just climbed Mount Everest,"

I said, gesturing to my outfit. "And besides, how do you even know he'll be here?"

"He is definitely coming," she said. "I talked him into it. There was a lot of down time while Ethan, you know . . . *orated*. Most of the other girls were being so embarrassing, getting all up in his face, so I think he appreciated that I was just being normal." She took the last mask off the wall and gathered them in her arms. "He's really chill, actually," she said, shuffling back down the hallway. "Not at all what you'd think."

"Oh," I said. "Great." I'll admit it bothered me, the fact that Liv had already bonded with Dave. It made it seem like she was gifting him to me, but in a backhanded way, like someone handing you a jelly bean and telling you they didn't like that flavor, anyway. Liv didn't really date other actors—her boyfriends were always visual arts majors who did shit like graffiti abstract paintings on found pieces of plywood and hosted pot-brownie bake-offs—but I'd been with her the day we found out Dave was transferring, and she'd lost her damn mind. We'd spent an hour googling him. Something was up.

"You *really* don't care if I talk to him?" I asked when Liv finally reappeared, staring down at her phone.

"Huh?" she asked. "Sorry, let me just finish . . ." She typed something quickly and then flashed me a smile. "I think I found a hookup!"

"For you?" I asked. If Liv already had someone lined up for *her* "party goal," it made more sense that she would relinquish the chance to get with someone famous enough to have been featured in a *Huffington Post* slideshow called "Child Stars Who Grew Up Gorgeous!"

"No, for *weed*," she said, rolling her eyes and drawing out the word into a singsong. "Jasper can eat a bag of dicks."

"Did Shakespeare write that?" I asked, and she laughed the way she had always laughed, since first grade, with her little nose wrinkled up like a rabbit.

"Fuck you," she said, and I started to relax. Whatever she was doing, I decided, it was probably good-hearted. And even if the setup with Dave ended up being horrible and awkward, it was better than competing with her for his attention.

I'd learned over the years that there was no competing with Liv. When she wanted something, she just took it. She didn't wait around for a starting gun.

Chapter Four

January 6
127 days left

IN NO TIME, the party had taken on a life of its own. A few dozen people were packed into the living room, draped across the couches, clustered around the alcohol, leaning against every available wall space. Hip-hop blared from the TV, which Liv had hooked up to her laptop, and Eunice, Lolly, and Maple were dancing awkwardly in the space where the coffee table had been, swaying and half-heartedly ass-bumping each other while trying not to spill their drinks. In the kitchen, a bunch of art kids were sitting on the counters, playing some budget version of beer pong where they tried to toss grapes into cups full of malt liquor; the floor was already covered in a sticky film of booze and dirt. And Liv's room had the door closed, with a towel stuffed in the crack underneath. She'd taped a sheet of paper outside, hand-lettered with the words *smoking lounge* in Sharpie. The Os had winky faces and cigarettes hanging out of their mouths.

You and Ethan had been the first ones to show up—you took pity on him and brought him back to your house for dinner since he lived so far away and didn't have time to go home first—but then it had started filling up and Liv had gotten distracted and you'd taken over door duties, hugging the girls and high-fiving the guys, showing them where to dump their coats and pointing them toward the makeshift bar. Since you and Liv were busy being Mr. and Ms. Hospitality for the night, that meant that I, by default, was Ethan's new best friend. We stood by the pretzels on the kitchen pass-through, talking about his favorite subject.

"She's just *so* good," he said, staring longingly at the hallway that Liv had disappeared down with Dave a few minutes earlier. After all of that cheerleading, she'd barely given me a chance to say hello to him before she'd whisked him away to introduce him to "the people you NEED to know." Given the fact that Liv hadn't brought him back yet, it seemed like I didn't fall into that category. OK, maybe that was unfair—I knew Liv was already drunk, and she always bounced around during parties, trying to talk to everyone—but being flat-out ignored was slowly curdling my pent-up anxiety into anger. I sipped my warm Coke and nodded, more to the song that was playing than anything else.

"She's got this . . . depth, you know?" Ethan went on. "And real vulnerability. You can't teach that stuff." He tipped back his cup and swallowed, wincing. Behind his glasses, his eyes watered.

"Do you even like that?" I asked.

"Gin was Tennessee Williams's drink," he coughed.

"And Snoop Dogg's," I said. Ethan pretended not to hear me.

"Did she say anything?" he asked. "About the audition?"

"Not really." I looked across the living room to where you were hanging out with Theo and Dominic, some of the other ballet boys. I tried to send you a telepathic SOS.

"Because we've never really worked together as director and actress," Ethan said. "We've just been friends, so this will be like a whole different"—he took another painful-looking sip—"relationship."

Just then, Liv and Dave came back into the living room. She was beaming and a little off-balance, while he was grimacing self-consciously down at the floor, in that way people did when they were moving through a crowd and just wanted to get the hell out without anyone noticing. Everyone's eyes followed him, and some people openly pointed and whispered as he passed by. This was the first time a lot of the Janus student body was seeing Dave in the flesh, so it was kind of like we were all on safari, catching a thrilling glimpse of him in the wild—wearing a knit cap indoors, no less, like some lost hipster DJ.

I felt bad for Dave, and not just because of the hat choice. No doubt Liv had promised him it would be an intimate gathering ("a select group of dope people," my ass), and now she was parading him around when he would probably rather be standing unobtrusively by the food, like any normal person.

As Liv started talking to one of Jasper's friends—she'd shunned him but invited his crew, of course, since otherwise no one would report back to him on how good she looked—Dave glanced up and locked eyes with me, and I gave him a half-smile of commiseration. I knew from experience what it was like to follow Liv around all night. I was debating whether or not to take matters into my own hands and beckon him over when Ethan started up again.

"Roth's pretty good, too. He told me he hasn't done anything lately except some failed pilots and commercials, but he's got this really understated"—gulp, wince—"gravitas. I don't know why he hasn't been cast in more movies."

I watched Dave's face as Liv thrust him upon a clique of drama girls, who smiled so hard it looked possible their cheeks might rupture. He seemed tense and uncomfortable, like he didn't belong. Or didn't *want* to belong.

"Maybe he doesn't want to be famous anymore," I said. Ethan laughed.

"Nobody here doesn't want to be famous," he said. In the middle of the room, Lolly tried to do a drunken pirouette and fell onto the couch. You rushed to help her up, and she held onto your neck longer than she needed to. Over by the TV, Liv was clutching Dave's flannel shirtsleeve, pulling him over to the next group, whispering something in his ear. Liv needed attention like most people needed air, but it wasn't like she couldn't get it from anyone else; I would have bet good money that Ethan wasn't the only guy standing around getting smashed and waxing poetic about her charms.

"My only reservation about casting the two of them," Ethan continued, as Dave said something that made Liv laugh with her head thrown back, tossing her black curls like she was selling shampoo, "is that they don't have the right chemistry. Rodolpho and Viola have this very magnetic, push-and-pull, love-hate thing going on. It's pretty intense, and it's really key to the production." I looked over at Ethan, ready to make fun of him, but then I saw the look on his face as he watched them, this sad stare that cut through all of his pompous showmanship. Ethan wasn't worried they had the wrong chemistry; he could see, like any other non-blind person in the room, that they had too much.

You finally made it over to me when Ethan's gin guzzling caught up with his bladder and he stumbled off toward the bathroom.

"It's about time," I said. "I was getting ready to set off a flare over here."

"Sorry. Mr. Director seemed to have your full attention, and besides, you could've come to me." You smiled mischievously and took a sip of your beer. "I don't know if you've noticed, since you seem to have a solid thing going with the pretzels, but there's this social gathering happening right now called a *party*. It's when people talk and dance and let loose and don't act like they're velcroed to the wall the whole time."

"Ohhhh, now I see." I took a step away from the wall and twirled around, bowing. "Happy now?"

"Very." You grinned.

"But seriously," I said, gesturing to the chaos going on around us. "I don't have anything to say to most of these people at school, so I don't see the point of letting them pretend they're my friends just because they're drunk."

"No, no, no, drinking doesn't make you *lie*," you said, holding up your bottle. "It makes you tell the truth. That's why they call it liquid courage."

"Mmmm hmmm." I cocked an eyebrow; I wasn't letting

you get off that easy. "Since when have you ever needed liquid for courage?"

You shrugged. "Hey, we can't all be as brave as you."

"Ha ha." I reached for your beer, and you gave me a sip. It tasted bitter and watery. I made a face.

"For real, though." You nudged me with your elbow. "What you did today . . . that was amazing."

"Thanks." Shame bloomed in my chest for the first time in a few hours; as intense as Ethan could be, and as oblivious as Liv was being, at least they'd kept me from thinking about my audition. "But I'm pretty sure I just threw away my shot. I should've kept my mouth shut."

"No way." You gripped my arm and looked at me, your eyes full of endearing—and maybe a little inebriated—sincerity. "You stood up for yourself. You stood up for all of us. And you're right: Things are changing. Someday every ballet dancer is gonna look like you and Ms. Adair will just be some old bag of bones mumbling her racist bullshit in a nursing home."

I laughed. "You sound like my dad," I said.

Your cheeks reddened, and you dropped your hand. "Uh, OK," you said with an embarrassed smile. "Not exactly what I was going for."

I didn't even notice how uncharacteristically awkward you were being because I was too busy getting worked up about whatever Dave and Liv were doing off on their VIP living room tour. I could have thanked you, or hugged you, or asked you what you meant, but instead I turned away, and so I'm left replaying our conversation over and over . . . like I'm a director watching a movie I made and know by heart, hoping that *this* time when I watch, the plot will change course.

I think I fixate on that moment now because it was the last one when it wasn't too late. It was the last second before the countdown was set in motion, to the end of life as we knew it.

To the end of a life.

Chapter Five

January 7
126 days left

THE FRONT DOOR OPENED, and a cluster of art girls who had been sitting on the floor in the entryway building a pyramid of empty cups quickly scattered to make room for two thick, wannabe-hard-looking older guys I didn't recognize.

"Oh, shit," you whispered.

"What?" I was clueless, until I saw Dante behind them. I'd met your cousin before, once or twice at your house. He called me Joyride, which made no sense, but which he seemed to find hilarious. He spotted us and grinned, sauntering over with a cocky, amused look on his face that immediately gave me goosebumps. It was the kind of this-should-be-fun look of someone about to start something.

"Well, now the party's here," you said with a grimace, taking another drink. You'd gone from charmingly off-guard to rigidly on edge in the span of seconds. It was like you knew we'd passed some point of no return.

"What up, cuz!" Dante cried, embracing you in one of those back-pounding bro hugs. He stepped back and looked between us, his smile widening. "Am I interrupting something? I hope?"

"No," you said quickly. Standing side by side, you and Dante looked like brothers. He was shorter and skinnier, and he'd shaved his hair down to a shadowy skullcap, but there was no mistaking the family resemblance.

"Nice to see you enjoying yourselves." He nodded at my cup and winked. "A little party never killed nobody, right?"

"It's soda," I said, gritting my teeth. Over by the door, one of the big guys kicked over the cup pyramid and laughed.

"That sucks." Dante threw an arm around you. "At least Little D got the real stuff."

"Don't called me that," you said. "And what are you, stalking me? I thought you worked Fridays."

"I *am* working," Dante said, taking your beer and finishing it in one pull. "I told you I'd get your fancy-ass school, with or without your help."

Liv. I felt my jaw tense. Dante was the hookup she had been so excited about. She'd gone behind your back. I took an angry swallow of Coke that just made me cough.

"Easy there, Joyride," Dante laughed, and I glared at him.

"She called you," you said. It wasn't a question.

"What can I say? Your girl knows what she wants." Dante smiled in a way that made me want to punch him. "Know where she's at?"

"Who are they?" You asked, nodding across the room at the guys by the door. They kept their hands in their pockets, and not in a laid-back way.

"Those are my associates," Dante said dismissively. "Don't worry about them. Just point me toward the lady of the house."

Liv and Dave were still standing by the TV, talking close, crushed together by the swell of people crowded around the speakers. He looked a lot more relaxed than he had a few minutes before. He might not have wanted to be at the party, but he wanted to be close to Liv.

"Just give it to me, and I'll get it to her," you said.

"You got a hundred bucks for me?" Dante held out his palm for a second and then burst out laughing. I wanted to move but there was nowhere to go except the kitchen, which had suddenly become the setting for a game of spin the bottle. Across the pass-through, I watched a junior girl with chin acne and electric pink braids make out with Matt Fareed, one of the senior actors, their eyes closed, their chins moving in long, slow ellipses. It gave me a flashback to sixth grade, at our first middle school party, when Liv had kissed Kris Harris like that, on the rug in his basement, while all of our parents ate pasta salad upstairs. Kris Harris, the boy I used to slip poems to under the desk when the teacher's back was turned, the one I'd asked her to talk to about me. I wondered if she ever had.

"Stop playing," I heard Dante say, and I remember thinking that even though he set me on edge, at least he would interrupt Liv's conversation with Dave. *That* was what I was worried about. I was so consumed with jealousy that I couldn't see what was really happening, right in front of me.

I wish I'd understood that the game Liv was playing was bigger than me, and more dangerous than cruel.

Maybe then I could have done something. Maybe then I could have stopped it.

Chapter Six

January 7
126 days left

ETHAN GOT TO LIV FIRST, as usual. While Dante was mixing up a rum and Coke, Ethan stumbled out of the bathroom and made a beeline for her, which gave me the excuse I'd been waiting for to run interference. I wasn't proud of myself as I crossed the room with the sole intention of ruining my best friend's game, but I was emboldened by what you'd said earlier, before Dante had showed up. You were right: I'd stood up for myself that afternoon, in front of all my teachers and my entire class, risking everything I'd worked so hard for. If I could do that, I could stand up for myself in front of anyone.

"Hey!" I said aggressively, stepping into the eight-inch gap between Liv and Dave. Ethan was on her other side, his hand on the small of her back. He'd only beaten me by about five seconds but was already holding court. Typical.

"I know I shouldn't say anything," he said, his consonants a little fuzzy from the gin, "but Liv is literally the *only* person who could ever play Vi. I mean, it was obvious, right, how much better she was than everybody?"

Dave looked down at me and raised his eyebrows. Up close, his eyes were a deep hazel green, flecked with copper. "She's, um, very talented," he said, going back to examining his beer.

"She's our generation's Angelina," Ethan said earnestly. "Only hotter."

"Shut up," Liv said, but I could tell she loved it. Hell, I probably would have eaten it up, too, if I'd had someone chasing me around all day telling me I was just a younger, cuter version of Kerry Washington.

"*There's someone here to see you*," I interjected, shouting over the deafening squeals that had erupted from the dancing girls as an old-school reggaeton track came on. "*Where have you been?*"

"Liv was just showing me around," Dave said. "Introducing me to what seems like the entire school packed into eight hundred square feet."

"It's actually twelve hundred, but there are some rooms I don't let anyone go in," Liv said. She bounced along with the music, chugging her drink. I hadn't seen her in a while, but I figured it had to be her fifth or sixth of the night. I handed her my water.

"Drink this," I said. "Pace yourself." She rolled her eyes, but took a sip.

"Hey!" A hand reached over me and tapped Liv's bare shoulder. Dante. I'm ashamed to say I was actually relieved. You followed sheepishly behind him.

"You're here!" she cried.

"You're looking beautiful as always," Dante said with a sly smile. "So, you wanna go . . . talk for a minute?" Ethan blinked at him angrily.

"*Yesssss*," she slurred, squeezing past us. "I'll be back!" she trilled as she led Dante toward the hallway.

"Who the fuck is *that* guy?" Ethan grumbled.

"My cousin," you said, side-stepping to avoid getting sandwiched by Lolly and Maple, who were energetically body rolling in your direction. "He's . . . leaving soon." You watched Liv and Dante go into her parents' bedroom with a pained look on your face.

"What are they doing?" Dave asked, seeing your expression and looking a bit stricken himself. I glanced over at the door; the two guys Dante had brought with him were still standing there, staring at their phones. They were acting like bodyguards, but they definitely didn't make me feel safe.

"You never know what Liv is up to," I said, feeling an immediate pang of shame at the intentionally misleading innuendo.

"Should I go check on her?" Ethan asked.

"Nah, man, I will," you said. "I guess it's my problem now." You ran your hands through your hair and started off after them, leaving me with the Olivia Gerstein Appreciation Committee—of which I was, at least temporarily, no longer an active member. Dave kept his eyes trained on the ground, and I knew it was only a matter of seconds before Ethan launched into either an ass-kissing reverie or belligerent diatribe, neither of which would do anything to diffuse the tension. So I did the only thing I could think of. I went boring, and I went hard.

"So . . . what neighborhood are you in?" I asked Dave.

"What?" He looked surprised, like he had only just noticed I was there. My heart sank. "Oh, um, Upper West. Eighty-fourth and Broadway," he mumbled. "Pretty quick ride from here on the 1."

"Cool," I said. "I'm uptown, too—Morningside Heights."

"I hate you both," Ethan groaned.

"He lives on Staten Island," I explained.

"Yikes." Dave winced. "That's got to be a rough commute."

Ethan laughed bitterly. "Well, if you're legally emancipated, I would make an excellent roommate . . ."

"Sorry," Dave said, not sounding remotely sorry. "I live with my family. Too much family, actually. So if you want to take one of them off my hands, maybe we can trade."

Ethan blinked and pushed up his glasses. "But wait, aren't you an only child?"

I cringed as I watched Dave realize how much homework we'd already done on him. He nodded and drained his beer, doing a quick sweep of the room, like someone looking for the nearest emergency exit on an airplane. "It's a long story," he said.

"Cool. So what's your plan for next year, man?" Ethan pressed, apparently drunk enough to completely ignore social cues.

"Don't know yet," Dave said.

"Did you apply anywhere? Like, Juilliard, or—"

"Nope."

"Liv's taking a gap year, too," Ethan nodded. "I already got in early decision to the Tisch dramatic writing program, so." He stared at Dave, waiting for an impressed reaction.

"You know . . . I think I'm gonna head out," Dave said, glancing down the hallway to where you were standing outside Liv's parents' room, jiggling the obviously locked doorknob. Admittedly I'd never seen a drug deal go down, but it seemed like too much time had passed. I hoped Liv wasn't messed up enough to make an even worse decision than inviting Dante in the first place. Or to not make a decision at all. But then you caught my eye and shook your head: *I got this.* I let out a breath and turned back to Dave.

"Nooooo!! You're *leaving*!?!"

For a second I was worried that pathetic banshee wail had accidentally come out of *me*, but then Eunice appeared on the other side of Dave, nearly tripping over an ottoman in her haste to harass him.

"Can I just tell you something?" she asked, grabbing Dave's arm, not waiting for an answer. "I seriously never, *ever* talk to famous people, but you are like, *so* amazing. I just had to say that, or I would hate myself."

"Wow," Dave said, his features resetting into an unconvincing smile, like a shaken Etch A Sketch. "Um, thank you." Lolly and Maple appeared behind Eunice trying to look casual, like they'd danced their way over by accident.

"You're so cute!" Eunice cried. "I've seen *Saving Nathan* literally a hundred times."

"Literally?" Ethan interjected. "You've *literally* seen it a hundred times?"

"OK, fine, like eight times," Eunice said, shooting Ethan a withering look. "Still, that's a lot. And I really, really love you."

"In it," Lolly said quickly. "She loves you in it."

"Oh my God, what did I say?" Eunice squealed, delighted with her Freudian slip. "I'm sorry, I'm just kind of starstruck."

"We all are," Maple said breathlessly.

"Don't be," Dave said, his plastic grin starting to wear thin. "Seriously, I'm just a regular person." He looked for an exit again, and I saw my opportunity. Dave was clearly waiting for Liv to come out and save him from his fans.

"Yup, he's just a regular person with a curfew," I said, taking Dave's arm in a way that I hoped wasn't as hungry or proprietary as the others had been. "Why don't we go find your coat?"

"That would be awesome," he said, glancing at me gratefully.

"Oh, sure, whatever, just leave me to the wolves!" Ethan called as we turned our backs. I hoped for his sake that one of the girls—or anyone, really—would stay and talk to him, take his mind off of Liv for a hot second. That boy was badly in need of a reality check.

"Thank you," Dave whispered as we snaked our way across the living room, dodging sloshing drinks and expressive elbows, ducking our heads against the current of double takes. I felt electrified by the attention, by everyone's eyes not only on Dave but on me, too. We were headed for the coats, so as far as anyone else knew, we were leaving the party . . . together.

I imagined Liv, finally emerging, stoned and bored, looking around for us, asking people where we'd gone. I could almost feel my phone buzzing against my hip as she furiously texted me. It gave me a wicked thrill.

"My pleasure," I said as we reached the kitchen. The bottle had rolled off into a corner, but a few couples had decided to continue the game anyway, sitting on counters and wedged against cabinets, their flushed faces pressed together under the bright track lighting. *My pleasure.* My real pleasure would have been to push Dave back onto the pile of coats in the laundry room and find out if his lips were as soft as they looked. And I hadn't even been drinking. We stepped through the tangle of bodies as quickly as we could.

Finding Dave's nondescript jacket in the sea of winter puffer coats could have been an SAT math question, it was that difficult. Mine was the only one that wasn't some variation on a muted shade of New York–cool black or navy.

"Red, huh?" Dave asked, pulling it out by a sleeve from the bottom of the heap. "I guess you must like to stand out."

"I don't have a choice." It came out cockier than I'd meant it—I was thinking more along the lines of feeling like an outcast and a long shot, more along the lines of 1 in 1,086, but Dave smiled and raised his eyebrows.

"I believe that," he said. I felt a tingle rush up my cheeks; I had to purse my lips to keep from grinning.

"I feel like I should apologize for everybody in there," I said, once I composed myself. "They're drunk. Which, I mean— that's fine, I guess, but you should know that not everyone at our school is like that. And *my* friends are definitely not like that." *Except Liv*, I almost added, but then bit my tongue. She hadn't always been that way. It had only been since things with Jasper started falling apart, around Thanksgiving, that she'd started coming to school hungover, and camping out in the nurse's office. And I gave her a pass because I had never had my heart broken. I thought maybe everyone did that.

"It's OK," Dave said, tossing me my coat. "Everyone at every school is like that, especially at a party. I just don't have any friends here yet, so it's a little intense." He leaned against the washing machine and looked out the window, which offered a beautiful—if tiny—view of Riverside Park, and the Hudson beyond, as smooth and gray as a piece of slate. The moon lit his profile like some old movie glamour shot. I wanted to ask him if he just walked around with a follow spot at the ready but then thought better of it.

"Must be strange to leave all that sunshine and sand for this icy hellscape, too," I joked. "This it, by the way?" I held up a black North Face windbreaker and Dave shook his head.

"I miss the seasons," he said. "And actually, I was born in the city. My grandparents still live here."

"Native, huh? Well, now I really like you." I smiled, caught his eye, and then looked away. Liv had taught me that move, back in middle school. I think she read it in some stupid magazine. Still, it worked: when I looked back at Dave, he was smiling, too.

"And here I thought you just liked me for my Papa John's commercial," he said.

"Please," I said, "No self-respecting New York girl eats Papa John's." Dave laughed. "OK—" I held up two more contenders. "If it's not one of these, I think you should just steal someone else's."

"You're amazing," he said, pointing to the leather bomber jacket in my right hand. "Seriously, thank you, Joy."

"No problem," I said, throwing it to him. "Want to—"
Want to ride home together?

That's what I was going to say. Buoyed by the caffeine, and the genuine smiles, and the banter, and the way the moonlight hit his eyelashes, and the way he said my name, I was going to take a leap unlike any I'd ever done in ballet. I was going to ask Dave Roth if I could walk him the five blocks from Liv's building to the subway, and then ride with him twelve deliciously slow local stops on the 1 train, and then—well, I didn't exactly know what then.

And I was never going to find out.

"You're *leaving*?!" Liv cried from the doorway behind me, sounding more like Eunice Lee than she would ever want to know. I spun around to see her looking back and forth between us, confused, her amber-shadowed eyes at a druggy half-mast. You were standing just beyond her in the kitchen, with an expression on your face like you just got slapped; something must have happened with Dante, but I was too swept up in my quickly unraveling fantasy world to care.

"Yeah, I've got an early morning," Dave said. "I would have come and said goodbye, but I didn't want to, uh—" He looked at me and raised his eyebrows. "—interrupt you."

"Oh, what, *that*?" Liv laughed dismissively. "That was nothing. And you are *not* leaving. I've barely gotten to talk to you!" She reached past me and grabbed for Dave's hand, but I intercepted her, pulling her in like I was going for a hug.

"Speaking of talking," I whispered, "Can *I* please talk to *you* for a minute?" I was expecting to get a familiar whiff of skunky smoke in her hair, but Liv didn't smell like weed. *Was she just wasted*, I wondered, *or had Dante given her something else?*

"Sure!" She grinned at me dreamily and then turned back

to Dave, who was still holding his jacket in one fist. "Why don't you go wait with the boys and I'll be right out," she said.

"Deserter!" I heard Ethan yell from the kitchen.

Dave laughed. "Well," he said slowly, "I guess *one* more beer won't hurt." He folded his jacket and shoved it on a high shelf next to a bottle of fabric softener. "So you don't have to go fish next time," he said, looking at me. *Next time.* Maybe—just maybe—I thought, there was hope for a walk home after all. Which only made me more pissed off that Liv had intervened.

"What the hell?" I demanded once the door was semi-closed (it couldn't close all the way, on account of the coat avalanche Dave and I had caused).

"What?" Liv was either playing dumb or too out of it to follow. Either way, it annoyed me.

"*You* were the one who told me I should go for Dave, but then *you've* been the one hanging on him like a spider monkey all night," I said. "And then, just when I'm actually having a moment with him, you break it up. So I'll ask again, what the hell?"

"I wasn't trying to break anything up," she said, the words slow and slurry. "I just want everyone to have *fuuuun*."

"I *was* having fun," I hissed. "I was having fun with Dave. I just wasn't having *your* kind of fun."

"What's that supposed to mean?" she asked, frowning a little.

She wasn't lucid enough to debate me, so I didn't bother sugarcoating it. "It means you're fucked up, Liv," I said. "And it's not cute. Bringing Dante here was a shady move. Did you even notice how uncomfortable it made Diego?"

Liv laughed derisively. "That's so weird, Mom," she said. "I thought you were in Puerto Rico with Tia Mari."

"Fine, then, don't listen to me," I said. "But if you like Dave, just say it. Don't use me to get what you want."

"I'm just being a good hostess," she said, still giggling, drawing out the last word like a child's whine. It was hard to be mean to someone who was so clearly out of it, but I couldn't help myself. The words were long overdue.

"No," I said. "What you're being right now is a bad friend."

Liv's face instantly crumpled; her moods were like quicksilver even when she wasn't wasted. "You . . . think I'm a *bad friend*?" she asked.

"Not always," I sighed. "Just—look, we can't really talk when you're like this, so I'm going to go home." I shoved my arms into my coat sleeves, avoiding her eyes. I knew that leaving meant giving up my supposed "party goal," but I wouldn't have felt right flirting with Dave knowing Liv was such a mess, anyway.

"Joy, please," Liv said, her voice suddenly small and pleading. "I don't want you to be mad at me."

"I'm not mad," I lied, to keep her tears at bay. "I just don't know why you can't let me have one crush without stepping in first to prove how much better you are." Unexpected tears sprung to my eyes as I moved past her and yanked open the door. On the other side of the pass-through, Dave and Ethan were engaged in another one-sided conversation. You were standing off to the side, looking as dejected as I felt, all traces of Mr. Hospitality gone. It was a special kind of hell to be plunged into personal drama while the rest of the party raged on so obliviously. "Get a fucking room," I muttered under my breath as I pushed by a couple groping each other against the fridge.

I tried on one of Dave's disposable smiles to say my quick goodbyes, pretending I was tired, but you saw right through it.

"Come on, don't go," you begged, following me to the door as I struggled with my zipper. "I'll deal with her."

"She needs to deal with herself," I said, kicking through the detritus of empty cups still littering the entryway. Dante and his "associates" had apparently left the building. "She's out of control." It seemed so surreal that just four hours earlier, Liv and I had been fanning out napkins and gossiping, taking pictures of cabinets so we would know where to put things back the next morning. But life wasn't like that; things got broken, and sometimes, no matter how hard you tried to force them, the pieces just didn't fit together anymore.

"Did something happen between you guys?" you asked.

"No," I said quickly. I couldn't bring myself to admit the truth. As hurtful as it was, I knew it would sound pathetic if I tried to explain it out loud—*We like the same boy!* I was too proud to own up to that level of pettiness. "She's just . . . embarrassing herself," I mumbled. "And I can't watch. I'm afraid she's going to do something stupid."

"Oh, shit," you said, suddenly looking over my shoulder with an expression that hovered somewhere between shock and delight. "Too late."

I turned around, steeling myself for what I was about to see. There was Liv, pressing him up again the wall, her arms around his neck, her tongue in his mouth.

Only it wasn't Dave she was kissing. It was Ethan.

"Looks like she just made his whole life," you laughed, holding a hand up to your grin, as Ethan eagerly wrapped his arms around Liv, dropping his drink on the rug in the process.

There was a part of me that wanted to laugh with you, to revel in the twist ending Liv had just thrown down. But I knew better—whatever she was doing, it wasn't fueled by liquid courage. It was classic, impulsive Liv, trying to make things right. It was her own backward way of saying sorry.

"What is she *doing*?" I whispered. Whatever Liv was trying to prove to me, it was only going to make things worse for everyone else. Ethan had worshipped her for years, even though it was obvious to everyone she wasn't into him. And as much as I'd hated seeing her all over Dave, I felt bad for him, too. He was standing there stunned, with a look on his face that made my heart ache.

I knew that expression; I'd been fighting it myself all day, ever since Ms. Adair had called me out before my solo. It was the look of someone watching something they desperately wanted slip between their fingers . . . and disappear.

Chapter Seven

January 9
124 days left

I WALKED TO THE FOUNTAIN on Monday with a creeping sense of dread, but for the wrong reasons. The anxieties stacked up inside me like layers of rock sediment, or maybe Dante's *Inferno* (Dante the thirteenth-century Italian poet, not Dante the twenty-first-century Manhattan drug dealer, although both of them brought to mind circles of hell). On top, the most all-consuming, was the Showcase cast list, which according to tradition would be posted on the bulletin board outside the auditorium after lunch, at the beginning of sixth period. I was fresh out of pointe class with Ms. Adair, and the way she'd treated me had made my blood pressure spike. It wasn't that she'd been cold or cruel, like I'd worried she'd be; it had been worse—she'd been *extra* nice, complimenting my form in front of the class, asking me to demonstrate a high arabesque, even commenting that my ribbons were laced perfectly. To anyone else I probably looked like a teacher's pet, but I had the distinct feeling that she was just killing me with kindness to set me up for a crushing blow she already knew was coming.

Underneath that, of course, was my fear of seeing Liv—or Dave, or Ethan . . . pretty much anyone except you (though I'd even been relieved to have had pointe class that morning so that you wouldn't be there, just to put off having to talk about any of the other three for a while). I'd lived the rest of my weekend in a sort of bubble, keeping my phone mostly silent, doing homework and helping my dad cook, watching dance movies on cable. I did check every few hours to see if Liv had texted, but amazingly, she never did. I knew she was alive, though, because she'd posted a photo on Saturday, of a toddler face-planting on a Slip'N Slide, accompanied by the hashtag #currentmood.

At the bottom of my pile of worries, throbbing faintly but unmistakably, was my right ankle. Something was wrong; it wasn't just sore, and no amount of ice over the weekend had made the gnawing pain go away. That should have been my first priority, I knew that, but it felt like denial was the only option. I couldn't stop dancing, not with Showcase and potential company auditions coming up, and telling anyone I was injured would only ensure that I would be taken out of the running. I couldn't imagine my parents not freaking out, since apart from a stable income, my health was the biggest thing we fought over about ballet. I'd had this Alvin Ailey poster above my bed since I was nine that pictured a beautiful dancer clutching her shoulders, facing the camera, in the middle of an acrobatic grand jeté. I loved it because she didn't look perfect and prissy; her face was almost in anguish, her hair flying out wild above her. To me, she looked like passion incarnate, but every time my mom saw the poster she'd say, "Look at that gorgeous body! I bet her joints are crumbling."

In class that morning my ankle had throbbed, but keeping it warm with an Ace bandage and leg warmers had kept the discomfort hovering just above tolerable. For the time being, I could shove it out of my mind. Unlike the drama with Liv.

I wasn't sure what the dynamic would be when we all met for lunch. It seemed possible that Dave wouldn't be joining us after the disaster that had been our collective first impression. You had texted me at two A.M. on Saturday morning to say that Liv was safely asleep in her bed and Ethan was passed out on the couch, but that was all I knew. So when I stepped into Lincoln Center proper and saw everyone, including Dave, clustered in our usual spot, interacting in a way that didn't seem (at least to the naked eye) openly hostile, it was a pleasant surprise. The weather had gotten nicer, too, so that the ice had melted into a slushy sheen on the pavement, and coats could be left partially unzipped without fear of frostbite.

"What up, girl!" Liv yelled when she saw me. She was sitting on the bench between you and Ethan, who was busy annotating one of his scripts with a mechanical pencil. You were wolfing down a hotdog and Liv was clutching a diet soda in one hand and her phone in the other. Dave stood in front of you, looking fine from behind in his bomber jacket and skinny jeans. When Liv called out, he turned and waved, shielding his eyes from the bright winter sun. I couldn't tell if he was smiling or grimacing. I wasn't sure if I was, either.

"Hey," I said cautiously, sliding onto the bench next to you.

"Hey!" You raised your eyebrows. "I didn't think you were coming. You didn't reply to any of my texts."

"Oh, sorry." I'd left my phone off since 10:15, when pointe had started. "You know Adair and vibrate." She had an ear like a bat, able to detect faint buzzing in a packed duffel from twenty feet away.

"Yeah, well, *check your shit*," you said in a low voice.

"Check what?" Liv asked, peering into her bag, which was Mary Poppins–sized, the better to hold the entire drawer's worth of makeup and up to four half-finished Smartwaters she carried on her at any given time. "Cast lists won't be up for at least another forty minutes." She fished out a lip balm and glared pointedly at Ethan. "Apparently they're being guarded like the fucking Oscar ballots."

"No special treatment," Ethan said, without looking up from his script. "People would talk." He smiled to himself and moved his right hand to Liv's legging-clad left leg. Dave looked at the ground. I unzipped my duffel and slipped my hand in, searching for my phone.

"What's the point of all that, anyway?" you asked, balling up your mustard-smeared foil. "I mean, can't we just get e-mails or something? Why's it gotta be posted in the public square like we're getting news in the Middle Ages?"

"Seriously," Dave said. "I'd rather get the call from my agent, even if everyone else still knows I didn't get it." I found my phone and turned it on, setting it in my lap alongside my container of yogurt and can of ginger ale. It looked like diet food but it wasn't—my stomach had just been weird all morning from nerves, and I would have sooner forfeited Showcase altogether than risked an emergency Number Two situation at school.

"Isn't your agent your mom?" Ethan asked. "That must make it weird." My phone buzzed to life against my thigh.

"No, she's my manager," Dave said.

"Aw, a momager!" Liv cried.

"Yeah, I guess," Dave said, shrugging. "It's not as cute as it sounds."

> 8:12 am: just saw e walking down the hallway like travolta in saturday night fever. asked how his weekend was and he said "transcendent." lol wtf

"Anyway, posting cast lists is all about building expectation," Ethan said, putting his pencil down. "Life-changing moments deserve a little drama." He looked adoringly at Liv. "Pun intended."

> 9:02 am: saw liv, she said her weekend was "boring." the plot thickens ... [crying laughing emoji]

And one from Liv:

> 10:13 am: NEED to talk at lunch. CRAZYTOWN. #helpme

"No offense, but I don't think *too* many lives are going to be changed by your play," Liv said, pulling down her cat-eye sunglasses. "And what about the losers? If you're gonna let someone down, it should be in private. Especially after all of that . . ." she shifted ever so slightly away from Ethan ". . . expectation." She shot me a look, hashtag "help me" in eye contact form, and I let out a breath I didn't even know I was holding.

11:12 am: lunch should be interesting at least. buy u some street meat?

My stomach lurched. I didn't feel like eating a dirty-water hotdog *or* talking to Liv—I definitely couldn't do either until I found out my Showcase fate. I had been trying to keep my expectations in check all weekend. I reminded myself how every single dance major was going to cross that stage one way or another, and that I could make the most of whatever I got. In my more confident moments I even sort of *hoped* they'd stick me in the corps, just so I could show them how good I was, and how they couldn't keep me down, blinding them even from the back row. But it was getting too close, and too real, for any of my lies to work anymore. If I saw the word *ensemble* next to my name, I knew I was going to be completely devastated.

"Yeah," you said. "Everyone seeing it makes it that much sweeter if you get what you want. But if you don't . . ." You looked at me, your eyes flashing with something I couldn't quite place. Concern? Pity? Either way it wasn't good.

"I think I'll actually be relieved if I don't get cast," Dave said. "I wouldn't feel right showing up last-minute and taking someone else's spot."

"There's no taking someone else's spot," Ethan said sharply, draping an arm around Liv's narrow shoulders. "It's either yours or it isn't." He smiled at her and she looked down at her lap, speechless for the first time in as long as I'd known her.

"Unless the person doing the casting hates you," I said.

"No way she hates you," you said. "She's cold like that to everyone. Nobody knows where they stand."

"Spoken by the only person who's got a lead on lock," I said. "At this point they should call it the *pas de duh*." Dave laughed, but you just stared out at Avery Fisher Hall, resting your chin on your fists.

"Believe me, I don't have anything on lock," you said.

"Does anyone?" Dave asked. I felt a twinge in my ankle, just as Liv squirmed out of Ethan's awkward embrace. You palmed the tin foil from your hot dog, aimed at a nearby trash-can, and missed. It seemed like the perfect metaphor for life at that particular moment.

By quarter to one I couldn't take it anymore and decided to go camp out in the dance hallway to await my fate.

"It's not gonna make a difference," Liv said, sounding almost annoyed, as I packed my uneaten lunch back into my bag. But even though I knew she wanted me to stay as her buf-fer, I tried to tune her out; she knew she was getting the lead in Ethan's magnum opus whether she made out with him or not, the same way she knew she would always get away with throw-ing blowout parties in her thin-walled apartment building. Liv never seemed to feel the threat of true failure. It was her most glaring character flaw.

"I'll go with you," you said, swinging your backpack up over one shoulder, and I tried to hide my disappointment. I'd had dreams all night long about seeing the cast list, weird, sur-realistic walks through a hallway stretched like taffy, where I'd come upon the sheet of paper, my eyes struggling to focus enough to read the fine print. In some of the dreams I'd find my name in a cluster near the bottom, one more body in an anonymous mass. In others, I couldn't find it at all. And while I was pretty sure (99 percent?) that I'd be *somewhere* on the list in real life, I didn't want you to be there to see my face when I found out. The only bright spot of the dreams had been that I was alone.

But as we walked back to school from the fountain, it seemed like you were mostly following me to gossip.

"Was that vibe weird to you?" you asked, trudging up the steps to campus, one bare brown knee poking through a rip in your jeans. "Like, is it just me or does Roth seem like he doesn't even want to be there but has no other choice?"

"Yeah, I don't know," I said, watching the rubber toes of my boots hit the marble, studying the sparkling gray stone for slippery patches. "People were kind of weird to him at the party. Maybe we seem comparatively normal."

"Sucker," you laughed. "That party was crazy, though. You were smart to leave when you did. It was all downhill from there."

"Why, what happened?" I feel guilty thinking back on it now; I wasn't really listening, and the Liv/Dave/Dante layers of angst had eroded momentarily. I was just going through the motions, holding that cast list in my mind's eye. It was like I was on autopilot, counting the steps until we reached the heavy green door that led into the basement offices, walked past the gym teachers' lounge, climbed the back staircase to the first floor, and walked down my dream-taffy hallway to the bulletin board around the corner from the auditorium entrance. This walk was all about the destination, not the journey, and for one of the first and only times in our friendship, I wished you would stop talking.

"People just got wasted and started doing stupid stuff," you said. "Someone put a cigarette out on the couch. There was definitely puke in the tub."

My insides shuddered again. "Did she come down OK?" I asked.

"Uh—" We were almost at the green door, but our favorite security guard, a lively middle-aged Liberian man we all called "Coach," was standing just outside, talking on his cell phone, so you stopped short a few yards away and lowered your voice. "Nothing too bad," you said, "but at a certain point she was barely standing and I had to kick people out so she could lie down in her room." Your face tensed; I could see the muscles harden under the skin. "Ethan wanted to go with her, but that seemed like an obviously bad idea, so me and Roth kept him out in the living room, talking about *The Crucible* or some shit, until he passed out."

He stayed the whole time? I was ashamed that that was my first thought, but it was. I'd assumed he'd left right after the Liv and Ethan Show. I certainly would have. Or, I guess, I *did*.

"Do you know what she took?" I asked. You broke eye contact and shook your head, looking down at the fountain, where Liv was now sandwiched between Dave and Ethan.

"I asked her why she called Dante," you said. "But she was so far gone, she kept swearing that her friend from middle school brought him and she had no idea he was coming."

"Right." The only person from middle school I'd seen at the party was Chitra Nagaraj, who had shown up at least an hour before Dante and had spent most of her time hand in hand with her girlfriend. Besides, he'd flat-out told us that someone had "called in an order." You'd been there. You knew. "She's lying," I said.

"Yeah, well, I wasn't gonna call her on it. Not in the middle of everything."

"Come on," I sighed. "Can you at least tell Dante not to sell to her?"

"We're not exactly close," you said, shifting uncomfortably.

"He's always at your house." I crossed my arms, trying to ignore Coach, who was off the phone and shooting me an enthusiastic thumbs-up. He was always trying to play match-maker, asking us when we were going to get married.

"Yeah, well." You squinted and tensed your jaw. "He shows up a lot of places uninvited."

"Whatever." I rolled my eyes. I thought you didn't care. I didn't know you already blamed yourself—that you would always blame yourself.

"See this patch?" you asked, pulling your backpack off your shoulder and pointing to a big, rectangular swath of fabric. "It's there because at the end of eighth grade, someone wrote 'faggot' on it in permanent marker, and then hung it from the basketball hoop down the street from my house." You laughed bitterly. "Guess who it was."

"Dante." I didn't realize he could fall even further down in my estimation, but now he was scraping rock bottom.

"He thinks I'm a joke," you said. "And even if he didn't, he wouldn't listen to me. He doesn't care who's buying, he just cares about making money."

I thought back to what Dante had said at the party—"*I told you I'd get your fancy-ass school, with or without your help.*" He must have asked you to hook him up with business, and you'd said no . . . I wondered bleakly what other punishments you'd had to endure for standing your ground.

"OK," I said, forcing a smile. "We can deal with it later. Right now I need to go be depressed by a piece of paper. You coming?"

"You underestimate yourself," you said, falling into step as I headed for the door.

"No, I *accurately* estimate other people's ability to underestimate *me*," I said.

You grinned. "Fair enough."

The cast lists weren't posted yet, even though it was only five minutes before the sixth-period bell. Since drama, dance, and music were all due to appear at the same time, there was a big group already gathered when we rolled up. Some people were talking excitedly, others silently stared at their phones, or at the empty space on the wall, as if they could somehow force the lists to manifest if they concentrated hard enough.

I spotted Theo and Dominic hanging with some dancers on the other side of the crowd, but when they waved you over you just leaned back against the wall by the yearbook office and stripped off your coat, letting it fall at your feet. Under your thin T-shirt, the muscles in your arms stood out, reminding me of one of those relief maps we used to study in elementary school; your whole body was tensed. You raised yourself up and down on your toes, bouncing like a boxer before a fight.

"Wait, *you're* nervous now?" I asked incredulously.

"You were so good—you *are* so good," you said. "If you don't get a solo, then this whole thing is rigged."

"Thanks," I said. "But I don't need you feeling sorry for me. Besides, if I don't get it I'll just live vicariously through you."

"What if I don't get one, either?" you asked. I gave you a hard side-eye but you just kept bouncing. "I've been lucky this far, but it's bound to run out someday. Maybe today is it." You swallowed nervously, and I reached out instinctively to hold your hand. We didn't touch that much back then; I wasn't tactile like that, and you always kept a little bit of distance from me, even though you were quick to wrap your arms around other girls you hardly knew, hugging them as you walked down the hallways between classes. It never felt like rejection, though, the way you gave me space. It felt more like respect.

"You and me—" I started to say but was interrupted by some manic clapping as Ms. Hagen rounded the corner with the drama list in her hands. I looked around for Liv, but couldn't find her. Ethan or Dave, either. They must have still been at the fountain, or slowly making their way back, too cool to rub shoulders with the overeager masses practically trampling each other just to put an end to the misery of not knowing. And while I wasn't proud, I was so desperate to know *something* that I ran up alongside all the drama majors just to see who got what.

Just like dance, the Drama Showcase was divided into half a dozen short performances (mostly scenes from longer plays) with just a few featured roles. My eyes scrolled down past *Waiting for Godot*, *The Zoo Story*, and *The Women*, to the bottom of the page, where "Boroughed Trouble, *an original play by Ethan Entsky*," was typed in bold caps. Liv got cast as Viola, which was no great shock. What I wasn't expecting was the name listed right above hers, next to the role of Rodolpho.

"Dave got it after all," I reported when I got back to the spot where you were still bouncing anxiously next to our bags.

"You're surprised?" you asked. "Even if he sucked, Ethan would have cast him."

"I just thought he might be . . . I don't know, jealous," I said. I leaned next to you, starting to feel hot and itchy in my down coat, resisting the urge to squirm. My heart thudded tirelessly in my chest. I knew it was just a muscle responding to a series of involuntary spasms, but it was hard sometimes to wonder why it didn't just give up. Why *I* didn't just give up. It was so exhausting to feel constantly like I was fighting for my future. If dancing was my destiny, shouldn't it have been easy? Inevitable? It didn't feel like destiny should require so much constant vigilance.

"Now, why would he be jealous?" you asked with a smirk. "He got the girl, didn't he?"

I smiled sadly and shook my head. I was about to open my mouth to say I couldn't see that ending well when my breath caught in my throat. Ms. Adair was coming down the hallway, the heels of her black boots clicking impatiently on the tile as she moved, her narrow hips swishing her wrap skirt back and forth like tiny, lapping waves. In her hands was a single sheet of folded paper. I felt dizzy and sick.

"Moment of truth," you whispered, squeezing my clammy palm just as the sixth-period bell rang.

"Sorry I'm late," Ms. Adair called out as she approached the group. "Believe it or not, we literally just finished." She reached the bulletin board but then paused, running her fingers along the crease in the paper. "It was a somewhat contentious decision-making process this year," she said. "But I hope you'll agree that every dancer got the part they . . . *deserve*." She turned and fastened the list to the board with two red pushpins. "I'll be in my office after four," she said, stepping aside to let the buzzards descend, "in case anyone has anything they need to discuss." She looked right at me when she said that last part, and then swished past us, clicking back down the hall as quickly as she'd come.

"I can't look," I said, my voice thick with nausea.

"Then I will," you said. A few yards away, Lolly leapt back from the list and started shrieking. She was happy about something. Of course she was. Of course she got it and not me. How could I ever have convinced myself otherwise?

I watched you move through the mob, my heart still going like a runaway train. It seemed like it took you forever to travel ten feet. That taffy-pull feeling came back, a pinhole focused on you, everything else starting to go gray. My fingers fumbled for my coat zipper. I wondered if I was about to faint.

But then I heard it: that wolf like whoop, your trademark celebration song. You ran back over to me, your face lit up like Christmas morning, and scooped my rigid body into your arms, swinging me around in a circle.

"We did it!" you said. "You and me, baby, pas de deux."

"You and me," I repeated, not quite believing. "But Lolly—"

"Lollipop got a solo," you said, stopping for a minute and

holding me at arm's length. "Dominic, too. But the grand pas de deux is all you and me. And get this—it's *Don Quixote*. I told you! I told you we killed it!"

Everything felt off-kilter, but all of a sudden in a good way, like stepping off a roller coaster, the rush settling into your bones as gravity pulls you back down. You hugged me again, laughing into my hair, and then I was laughing, too—crying, almost—letting it all wash over me: the relief, the giddiness, the pride and amazement.

I was one step closer to beating the odds and realizing my dream. But there was something else happening, too. I couldn't place it then, but I know it now.

That was the moment I first felt it. That obvious, unstoppable truth.

You and me.

Act Two

Dave

Chapter Eight

February 2
100 days left

I WAS PREPARED for New York to change me. I *needed* it to. I didn't just want to live somewhere different, I wanted to be someone different. First and foremost, not a dick, which seemed to be the general consensus at Harvard Westlake before my untimely departure.

But that was behind me. No more faking it in a city of fakes. No more dry L.A. heat, no more freeway traffic, no more awkward auditions for too-tan casting directors who raised their eyebrows at my résumé, jotting down notes next to my *Saving Nathan* credit, probably some variation on *LOL*. No more Daphne—my agent—leaving me voicemail messages that started with long, dramatic sighs, which I would immediately delete because I knew what that meant without having to listen to the words that came after. No more Mom pushing me to go out for humiliating acne commercials or community theater productions, telling me I just had to keep my name out there. I once heard her on the phone with my dad, after they split but before Dad and I left, telling him my brand was failing. My *brand*. I never wanted to be a brand. I didn't even really want to be an actor anymore. So as messed up as everything had gotten, I was kind of excited to start over. I was ready for a change.

I just wasn't ready for you.

Less than a month in and I was more miserable than I'd ever been. I thought a new school would be the best part of the whole deal, some nice, boring white noise to numb me for the quick five-month slide to graduation—that had been the point of the string-pulling, just making sure I'd get left alone—but then I'd seen you, and been stupid and helpless, and before I knew it I was memorizing lines and learning blocking and spending my days the opposite of numb: pent-up and pissed off. Ready to burst.

It didn't help that at end of every rehearsal I went home to find Dad dozing on the fold-out couch at 5 P.M. while Nana and Pop-Pop watched *Jeopardy!* in the kitchen, with the volume so loud I could already hear it by the time I got off the elevator. They'd mute it just to ask how my day was, and I'd shrug and mumble something about hating it, before grabbing a snack from the fridge and storming off to the geriatric "man-cave" that had become my bedroom. I was basically playing the part of the tortured, brooding teenage son in any TV drama; too bad no one was filming or I could have added it to my reel.

They were putting us up indefinitely until Dad found a job, but based on his tendency to fill his days going to yoga and/ or drinking scotch while reading books with titles like *Daily Meditations for Codependents*, that seemed unlikely to happen anytime soon. And it was easier to tune them out than to try to explain everything. About Mom and how weirdly cheerful she was being. About how much it stung every time she e-mailed one of her updates full of exclamation points and smiley faces and casually dropped names of promising up-and-comers she was working on signing. About how it took my supposed friends back in L.A. days to return my texts, which had been getting increasingly pathetic. And, speaking of pathetic, about how I was developing a serious crush on my costar in the school play, who had everything I'd ever wanted in a girl, except for the one thing I didn't, which was a boyfriend.

Or, pseudo-boyfriend—it was really fucking hard to tell— but either way he was my director and so I was confirmedly, completely screwed. Which meant that nothing had changed, really, which might have been the worst thing of all.

"On a night like this, you can see the whole city," I said. We were sitting next to each other on the edge of the stage, our legs dangling into the empty orchestra pit. You were wearing a thin, fuzzy sweater that rubbed gently against my bare forearm whenever you moved, raising my body temperature by a good three degrees. The top of your head was just about in line with my nose, which is how I knew that your hair smelled like lavender and honey. It made it hard to focus, and really, really hard not to hate Ethan.

It had taken me exactly one read-through to realize that *Boroughed Trouble* (pun most definitely intended) was an extremely thinly veiled wish-fulfillment fantasy about you. Sure, it was *technically* about an Italian immigrant building the Queensboro Bridge in 1905, and the two characters were strangers, which threw me off initially, but the way the beautiful and enigmatic Viola fell for the lonely, underappreciated Rodolpho (who *wrote plays* when he wasn't building bridges all by himself in the middle of the night) started to imitate life a little too closely. Especially after you guys started . . . doing whatever you were doing. I didn't bother asking. I didn't want to know.

"Sometimes," you sighed, "I wish I couldn't see it at all. I long for the mountains back home." You leaned into my shoulder, dropping your hand into my lap, where you found my fingers and curled yours around them, massaging my palm. I gulped, which wasn't in the script. You were turning me into a method actor.

"How can you say that?" I asked, my heart beating furiously in anticipation of what I knew was about to happen. "It's so much better here. There's so much opportunity."

"Sewing underclothing in a stifling factory until my fingers bleed doesn't seem much like opportunity," you said. "The conditions were better traveling steerage."

"That can't be true," I said, drawing away from you despite my body's vehement objection. Rodolpho was not supposed to make the first move on Viola. It was crucial, Ethan argued, that *she* be the one to seduce *him*. I tried not to think about whether he'd added that part before or after the party.

I still hadn't recovered from the moment you'd come out of the coatroom and pounced on him. The night had gotten weird, for sure, but I'd thought we'd had a pretty promising start. You'd been so cool and unassuming at the auditions, the only person who didn't seem to care who I was, or was supposed to be. And then, at your house, you'd somehow sensed that if left to my own devices I'd retreat into the corner to play chess on my phone for hours. "This is going to suck no matter how you do it," you'd said, handing me a beer and giving me a reassuring smile. "So let me introduce you to everyone now and then you can come back Monday morning not feeling like the new guy." It was like you'd instantly understood, without knowing me yet, exactly what I needed. Until you'd started making out with someone else.

"Your line," you whispered, without moving your lips, which I noticed because I'd been staring at them. You rubbed your thumb against my palm and I almost bolted upright.

"Besides," I stammered, gesturing out to the imaginary cityscape in front of us. "This is just the beginning. You speak as if this is the end."

"Maybe I wish it was," you said, your voice turning hollow and pained. I looked at you, forcing my face into an expression of concern as my eyes traced your profile, taking in your thick lashes, your perfect skin, the tantalizing curve of your mouth, which was trembling as you stared out into the empty seats, preparing to deliver the monologue that led to the part of the play I'd been waiting to practice ever since I'd taken my script home the day casting was announced. I'd chewed as much gum as I could stomach before we'd started rehearsal, but that had been at least an hour ago. I ran my tongue over the roof of my mouth, checking for any traces of the ill-advised vegan burrito I'd had for lunch.

"I just want to feel something," you said, looking down at

the "water." "I want to feel something other than homesickness. I want to know something other than sadness. I want to see something besides my mother's face as she lay dying. I want to touch something other than a sewing needle." You looked up at me, raising a hand to my face and tracing a line from my temple to my Adam's apple. I swallowed thickly, working hard to look confused and reluctant instead of crazy with pent-up lust. "I want to feel something . . ." you said again, starting to pull me in by the back of the neck. I started to close my eyes, ready to feel what *I'd* been waiting to feel since the first day we met, what I'd been imagining while lying in the dark on my slowly deflating air mattress every night for weeks, when—

"Cut!" Ethan yelled from the back of the auditorium. Fucking Ethan. I'd almost forgotten he was there.

You dropped your hands to the lip of the stage and turned away, letting out a slow, shaky exhale. I thought for a second you might be relieved, but then you glared out at Ethan with an expression of unmistakable contempt.

"What the hell?" you said. "I was in the zone. You couldn't just let me finish my fucking lines?"

"It's not your delivery, babe," Ethan said, bounding down the aisle steps two at a time. He had taken to calling you exclusively *babe* or *baby*. "I just don't think we need to rehearse the, um . . ." He frowned down at the script he had bound in a leather binder with a leather strap that tied around the front like something out of the nineteenth century. I was frankly pretty surprised he hadn't written the thing out with a quill.

"The what?" you demanded, crossing your arms defiantly. "The climax of the whole play?"

"Climax is a strong word," Ethan said, frowning. "If any-thing, the climax is when Rodolpho jumps off the bridge after Viola leaves." *Boroughed Trouble* ended with a tragic suicide twist, which lent the whole art-imitating-life aspect a pretty creepy vibe.

"But that's the *end*," you said. "The climax can't be at the end."

"That's what she said." Ethan grinned. It made my skin crawl to think about his hands on you.

"Oh my God," you groaned.

"That's also what she said."

"Please, seriously, *stop*." You grimaced and covered your face with your palms. Ethan's smile disappeared, and I had to admit, when I repressed the mental image of the two of you sucking face by the pretzel bowl, I felt kind of sorry for the guy. Any time he touched you, you wriggled away, and all you did during rehearsal was challenge him. Don't get me wrong, I agreed with you—Ethan could be pretty pretentious, and the script some-times read like a fanboy mash-up of his favorite scenes from clas-sic plays. But that didn't change the fact that he was the director, or that he was directing me playing some imaginary version of him meeting you, playing . . . well, basically just you. All while I fell for you in the process of rehearsing the play about you fall-ing for him. It all would have been weird enough without the kiss Ethan had written into the script, but it was *extremely* weird with the kiss. I didn't know how much longer I could stand it.

"I just think," you said, your fingers—topped with bitten-down, gold-painted nails—migrating into prayer position in front of your lips, "That the kiss is a pretty important part. I mean, she ran onto the bridge to kill herself because her mom died of consumption and she's stuck in some old-timey sweat-shop making Prohibition panties—"

"Prohibition was actually 1920, so—" Ethan interrupted, but you shot him a look that shut him right up.

"Regardless, she's ending it all because everything sucks," you said. "But then she meets this guy who manages to show her that all is not lost, and there's love out there for her—" you glanced at me and I could swear the corners of your lips turned up ever so slightly "—and that kiss is the moment that she takes life into her *own* hands for the first time, and takes what *she* wants instead of what's been forced on or expected of her. So the way *I* see it, the kiss is her making the choice to live. Which I'd say is a pretty fucking important moment. Wouldn't you?" You raised your eyebrows expectantly, and Ethan just stared at you with the exact same dumbfounded admiration I was trying so hard to repress.

"That's *exactly* it, babe," he said excitedly. "But it's a spur-of-the moment choice, one that she doesn't see coming, and I want it to feel urgent and sudden. That's why I don't think it should be rehearsed." He turned to me with a smug smile, and it was all I could do to keep from throttling him. Still, I nodded, slowly, like I totally understood.

"Yeah, we probably shouldn't practice it," I said. And as it came out of my mouth, I realized that I meant it.

I didn't want our first kiss to be on a stage, in front of Ethan, or in front of anyone. I didn't want it to be public and I didn't want it to be planned.

When I kissed you for the first time, I wanted it to matter. And I wanted you to know it.

Chapter Nine

February 2
100 days left

I WAS HOPING we would walk to the train together. We'd taken to splitting off while Ethan stayed behind to type up his notes for the next rehearsal, and those two blocks from campus to the 66th Street subway station had become the best part of my day. It was a perfect distance, not long enough to get into a real conversation that might lead to uncomfortable questions—like *Hey, have you seen Ethan naked?* or *Do you live in your grandparents' rent-controlled apartment? Because you smell a lot like Ben-Gay and a Golden Sands Yankee Candle*—but just long enough for little jokes and sidelong glances, long enough for me to grab your sleeve as the traffic whizzed past on Broadway. Long enough for you to smile and push the hair out of your face and say, "Relax, I grew up here. I'm not about to get flattened into a *New York Post* headline." Long enough to get me through to the next time I saw you.

But that day, you had other plans.

"I promised Joy I'd get coffee," you said as we spilled out through the heavy front door onto Amsterdam Avenue, the bitter wind whipping your scarf around your face. It was less than two weeks to Valentine's Day, and all the store windows were plastered with giant hearts and winking Cupids. As if anyone needed the reminder.

"Cool, cool," I said, shrugging like it didn't make a difference.

"I feel like I've barely seen her," you said. "She's been ghosting during lunch lately."

I nodded, or at least sort of wobbled my chin noncommittally. I liked Joy but hadn't really spoken to her one-on-one since the party, when she'd saved me from the Drunk Girl Chorus. Selfishly, I mostly wanted to get to know her better so that I could get closer to you.

"Tell her I say hey," I said. You cocked your head and narrowed your eyes.

"How many Y's?" you asked.

"What?"

"You know." Your lips parted slowly in a sly smile. "Just 'hey,' or, like—" you wiggled your eyebrows lasciviously "'—heyyyyyy'?"

"How about just 'hi,'" I laughed.

"'Hi' or 'hiiiiiiiiiiiii'?" You were cracking up, but I wasn't sure what you were doing. You were acting like I was into Joy, which had come out of nowhere. And sure, she was cute and seemed cool, but she wasn't the one who—as Nana would say—had her hooks in me. The expression always made me think of meat processing, but if you could get past the gross

visual it made sense. You'd gotten under my skin, and there
wasn't anything I could do about it. You felt—and I know this
is a terrible analogy given what happened but I really don't
know how else to say it—like a drug.

"The first one," I said.

"Got it," you said, giving me a little salute before turning
south on Broadway, toward Starbucks. "See you tomorrow,
Rodolpho." I watched you walk for a few seconds, shamelessly
hoping you'd look back, but you just stomped ahead, your
bag bouncing precariously on your shoulder, one strap hanging loose, as if everything could spill out onto the street at any
second.

Not knowing where we stood, I felt just as unstable.

I decided on a whim to walk home. It was only a mile or so,
and I was in no hurry to get there. Besides, the weather was
so beautiful: black ice on the ground, yellow snow frozen in
custardy clumps on the curb, the sky a dumpy shade of pigeon
gray. Every day in the New York winter felt like an eternity, but
I didn't mind; I would've made it stretch on and on to infinity if
I could. After graduation (or "commencement," since teachers
were always bending over backward to convince us that this
was just the *beginning*, like that was somehow comforting), my
life would become a big, empty nothing, the future greeting me
not with an excited *heyyyyyyy* or even a casual *hi* but with that
terse, punctuated "hey." people text when they're mad at you
and want to make you guess why.

I doubled back down to Amsterdam, shoving my numb fingers into my pockets. I wasn't in the mood for the crowds on

Broadway. I walked fast, keeping my head low, just like at school, only now there was no one trying to talk to me, only the sharp, apathetic air that slapped at my cheeks, burned in my lungs, and came out of my mouth in short, crystallized puffs. Everything felt shaky, temporary—like Mom, like money, like my so-called career, or even my confidence lately. I thought we had a vibe, but you teasing me about Joy made me think I'd made the whole thing up. Maybe you really were into Ethan. Maybe he wasn't the delusional one. I was debating exposing my hands to the elements so that I could dig out my headphones when I heard the dull thud of a basketball on pavement and glanced over to see Diego shooting hoops on the 70th Street playground courts.

"Hey!" I called, grateful for an excuse to lengthen my commute. Coming home at five o'clock had turned into five thirty had turned into six. I could always blame rehearsal, not that anyone bothered asking me to explain anymore.

Diego started, scooping the ball under one arm, but then relaxed when he saw it was me.

"Hey, man, sorry," he said, as I crossed the blacktop. "I've gotten chased out of here a few times by bored cops."

"Really?" I asked, dumping my bag next to his at the base of the hoop.

Diego dribbled the ball back to center court. "Yup," he said. "Apparently there's a thin brown line between playing ball—" he feinted back and made a perfect three-point shot "—and loitering," he finished.

"Well if you're loitering then I guess I am, too," I said.

Diego smiled and tossed me the ball. "You don't want to go home, either, huh?" he asked.

I dribbled ham-handedly, wishing I had spent more time playing sports like a normal kid instead of sitting in casting offices running lines with my mom. "My dad works late," I lied, making a clumsy attempt at a layup that hit the underside of the hoop with a metallic clang.

"My mom, too," Diego said. He nodded after the ball, which had rolled meekly off into a corner as if it were embarrassed to be seen with me. "Want to go one-on-one?"

"You need an ego boost?" I laughed.

"Nah," Diego said. "I want the company. How about HORSE or something? Just for fun?"

I rubbed my hands together, feeling the tingle of blood starting to flow again. Even if I completely embarrassed myself, at least it would warm me up. "OK," I said. The last of the light was gone from the sky, anyway, so everything was starting to look dim and pixelated, comfortingly obscure.

"You first," Diego said, throwing me the ball. He jogged back to the hoop and I trudged over to the free-throw line. "You probably need to blow off some steam after rehearsals with William Fakespeare."

I laughed, bouncing the ball once, hard, just to feel it rebound into my hands. "He's all right," I said. "And Liv gives him so much shit, I actually feel kind of bad for him." I took a shot, which fell short of the basket by a good inch or two.

"That's H," Diego said, deftly catching the ball before it hit the ground. We switched positions. "You can't say he doesn't kind of deserve it, though." He grinned and aimed.

"Maybe," I said, watching the ball sail through the dark. It spun around the periphery of the hoop a few times before veering off to the left.

"H for me, too," Diego said. "See, I'm not that good."

"Or you're letting me off easy," I said.

He laughed, brushing the hair out of his eyes as we swapped again. "Sure, I'll let you believe that," he said. I dribbled the ball back out to the line just as the lamp came on at the opposite side of the court, sending my shadow stretching out in front of me.

"Must be six," Diego said. "They're on some kind of timer."

"You come here a lot, then?" My next shot miraculously made it through the net—not exactly a swisher, but good enough—and I jogged back to the hoop on a swell of pride.

Diego shrugged. "Beats going home sometimes."

"Yeah, I know the feeling."

He leapt up and threw the ball in a perfect arc into the basket. "See? I'm not letting you win, Hollywood."

I winced a little at the nickname. I knew it was a joke, but I also knew that Diego, and all of you probably, thought I was rich. Outside of L.A., it was a common misconception that one movie gig meant you were living the life, even though the truth was that I hadn't been paid that much for *Saving Nathan* to begin with, and the money had been siphoned from savings a few years back to start Mom's agency. At my old school, I was one of the least rich kids, and a flat-out joke once Dad and I moved into Oakwood Apartments, the infamous housing complex in Toluca Hills where wannabes from places like Nebraska and Tennessee moved when they were just starting out with a dollar and a dream—"starting out" being the operative phrase. When you *ended up* in a place like Oakwood, it was a sign that something had gone horribly wrong.

I missed the next shot, overthrowing so aggressively that the ball ricocheted back at me in a straight line.

"Don't try so hard," Diego said. "If you want it too much . . ." He grabbed the ball and spun around, shooting so fast it didn't even seem like he was aiming. It sailed through the net with a satisfying swoosh.

"See now you're just showing off," I grumbled as he ran to retrieve the ball.

"Nah, just lucky." He smiled and tossed it back to me. "I was gonna say that if you want it too much you'll overshoot, but that's not always true. I mean, look at Ethan, right?"

"Yeah, I guess," I said, dribbling a few times before taking a shot that rebounded swiftly off the hoop. My pulse raced; thinking about Liv and Ethan together gave me something akin to 'roid rage. "I don't really know what their deal is."

"Seems like they're talking," Diego shrugged. "Anyway, I hope so. It's inspiring to think he finally made it out of the Friend Zone." He dribbled and took a shot that glanced off the rim.

"I never have," I said. That was true, mostly. I'd been friends first with a few of my girlfriends, but not *real* friends, just that vague in-between stage when you're hanging out and flirting and calling it friendship. Kind of like how it felt with you. I took a deep breath and launched the ball high into the air. *If it makes it in, she likes me, too,* I thought—so stupid and pointless, but I couldn't help myself. It swished through the net and I grinned like an idiot.

"Well if you can't, there's no hope for me," Diego said.

"Wait," I said, walking backward as we swapped positions again. "You're a straight guy who dances. You're telling me you can't get girls?"

"Some girls," he said. "Not *the* girl." He reached the line and made his shot, which bounced gently off the backboard and dropped through the hoop. Diego's eyes lit up, and I wondered if he'd made some secret bet with himself just then, like I had.

"So it's someone specific," I said.

"Don't jinx it," he laughed.

"No names," I promised, even though it didn't take much deduction to figure out that it could really only be one person. Every time she went anywhere, he followed her. You'd told me that she was the only reason we collectively agreed to freeze our balls off on the fountain bench every lunch period. And that night at your party, after she'd left, he'd kind of checked out, getting drunk and quiet and all but ignoring the cute girls begging him to dance. Then again, I had checked out, too. That had been right after the kiss. I grimaced and took my shot, barely making it after a few teasing rolls around the rim.

"I've been in love with her forever," Diego said, catching the ball and staring at it for a minute, as if he was trying to decode some message in its grooves. "It's messed up. I've never been able to make a move. And I feel like time's running out." He walked back to center court and dribbled slowly. "It's second

semester, senior year. It's now or never, man. But every time I try
to tell her . . ." He threw the ball wildly, barely hitting the bottom corner of the backboard. I couldn't tell if it was on purpose
or not. ". . . I brick the shot," he said.

"But you spend a lot of time with her, right?" I chased the
ball past the chain-link fence that separated the courts from the
playground, grabbing it just before it disappeared underneath
a slide. I walked back panting, and we stood at the base of the
hoop for a minute, catching our breath.

"Yeah," he said. "We have a great thing going, but I literally
have no idea if she would be into it or recoil in horror if I tried
something."

"Only one way to find out," I said, but I knew it was easier said than done. I'd wondered the same thing about you—
what you would do if I grabbed on to your hand instead of
your sleeve on our walk to the subway. What you would do if
I pulled you in and kissed you, with all of Broadway watching.
No matter how you reacted, it would change everything. We
could never go back.

"What can I do, though?" Diego asked helplessly. "Do I just
ask her out? Like, hey, I know we've been friends for years but
let's go on an awkward date now?"

"Maybe it wouldn't be awkward," I said. Buoyed by hope, I
walked out to the line and tried to do that thing Diego had done
where he just turned and threw in one motion. Unsurprisingly,
it didn't go anywhere near the basket. "H-O-R-S," I said.
"Prepare to win."

"Not necessarily." Diego caught the ball and dribbled past

me. "Weren't we just discussing how I've got no game?" He took a balletic jump shot and sank it.

"Fuck you," I laughed.

"Sorry," he said.

"No, it's OK," I said. "I've definitely got no game. I can admit it." I looked up at the hoop, glinting silver in the floodlights.

"Moment of truth," Diego called. "No bricks!" I paused my dribbling to give him the finger.

Moment of truth, I thought. If Diego was willing to risk his friendship with Joy, then I could definitely risk my friendship with you, and my nonexistent friendship with Ethan, right? It seemed like it should have been an easy choice, but it wasn't. Diego felt a ticking clock? Well I felt the opposite: like I was floating aimlessly in a lazy river that slowed everything to half-speed and kept me from making any decision that might possibly move my life forward in any way.

Enough stalling, I told myself. *If I make this shot, I make a move.*

I held my breath and listened to the sound of the ball on the pavement, a thick, muffled smack followed by a sharp, ringing recoil. On the next bounce, I shifted my weight and palmed it into my right hand, springing up and extending my arm and pushing it off my fingertips with the tense focus of every muscle in my body.

If I make the shot, I make a move. But if I miss, I let her go.

The ball sailed into the hoop—and then spun right back out.

I missed. Not a brick, but a so-close-I-could-almost-taste-it miss, which felt even worse.

I walked back to get my stuff, the weight of the promise I'd just made to myself crushing me deeper with each step.

"Sucks, man," Diego said, shoving the ball into his duffel. "You were robbed."

I pulled my bag over my shoulder and looked up at the floodlights. Inside the beams, tiny snowflakes were starting to fall, dancing, almost—swirling in circles so tight they were almost touching before melting invisibly into the pavement.

"No," I said, shaking my head. "You were right. I wanted it too much."

"Forget about it," Diego said, patting my shoulder. "It was just one shot. We'll do a weekly scrimmage, turn you into a baller in no time." We flipped our collars up against the cold and cut across the court back to Amsterdam, where taxi tires were already grinding the new snow to brown slush that splattered silently against the curb.

After Diego broke off to go to the train, I kept walking, all the way home until my legs went numb. I felt more depressed than ever, but I didn't know why. I mean, I hadn't really needed a game of HORSE to tell me that going after you would be a bad idea; I already knew it. Which, I guess, was the problem.

Just because you know something is wrong doesn't mean you won't do it anyway. I know you know that feeling. I think all of us did.

By the end.

Chapter Ten

February 11
91 days left

I PRETTY QUICKLY ACCEPTED that not wanting you was an impossibility—or, at least, an idiotic plan that was both painful and completely futile, like that guy from Greek mythology who pushed the boulder up the hill and had to watch it roll back down, over and over. Ethan probably knew his name, not that I would have asked. With each passing day I resented him a little bit more. I couldn't help it. He had brought me into the group, introduced me to you, and then cast us together in the fucked-up period piece fan fiction he had written about you—for *you*—which culminated in my sitting next to you every day for two hours, trying to make real feelings seem pretend and building to a climax that would never, and could never, happen. Wasn't that Greek guy being punished by Zeus for something? I guess that would have made Ethan a god. Based on how hard he was power-tripping, it wasn't such a stretch.

"OK, everyone owes me thirteen bucks for their ticket,"

he said. We were huddled in front of Film Forum at 7:30 on a Saturday night to see *Jules et Jim*, a French New Wave movie from the 1960s that Ethan claimed was "mandatory viewing" to understand what he was "trying to accomplish" in *Boroughed Trouble*.

"What?" Diego bounced from foot to foot, his high-tops a few inches deep in snow. "You begged us to come, man. I thought this was a freebie."

"You should pay *us* for having to read subtitles," you said, your face barely visible from under an enormous faux-fur hood. "Joy even had to wear her glasses!"

"Yeah, you know, a night out in the city, I like to dress it up," Joy laughed. She was wearing bright red earmuffs to match her bright red coat, and every time Diego looked at her I could see a change in his eyes, that shift in focus of finally spotting the person you've been looking for in a crowded room. It made me resent him, too, because I wanted to be able to look at you like that, not have to fight the impulse with every muscle in my frostbitten face. My old teacher Mr. Cunningham used to say that my body was just a vessel for the role to live inside. It was the kind of pompous theater-speak I hated, but it was true; an actor's body was supposed to be a vessel, and so that night I was trying to make mine totally and completely empty.

The theater was packed, mostly with old people. By the time we got popcorn and soda and paid Ethan back in exact fucking change, it was so full that we ended up having to sit in separate groups. There were two seats open in one row near the middle, but when Ethan staked his claim, beckoning you—a.k.a. *babe*—to join him, you acted like you couldn't see him and squeezed into the three-seater behind him, next to Joy. Diego started in after you, leaving me to sit next to our illustrious director, but then Ethan quickly insisted that since he might need to point out important scenes to us, it was crucial that we all be together, which then meant that four of the five of us had to get back up, make everyone *else* in the rows stand up, and switch places. You also got up to go to the bathroom twice, so by the time the lights dimmed I was confident that at least 75 percent of the theater hated us, but that was OK, because I hated everyone, too.

Not only did I have a front-row seat to Diego having a pseudo-date with Joy, but Ethan made you scoot down so that he was in the middle ("Do you mind, babe?") and I was on the other side of him, smelling his aggressive body spray and watching him try to hold your hand every time you reached for the popcorn. ("It's gluten-free, babe. I checked for you.") The fact that you still seemed to reject his public displays of affection was cold comfort. I didn't mind so much that I didn't understand French, but I found myself wishing I couldn't speak English, if only to spare myself the torture of eavesdropping on Ethan's version of sweet nothings.

"You said, 'I love you,'" he whispered as the same words appeared on a black screen, over a French woman's voice. "I said, 'Wait.'"

"I said, *shut up so I can watch*," you whispered back, and someone behind us made a loud shushing noise.

Then the credits started, with some carousel music playing over a montage of seemingly unrelated stuff: a woman laughing, two dudes trying to open a gate, a kid throwing a dart, an hourglass, a painting. My eyes were already starting to glaze over. One of my dark secrets as an actor was that I really wasn't all that into artsy movies. If I was going to fork over thirteen bucks, I wanted to see some CGI explosions—or, at the very least, the Rock looking constipated with concern for the fate of mankind. The only thing that would have made this worth it was two hours of sitting next to you in the dark. Alone.

I looked down at Diego and Joy. They were sharing a box of popcorn and some Sour Patch Kids, each holding one, so that the other person kept having to reach into the opposite lap. Every few minutes one of them would whisper something to the other one—not a loud stage whisper like Ethan's, but the kind when your mouth has to be almost *inside* the person's ear—and laugh, their shoulders shaking in silent tremors. I seethed with jealousy.

It definitely did not help that *Jules et Jim* turned out to be about a love triangle where both of the main guys were obsessed with a woman named Catherine, who basically had the market cornered on Manic Pixie Dream Girls before anyone had invented them. She drew on a mustache just for kicks and fell into rivers and was sad and gorgeous and batshit and whimsical. But it was obvious it wasn't going to end well: anyone could see it coming. (OK, so I guess I was paying a *little* bit of attention, when I wasn't watching your right arm out of the corner of my left eye, trying to predict when your hand was about to dig into Ethan's popcorn so that I could put mine in, too. If I had put half as much effort into my calculus homework, I could probably have worked for NASA. But you never ate the popcorn, anyway. You just kept drumming your fingers on your jiggling knees. I thought it meant you were bored.)

But halfway through the movie, we'd never touched, not even "accidentally," and I was swiftly spiraling into a dark and fragmented place that felt less New Wave and more Fifth Wheel. Loneliness was bad enough when I was actually, physically alone, staring up at Pop-Pop's presidential memorabilia covering the walls of my makeshift bedroom, passing time like treading water and praying for someone (you) to send a hopeful ping into the void with a text . . . but being lonely in a group made me feel even worse. Luckily I had also drained a large soda and was about to piss myself if I didn't get to a bathroom soon, so I got up and edged my way out of the row, causing a chorus of groans from about half the theater. As I tripped over the clogs of the woman sitting in the aisle seat, who had refused to stand or even tuck her knees up, I glanced back to see Ethan wrapping his arm around your shoulders. And then, just like any good girlfriend would do, you leaned into him and whispered something in his ear.

You both laughed.

"You've reached the voicemail of Allison Anders, formerly Allison Anders Roth, of AAR Artists. Please leave me a message and I'll get back to you as soon as I can, or you can reach one of my assistants . . ." I held the phone away from my ear as my mother's disembodied voice read out a series of names and numbers. I thought about hanging up. I'd decided to call her mostly out of boredom, anyway, since I'd been sitting in the

lobby for an hour, unable to face the Molotov cocktail of lust and angst that awaited me back in the theater. I'd played four chess games already and was down to 5 percent battery on my phone, which was an even more compelling argument for hanging up on Mom's voicemail. But then I realized that she would see the missed call even if I didn't leave a message and would probably start concern-texting me a series of standalone question marks. So I waited, as instructed, for the beep.

"Hey Mom," I said, getting up and pacing across the geometric lobby carpet. "It's your most important client. Haha, just kidding, it's your son." Just then, the double doors to the theater opened; the movie was letting out. "I guess I . . . um, just wanted to say hi," I said, stepping back against the wall by the men's room, keeping one eye on the stream of people moving toward me. "And that it's like the Arctic Circle here, and that—" I felt someone watching me and noticed a girl a few feet away, zipping up her coat with a don't-I-know-you? look. I cleared my throat and lowered my voice.

"I, uh . . . miss you," I said, trying to sound nonchalant. "But I'm actually at a movie right now with some friends, so I guess that's a good sign. Except for the fact that I'm outside calling my mom, so . . ." I laughed gently, shaking my head. I definitely should have hung up when I got her voicemail. I hadn't wanted to leave her a dumb, rambling message. I hadn't wanted to leave her any message at all. I'd just wanted to hear her voice.

"Anyway, I know you're really busy," I said, "so you don't have to call me back. I'll talk to you later."

I ended the call and slipped my phone into my back pocket just as Ethan came out of the theater and spotted me.

"What the hell, dude?" he cried, tossing me the coat I'd left crumpled on my seat when I made my escape. "You missed half the movie!" You, Diego, and Joy followed a few steps behind him, looking restless, confused, and puffy-eyed, respectively.

"Sorry," I said. "I had to—"

"Take an epic dump?" Ethan asked, loud enough that a few strangers laughed.

"Um, *no*. I had to make a phone call." That was true. "To my agent." That was not true.

"Oh," he said begrudgingly, looking annoyed he couldn't be more annoyed.

"Consider yourself lucky," Joy said, wiping her eyes. "That was so sad."

"What happened?" I asked.

"Don't tell him!" Ethan said. "This is the kind of film you have to see from start to—"

"She drives her car off a bridge," you cut in. "With Jim in it."

"Babe!" Ethan said sharply, and you shook your head at him like someone training a dog. I felt my shoulders relax.

"And she makes Jules *watch*," Joy whimpered. She looked up at Diego, her lower lip quivering. "Did I get snot on your arm at the end?"

"It's OK," he said, smiling down at her. "This shirt is so old, it's basically Kleenex."

"I mean, who would do that?" Joy asked, her eyes wide and watery.

"A crazy person," Diego said.

"See, that's what I take issue with," you said, pulling on your coat while simultaneously dodging Ethan's attempts to help. "Why does the *woman* have to be some unhinged sociopath?" You rooted around in your purse and fished out a container of Tic Tacs. "That's just straight-up misogyny."

"Truffaut is not a misogynist," Ethan said, rolling his eyes. "He's a genius. Have you seen *The 400 Blows*?"

"Nah, I think my mom blocks those channels," Diego joked.

"Anyway," Ethan continued, ignoring our snickering, "Catherine doesn't do it because she's crazy, she just realizes she can never have him, or the kind of life she wants. It's about the choices you make when you feel desperate and trapped."

"I felt trapped watching that," you said, rolling your eyes and jiggling your jaw from side to side. "I'm going to the ladies' room."

"You have to see it," Ethan said, turning to me as you scampered off, clutching your bag. "I think you could really use it for Rodolpho's motivation at the end."

"Hold up, does your play end with murder-suicide, too?" Joy asked. "Because I thought ballets were depressing, but damn. This was worse than *Swan Lake*."

"It's . . . more nuanced," I said, mostly for Ethan's benefit. Really I wasn't sure I understood how someone could hurl themselves off a bridge just from wanting someone. I mean, I wanted you, but not *that* badly. Yet. Maybe Ethan was right, and I needed to study some unstable types, although people watching was more my speed than movie watching. It had always been a habit of mine, since I was little, to pick someone out of a crowd and try to imagine what it would be like to be them, sort of a Choose Your Own Adventure—I'd start with the shoes or the walk or some other detail and then let my imagination spin out from there. There were a dozen people standing around me in the lobby at that moment who I could use: The middle-aged man with the pleated jeans and slight limp, who would go home to Queens to care for his disabled brother; the twentysomething hipster couple with matching asymmetrical pixie cuts who might get into a fight on the train, and then, back on the sidewalk, she'd walk ahead of him, fighting tears, while he silently smoked a hand-rolled cigarette. Most of my made-up stories had depressing trajectories, which was something my therapist in L.A. would have called "worth exploring."

"Hey, Roth, you coming or what?" Ethan called.

I hadn't noticed that everyone had started walking without me and were almost at the exit. Diego, who had put on Joy's earmuffs, seemed to be doing some kind of impression of her, and she was snatching at them while Ethan laughed.

I felt you next to me before you said anything—as you pulled your hood up, the fur brushed my cheek, soft and prickly at the same time. I almost jumped.

"Think they'll ever do it?" you asked, looking up at me with eyes that seemed anime-wide all of a sudden.

My cheeks lit up with heat. "What?" I sputtered.

"Joy and Diego," you said. "I mean, it's so obvious."

"I don't know," I said, pulling my hat on. "He's taking his time, I think. Waiting for the right moment."

"Waiting is overrated," you said with a smile.

"Jesus Christ, come on, you need a formal invitation?"

Ethan yelled. He was already holding the door, and a gust of frigid February air snaked into the lobby. We started down the carpet.

"For future reference," you whispered, "if you're ever planning a jailbreak, you could at least take me with you."

"Yeah well . . ." I shrugged apologetically. "Every man for himself, I guess."

You scrunched up your nose in playful indignation as we reached Ethan and he cut in, taking your arm as you stepped gingerly out onto the ice of West Houston Street in your high-heeled boots. I felt my spirits lift in a way that felt like both a relief and a warning.

I couldn't make the feelings I had for you disappear, but I could leash them temporarily. At least until the play was over, I told myself.

It's hard to think back to when it all felt like such a game. I didn't realize then that you were right—that waiting wasn't always a virtue.

Sometimes, waiting is just the difference between being able to save someone, and being too late.

Chapter Eleven

February 12
90 days left

"LAST-SECOND CLUB SWITCH *there by Mickelson . . . he's got the ball below his feet, an awkward stance in this fairway bunker . . ."*

We were in the living room the next morning, Dad, Pop-Pop, and me, watching golf on ESPN despite the fact that I would literally have preferred to do anything else, including my art history homework or bringing dirty boxer shorts to the building's basement laundry room, which could have been used as a location for one of the *Saw* movies with zero set decoration.

But I was too lazy to do either of those things, and my coffee—despite being served in a truly humiliating mug emblazoned with my seventh-grade portrait—was still hot. And if I was honest with myself it was actually a *little* bit nice to be sitting on the couch with my dad, both of us bed-headed and bleary-eyed, with our tube-socked feet propped up on the coffee table. It felt almost normal, until I turned to look out the window and saw the snowy cityscape instead of Mom's lilac bushes.

I felt for my phone on the cushion beside me as the golfer stared intently at the tiny hole onscreen, adjusting the belt on his bright orange pants. Riveting entertainment. I knew Mom had sent a bunch of texts the night before, around 10:30 L.A. time, when I was already passed out; I saw them lined up on my lock screen when I woke up, to check if there was anything from you. (The night before, at dinner, you'd casually asked for my number "in case you want to run lines sometime," which had made my entire night. I'd chosen not to tell you that I already had your number programmed into my phone, and that I'd even given you your own ringtone.)

"You know, it *is* possible to live without that thing attached to your hand," Dad said. He had a thing about phones, a recent and incredibly annoying thing he had picked up on a meditation retreat. Apparently being too "plugged-in" interrupted the mind's ability to be silent, which was the key to true knowledge. Or something.

"I'm not even doing anything," I said. "I'm just holding it."

"But holding it means you're waiting for it to do something, and if your attention is focused on that, it can't be focused on *this*." He gestured to the cluttered living room.

"What, like golf and Nana's vitamin collection?" I asked. Dad gave me a withering look.

"Well if you're going to 'just hold' it, would you do me a favor and text your mother back?" he asked. "She's getting on *me* now."

"Jesus, it's been like twelve hours. Tell her to chill." I wished

I hadn't called her from the movie theater. I never actually called her, let alone left her a message, so she probably assumed I was out on a ledge somewhere.

Dad held up his hands—or one hand, anyway; his other had his coffee mug in a death grip. "I'm staying out of it," he said. I turned off the phone and tossed it onto the coffee table, on top of a stack of *New Yorker* magazines.

"Happy now?" I grumbled.

"Would you look at that, a double bogey," Pop-Pop said. "He's off his game today." I looked at the TV but all I saw was a big, green nothing. I couldn't even guess where the ball was supposed to be.

Nana got bacon and bagels from Zabar's like she did every Sunday, and by one o'clock the table was set with a spread that could have fed a reality show family with three sets of triplet farmhands. Golf was off and the radio was on, tuned to some jazz station. It wasn't exactly the stuff crazy weekends were made of, but at least it was dependably uneventful. I was on my second plate—and second hour of phoneless daydreaming—when the doorbell rang.

"Did you order a package?" Pop-Pop asked Nana, looking up from his section of the newspaper.

"Who delivers on a Sunday?" She took off her reading glasses and walked over to the buzzer while I went back to my bacon. I'd barely registered the exchange; my parents used to joke that every time they talked, it sounded like the grown-ups in the *Peanuts* cartoons, just a bunch of dull, wordless *wah wah wah*s. So when the doorman's voice crackled through to say that someone named Libby was there to see me, it took me a few seconds to catch up.

It felt like slow-motion, Nana's barely contained look of delighted surprise, the way she said, "It's for you, Davy," using the nickname that made me feel like I was six years old again and sitting with her in the planetarium at the Museum of Natural History, counting the minutes until the show was over and we could go to the gift shop for astronaut ice cream. Then the mental dominoes started falling and I realized that I didn't know a Libby, and that it had to be *you* standing downstairs in the lobby, talking to Bobby the weekend doorman, and that Nana was already telling him to send you up, and that I was still in tube socks and boxers, and that Dad was doing tree pose in spandex bike shorts like some sort of statue erected in the center of the living room to commemorate the utter humiliation of my life.

"Call back!" I pleaded, leaping up. "Tell him I'll come down!"

"Who is this girl?" Nana asked. "One of your school friends?"

I didn't answer. I didn't have time. "Dad!" I yelled, sprinting into my room. "Put on regular pants!" I ran my fingers through my hair, taking in my unmade bed with the faded Mets comforter, my open suitcase of dirty clothes, the framed bumper sticker over the dresser that read IMPEACH TRICKY DICK. I grabbed the nearest pair of jeans and pulled them on, shoving my feet into my boots so fast I almost tripped over a dusty medicine ball. My T-shirt didn't smell great, but I pulled a sweater on over it and hoped for the best.

I got back to the living room just in time to see Dad roll-ing up his yoga mat, still in the bike shorts. "Come on!" I said. "This isn't funny."

"It's a little bit funny," Pop-Pop said. He hadn't moved from the dining table and was watching me with a glint of amuse-ment in his eyes.

"You didn't mention you were having company," Dad said. "A heads-up would have been nice."

"I didn't know!" I shouted. I vaguely remembered telling you, probably overeagerly, that I was up for rehearsing one-on-one, any time, any place. But I think I'd also promised Ethan I would go to Staten Island, and that was definitely never going to happen, just like you, in my grandparents' apartment wasn't supposed to happen.

"Relax, honey, we're excited to meet your friend," Nana said. "But Kevin, you really should change."

"Don't act excited," I said. "Don't act any way. Just—" *Don't exist. Evaporate, please.* "—be normal." I swallowed nervously as I heard the telltale chime of the elevator doors opening. Out of the corner of my eye, I could see Dad stepping back into the sweatpants he'd slept in. It wasn't much of an improvement, but it would have to be good enough.

Nana, displaying a staggering lack of smoothness, opened the door before you'd even had a chance to knock.

"You must be Libby," she said. I shoved my hands into my pockets and then took them out again, crossing my arms over my chest. No pose felt casual.

"It's Liv, actually." You appeared in the doorway, so improb-able in the space that you looked like a hologram superimposed over the fading floral wallpaper. You were glowing, your cheeks rosy from the cold. Nana took your coat and you stepped into the apartment. If what you saw surprised you, it didn't register.

"Hey," you said.

"Hi." We locked eyes and I smiled dumbly. "I would've come down if I'd . . . um." I could feel my family staring at us, which made me even more self-conscious.

"No, it's OK, I'm early," you said. "I like your place."

"Thank you," Pop-Pop said, standing up.

"Sorry, Mr. Roth," you said, moving past me to shake his hand. "I mean, I like *your* place. It's really homey."

"Call me Phil," Pop-Pop said. "Also known as 'the actor's grandfather.'" I gritted my teeth; this was just as embarrassing as I'd feared. And I was still tripping over your apology that you were early. Early for what? How could I have made a date with you and forgotten about it? We hadn't even been drinking.

"I'm Barbara," Nana said. "Davy's grandmother."

"Which makes you . . ." you said, turning to my dad with an expectant smile.

"Dave's dad," Dad said, extending his hand. "Although I would also accept much-older brother."

"I'm an only child," I said quickly, and everyone laughed.

"Are you hungry, Liv?" Nana asked. It was a rhetorical question, since she was already making a plate. Within minutes, you were perched on the couch in your socks, balancing food on your knees and drinking coffee out of a mug printed with the title of a failed pilot I'd shot a few years back. I sat next to you, more awkward in my own (sort of) apartment than I had been at the movies. I felt like a goalie, my whole body on edge, ready to leap up at any second to block a dangerous shot.

"So how do you two know each other?" Dad asked. I'd been so preoccupied with his pants situation that I'd failed to notice his scraggly five-day beard growth or the shirt he was wearing, a souvenir from the Jewish Museum in San Francisco, printed with the words YO, SEMITE under a picture of trees.

"We're in Showcase together," you said.

"The play," I practically screamed.

"See, he doesn't tell us anything," Nana said. "Do you two play friends, or . . ." Her eyes twinkled.

"Strangers," I said, before she could finish. It was like I could only speak in two-syllable barks designed to stop conversation in its tracks.

"We meet on a bridge under cover of darkness," you said, leaning in conspiratorially, raising an eyebrow. "At the turn of the century."

"Interesting," Pop-Pop said. "Do I know this play?"

"Nope, it's an original," you said. "This guy, Ethan, wrote it—" You kept talking, but I stopped listening. *This guy.* You didn't call your boyfriend *this guy.* I floated silently to the ceiling.

You held court, with Dad and my grandparents in the palm of your hand. I remember watching them fall for you, all of them leaning in, warming themselves on your glow like you were a fire in the middle of winter. You told them all about growing up in the city—you lived just a few blocks from where Nana and Pop-Pop met at the Village Vanguard, which made them like you, and ID'd Thelonious Monk on the radio, which made them love you. You even handled awkward questions—"Are you Jewish?" Nana asked bluntly at one point, as if she could actually see the chuppah in the distance—with ease.

"Jew . . . *ish*," you said wobbling your hand. The gold polish was gone, replaced with a dark, mossy green. Still bitten, though. For some reason that detail always stood out. It meant you had . . . I don't know. Appetites, I guess. "My mom's Puerto Rican," you went on—hopefully not noticing my flop sweat—"so we eat *pasteles* at Pesach."

"We'll have to try that," Pop-Pop chuckled. The conversation kept going like that until Dad gave me a super conspicuous nod of approval and I finally decided to call the game.

"So, do you, uh . . . want to run some lines?" I asked, standing up so fast I almost toppled the coffee table.

"Yeah, we should probably get to it," you said. "It's past two." You held up your palm, which had *D, Sun, 2pm* written on it in purple ink. I must have looked confused, because you laughed and said, "Good thing one of us remembered."

"We might need to get your head checked," Dad laughed.

That's not me, I should have said. I knew I would never forget a date with you. I knew it and I said nothing. All I wanted was to get you alone. I didn't know what I'd done to deserve the luck of you showing up on my doorstep out of the blue, but I wasn't about to question it.

That was my first real mistake.

"Sorry about the mess."

We were sitting on opposite ends of my air mattress, which

made squeaky little farting noises every time we moved, giving
me great motivation for my character being moved to swift and
unexpected suicide.

"It's really fine," you said.

"We're getting our own place soon," I heard myself lie.
"This one's kind of small."

"I like it. It feels like people really live here, you know?"
You leaned back on your elbows, a loose tendril of hair grazing
my pillow. "My house is like a museum." You ran your fingers
over Pop-Pop's line of presidential figurines, standing guard at
the headboard like a chorus line of historical chaperones.

"I remember it being more like a zoo," I said, trying to find
a casual place to put my hands.

You laughed. "That only happens when my parents go out
of town. Like once a month."

I raised my eyebrows. "Lucky."

"I guess," you said. ". . . It's kind of lonely." You looked at
me sheepishly, the hint of a smile in your eyes. "I had like five
imaginary friends."

"So you've always been popular, then."

"I wasn't creative, though," you said. "Their names were all
Fifi. Fifi I, Fifi II, Fifi III . . ." You laughed and shook your head.
"I had a harem of clones."

"Mine's worse," I said. "I had an epileptic dog named
She-Bo."

"No!" You cracked up.

"Yup. And he was real."

"*She*-Bo was a *he*?" You had to put down Millard Fillmore
to wipe tears from your eyes.

"*Genetically* he was a he," I said, grinning. "I don't know how he self-identified."

"Stop it, I'm dying." You took a deep breath, but it failed to control your giggles. I'd never seen you so uncomposed. It was fucking amazing.

"You're—" *You're beautiful*, I wanted to say. But I couldn't. I didn't want to be that guy anymore. I was actually trying to keep friends.

"Hey." You sat up straight, and your sweater slipped down over one golden shoulder. Your face was still flushed from laughing, your eyes warm, dark pools that I gladly would have drowned in if you'd asked me. Did you mean "hey," or "*heyyyyyy*"? My heart beat wildly against my ribs.

"Isn't that the lady from the lobby?"

"Huh?"

You leaned in closer, and I realized you were looking past me, to the radiator cover by the window. On it was framed picture of Pop-Pop and Roberta Zeagler, the founder of our school, whose giant wrinkled face hung over the water fountain by the security desk. I saw her every day, but didn't even think about it anymore, because she was just my grandfather's old friend who had died before I was born, just a name that meant nothing—except when it got me a second-semester transfer to an elite New York school I probably couldn't have acted my way into, anyway.

"Is it?" That was the best I could do, feign stupidity.

A few awkward seconds ticked by until you shrugged and smiled. I could tell you knew but kept silent to spare my feelings. It was kind. Maybe that's why I was so eager to return the

YOU IN FIVE ACTS

favor later on, so eager to turn away so I couldn't see what was happening right in front of me. Except, cowardice feels different from kindness. You can tell by the sting. You can tell by the shame.

"Should we . . . ?" you finally said.

". . . Oh, right. Yeah. Let's rehearse." I'd forgotten completely about the script on my lap. I hoped I could remember how to read.

"Anything but the . . . you know," you said, smiling down at your knees.

"Yeah, that would be weird to do without . . . someone else here," I said, attempting a laugh that sounded more like a grunt. My breathing was getting fast and shallow. As if on cue, your phone pinged.

"Ethan?" I asked.

"No," you said, frowning at the screen as you typed something quickly with one thumb. "For once. I just forgot about something else I was supposed to do today."

"We can run lines any time," I said. "So, if you need to—"

"Nah, I'd rather be here." You curled your legs underneath you and shot me a smile that made me forget everything else. I needed something to do, fast, to distract me from the fact that I wanted to kiss you so badly my head felt like it might explode.

I flipped open my script to a random page and started reading. "The stars are like diamonds in the dark," I said, substituting volume for any kind of emotion. "They're the only things in this city that are free."

"Oh! Um, ok . . ." You flipped through until you found the right page. "Catch one for me, and we'll be rich."

"We?" I asked, making tentative eye contact with you. "A moment ago you called me a stranger."

"That was a moment ago," you said, looking up at me with a coy half-smile. I wasn't sure if it belonged to you or to Viola. "In this moment I feel differently."

"How can so much change in one moment?" I asked. "The world is the same. I am the same. You are the same. Nothing has changed except the time."

"Time changes everything," you said solemnly. Then you threw your head back and laughed, breaking character. "Oh, God. How did we get ourselves into this?" you groaned.

"I know, right?" I smiled. "Maybe we can ditch Ethan and just rewrite the script."

"I wish," you said, not looking at me.

"Should we keep going, then?"

"Why don't we just improvise?" You chucked your pages on the rug and raised your eyebrows, and I'll admit for a second I thought you might be thinking what I was thinking.

"What do you mean?" I asked, half expecting my voice to crack like I was twelve.

"Let's pretend we're on a bridge," you said. "What would you say to me?"

I looked at you cautiously; it felt like a dare. "As Viola?"

"No," you laughed. "Just as me. Or even better, a stranger. If you met a stranger and you were the only one around for miles, what would you tell them?"

"Wow, I don't know." I leaned back against the wall, feeling the mattress wheeze under my weight, knowing that every second it was getting closer to the floor but not caring. "Everything, I guess."

"So tell me everything," you said, leaning forward until your elbows were balancing on your knees. "Start at the beginning."

So I did. Just like I'm doing now. I started at the beginning and told you everything. About getting famous too early and letting it go to my head. About treating girls like shit and my friends only marginally better. About the divorce and the career flameout and how it caught up with me in Toluca Hills, ending in a school suspension after I got wasted during lunch and thought it would be a good idea to sneak into the gym and throw empty beer cans into the lap pool. I confessed it all, and you listened without judgment.

But there's something else I need to say that I didn't know yet on that Sunday afternoon:

Forgive me.

Chapter Twelve

February 24
78 days left

A FEW WEEKS LATER, I did something even scarier than letting my guard down with you: I went to Staten Island. When I said OK (the third time he asked) Ethan reacted like no one had ever gone to his house before . . . because apparently, no one had ever gone to his house before.

"Hell no," Diego said when I asked about it during our second, slightly less humiliating scrimmage. "If the subway won't go there, neither will I. It's a practical rule, not a prejudice."

You were less diplomatic. "There's a borough hierarchy," you explained at the end of rehearsal on Friday, as I was gathering my stuff to go with Ethan to the ferry. "You should only travel to the ones that rank above yours."

"So we can never leave Manhattan?"

"Brooklyn and Manhattan are basically even now," you said, your brows knit together adorably like you were crunching actual numbers for a Buzzfeed quiz on the sexiest borough.

"Parts of Queens are catching up. The Bronx is far, but at least you don't have to take an orange boat."

"Hey, great poems have been written about that boat," Ethan said. "Also Method Man grew up there, and my house could fit three of your apartments, so." He was in a great mood, not only because I was going to be the first friend to come over since middle school (it was going to be a sleepover, because Ethan didn't trust that I would actually make it unless he personally escorted me) but because rehearsals had been going especially well ever since your surprise appearance at my apartment. Not that he knew about that. He just knew that we had a different rhythm. Like two people who had been texting pretty heavily for the better part of two weeks.

It had started out slow—a few hours after you'd left, I wrote something like, **Thanks for listening to me play my tiny violin.** You didn't respond right away, which sent me into a brief panic, but then around ten P.M. you'd texted, **U are fucking awesome and I love ur violin—play you mine sometime?** which had the approximate effect of six 5-hour Energy shots taken back to back.

Then it was on, kind of. Really it was on and off, over and over, like a little kid playing with a light switch. We never talked much at school, but walking to the subway after rehearsals had become pure torture. Neither of us could say anything without a teasing smile, and it had gotten to the point where I could barely look at you half the time, because being with you made me feel drunk, which was almost the same as feeling brave, which brought me dangerously close to telling you how I felt. I could restrain myself for the duration of the ride to 86th, at which point I usually texted you some stupid joke with a winking emoji just to keep it going. (There was always plausible deniability with the winking emoji—it was just silly, unless it wasn't, and who could tell?) Then I'd wait for one of your middle-of-the-night missives, never bothering to wonder why you were always awake at two or three or even four A.M. They'd always wake me up because I deliberately turned the ringer volume to the loudest setting, just in case. I barely slept.

Valentine's Day was a landmine. I didn't see you all morning but couldn't resist sending a text: **Do you think Hallmark knows how gross-looking real hearts are? [wink]**. Then, when I showed up at the fountain for lunch, you were holding a gigantic bouquet of roses and wearing a necklace Ethan had gotten you, a little heart pendant with cute penmanship spelling out the words FUCK OFF.

"It's what you've been telling me for years," he said with a self-satisfied grin, but instead of rolling your eyes like you usually did, you actually hopped up and kissed him on the cheek. I felt like someone had sucker punched me; I hadn't really believed you were dating him until that second, and suddenly it was right in my face. FUCK OFF.

Dad says that when I was a kid and something didn't go the way I wanted it to, I'd cross my arms defiantly and scream that the day was ruined. Of course it was bullshit, and the next second I'd be playing Legos and popping fruit snacks like it never happened. But that day, Valentine's Day? That was ruined. I was a dick to everyone all afternoon. I took the message of the necklace literally. I blew off rehearsal, bought some weed from a guy in my English class, and went home to get baked.

It felt great, not feeling anything. For once I didn't wake up when your reply came at 3:46 A.M.: an animated gif of Audrey Hepburn from *Breakfast at Tiffany's*, sitting on the windowsill, one foot in her apartment and one on the fire escape, strumming her guitar. *Wherever you're going*, the text on the photo said, *I'm going your way*.

After that things went back to normal, normal being a total mindfuck. Our scene work was better than ever, off the charts.

I felt bad that I was going to Staten Island because Ethan was so excited about it, and because I was basically just using it as a recon mission to see if I needed to feel bad about being infatuated with you and to find out if he had seen you naked. But apparently there was a guest bedroom, with a real mattress and (presumably) no old-man smell, so at least, I told myself, that was something.

I'd imagined that the boat ride might be kind of cool—the big city dwindling down to a speck in the distance, Lady Liberty looming large—but when we got there at 5:30 the ferry terminal was completely mobbed, so much so that I wondered briefly, as I filed onto the boat behind him, pressed so tight against his back by the crowd that some of his hair got in my mouth, if Ethan was giving me some kind of method lesson for the play about the immigrant experience.

"At rush hour on a Friday, it's worse than the subway!" Ethan shouted.

We stumbled to the western side of the boat, where we stood shoulder to shoulder with businessmen in big-shouldered wool coats holding sloshing cups of foamy beer in their hands.

"I can't believe you do this every day, man," I said.

"I don't," Ethan said, rubbing his hands together. "I take a chartered bus."

"Then why the hell—"

"The experience!" he said. "This is an *experience*. The bus is just a bus."

He was leaning out and grinning so aggressively that I was afraid he'd yell, *"I'm the king of the world!"* when we started to move, but instead he pointed to a tiered building on the east side of the skyline and told me that his mom used to work as a secretary there. "Just like in *Working Girl*," he said proudly. I'd been a decade off on his movie reference.

The ride was twenty-five minutes, but cold enough that we didn't talk much. Ethan seemed genuinely psyched to have me over, which was kind of endearing, although some of the stuff he said ("My dad's really old. Most people think he's my grandfather, but he's not!" or "I have the *sickest* Blu-Ray set-up. There's a 90-inch HD TV, so you can watch *Citizen Kane* and see the outline of Orson Welles's bald cap.") still made me nervous. From the boat, Staten Island looked flat and desolate, kind of lonely. It was weird to think that New York City had this other big island in it that most people barely even noticed.

Ethan's dad *did* look really old when he met us at the ferry terminal. He was wearing a plaid golf cap and had a transistor radio around his neck, like someone carrying a giant boombox but even less cool. He was short like Ethan but much thicker, with tan skin and white hair, and he squeezed my hand so hard when we shook that my knuckles cracked.

"We're so happy to meet one of Ethan's Janus friends," he said as we lobbed our bags into the trunk of his sweet Mercedes. Only instead of Ethan it sounded like *Eh-tahn.*

"Ignore the Russkie accent," Ethan said.

"Ignore my impolite son, *Dah-veed,*" Mr. Entsky said. He motioned for me to get in the front seat.

"This is a great car," I said, running my fingers over the dash. I instantly missed my old Saab—well, Mom's old Saab that had been mine for a brief but memorable period during which I completely underappreciated it, ignorant as I was to the coming vehicular famine.

"Thank you," he said, pulling out of the labyrinthine parking lot into traffic. "So, tell me, how is my son's play?"

"You . . . haven't read it?" I asked, stalling.

"I've read it, I just want to know what you think." I saw him wink at Ethan in the rearview mirror.

"Dad," Ethan groaned.

"I think it's really strong," I lied. "Really interesting and . . . layered." Thanks to years of getting rejection phone calls from Daphne, I was a pro at using vague buzzwords that sounded good but actually meant nothing.

"Well," Ethan said, grinning down into his lap, "I mean, I wrote it, but you guys are bringing it to life. Everything's coming together. I actually think with a few tweaks, I can take it all the way."

"All the way?" I asked.

"Broadway!" Ethan said. "It's nothing but revivals now, and the original stuff is hack work."

"He wants his name in lights," Mr. Entsky said, smiling, and

I just nodded and tried to look like I was really into the passing scenery. I wondered if he knew that *Boroughed Trouble* was a Frankenstein monster made of characters and scenes borrowed from other playwrights. There was even an Italian immigrant character named Rodolpho in *A View from the Bridge*. Ethan hadn't even bothered to *steal* stealthily.

"I sent the script to a few agents," Ethan said. "And just so you know, dude, I'm inviting some VIPs to the performance. Stephen Karam, Tracy Letts, Lin-Manuel Miranda . . ." Ethan listed them casually, like they were old friends. But I let him have his fantasy. If anything, it gave me hope. If he was that deluded about the play, then maybe he was deluded about you, too. Maybe it really was all one-sided.

"You know, it was your movie that inspired him to be an actor," Mr. Entsky said as we turned onto a broad, tree-lined street.

"Oh," I said, gritting my teeth—my automatic nervous system response to anyone bringing up my one-hit wonder.

"Dad, come on," Ethan said, annoyed. "You know that's not true. It was the regional tour of *Newsies*. And it doesn't matter anyway, since I'm not an actor anymore."

"No, no, I remember it," Mr. Entsky said. "We took you to see it and by the end, when the little boy died, you and your mother were both crying, and afterward you started begging us to take you on auditions." He glanced over at me for a reaction and I tried to arrange my face in a way that I hoped would read as flattered. Inwardly, though, I was cringing. Why had I thought that going to Ethan's would be anything other than horribly awkward? Why hadn't I just said no like everyone else and spent the night lying in bed with my phone, waiting pathetically for you to text?

As if on cue, my phone vibrated in my coat pocket.

Regretting it yet? you'd written, with a grimacing emoji.

You have no idea, I typed back, with a wink.

Ethan's house was insane, not in the floor-to-ceiling photo shrine way of a secret serial killer, but in the columns-in-the-front, pool-in-the-back way of a secret rich kid. It looked more like the houses I was used to seeing in L.A., set back from the street, with a sprawling lawn and a circular driveway. His mom, a New *Yawk*–accented redhead who looked tired but significantly younger than her husband, met us at the front door and immediately ushered us into the kitchen, where she'd laid out bowls of candy and chips alongside trays of cheese and salami and cut-up vegetables arranged in rainbows.

"You can each have a beer if you want," she said, leaning against the pristine counter with a smile. "And Dave, let me know what you like on your pizza."

"Can we take this stuff downstairs?" Ethan asked, grabbing a fistful of M&M's. "I want to show Dave the basement."

I reached for the offered beer, figuring I'd need it to dull my jealousy. Ethan had you *and* his own wing of a mansion? It was like he was fucking Batman.

"Come on," Mrs. Entsky—"call me Audrey"—said, with a playful frown. "I put this stuff out as bait to keep you up in the sunlight with the rest of the humans for a few minutes. Humor me."

"Dad embarrassed me enough in the car," Ethan said, shoveling some pretzels into his mouth.

"Well, at least tell me what you talked about," she said. "What's the latest at school? How's the play going?" Her eyes lit up and she turned to me. "Dave, do you know Liv?"

"Mom!" Ethan said sharply.

"I've been hearing about her since Day One," Mrs. Entsky beamed. "Ethan's been smitten with her from when he was—" she lowered her hand to waist height "—and now they're *together*. I mean have you ever heard of a sweeter thing?"

"Nope." I hung my head, staring into my beer.

"You know I've never met her," Mrs. Entsky said. "I almost thought he made her up."

"*Mom*," Ethan growled again. "This is exactly why I want to take Dave downstairs, you sound like a drunk morning talk show host."

"If you're going to insult me you can make your own food," she snapped. "And since when do you not want to talk about her?" She turned to me. "I swear, he wants to sit here and chat like we're girlfriends most of the time."

"Jesus Christ, Mom," Ethan said. "OK, *I'm sorry*. But can we please just go? Dave and I need to work on his new scene."

Great, I thought miserably. The only thing that sounded worse than gossiping with Ethan's mom about you—or watching another old movie while he provided a steady stream of commentary—was learning a new scene. I was only interested in the play if you were in it. Reading lines with Ethan would feel like banging my head against a wall.

"Well, of course, honey," Mrs. Entsky said. "The play's the thing, right?"

"I guess, if you take that line completely out of context," Ethan sighed.

My phone buzzed again; I'd slipped it into my back pocket when we'd gotten out of the car.

Send pics! you'd texted. I glanced at Ethan. He hadn't looked at his phone since we'd gotten on the ferry. Which meant you were only texting me.

"Is everything OK?" Audrey asked.

"Oh, yeah, just my dad checking in," I lied.

"Tell him we'll take good care of you," she said. "I'm making popovers tomorrow morning."

"You coming?" Ethan called. He was already standing by a door down the hallway, beckoning impatiently. I turned my phone off. I didn't know what to write back just yet, and besides, I'll admit, it felt good for once to be the one keeping you waiting.

"Don't worry, there's no new scene," he said once we were safely out of earshot, down the stairs and around a corner into a carpeted, windowless den with a big leather sofa and a huge television sandwiched in between two bookcases lined with DVD box sets and collectible action figures staring out stoically from their original packaging.

"Cool," I said, "I wasn't sure if you asked me out here to work or just hang."

"I wouldn't make you come all the way out here just to rehearse," Ethan said, crouching down to open a cabinet under the TV. "I'm not that much of an asshole, am I?"

I walked over to a frame hanging on the wall. It was a Little League portrait, one of those preprinted cardboard things with the team photo in the middle and then a little oval picture of the kid by himself inset at the top. Ethan had a bowl cut, a missing tooth, and glasses that looked like goggles. You'd told me a few times that he'd been shy as a kid. Not like me. Mom always said I'd walk into a casting office at six years old like I owned the place. If one of us was an asshole, it definitely wasn't Ethan.

"Who do you want to be?"

"Huh?" I spun around to see Ethan holding two Xbox controllers.

"*Destiny*," he said. "Ever played it?"

I shook my head. "My parents never let me have a system," I said.

"Jesus." Ethan stared at the TV, pressing buttons and switching between screens with lightning speed. "My parents gave up when I was like seven. My dad had a hip replacement and they were desperate for me to do anything by myself. Hence my lair."

I sat on the couch next to him and picked up the controller, feeling like some sort of Amish kid on a Rumspringa. I'd played at friends' houses before, but not enough to get good. Still, I figured I'd rather have fun sucking at Xbox than whatever the alternative might be.

"It's standard POV shooter stuff, like *Halo*," Ethan explained. "You can be a titan, a warlock, or a hunter, and then within that you can be human, a sort of *Avatar*-looking alien, or a humanoid machine."

"What do you recommend?"

"Well, depends what skills you want to have. A titan's like

a big tank—you can take a lot of hits and Hulk out on people. A hunter's faster and better at shooting, and then a warlock just sort of fucks shit up with spells, and can drain life force and stuff like that."

As he spoke, Ethan selected the blue-skinned alien warlock character for himself. He wore a long black coat and had some sort of magnetic energy ball in his hand.

"I guess I'll be . . . a hunter," I said.

"Human or machine?" Ethan asked, reaching over to correct my button-pushing.

"Uh . . . human?"

"That's the most fallible," he said. "Just so you know."

"I'm prepared to die quickly," I laughed.

"That's good, Roth, because you are going *down*," Ethan said, hunching over his controller.

Within the first fifteen minutes, he'd sucked my life force three times, but I was weirdly more relaxed than I'd been in months. I think it was the fact that my mind was completely blank. No family, no school, no play, no future, and I didn't even have to worry about whether I was impressing anyone. I was just running around some dystopian planet trying not to kill myself by accident, which was a pretty satisfyingly low mental bar. I almost forgot why I'd been afraid it would be awkward in Ethan's house, until he reminded me.

"You've had, like, a lot of girlfriends, right?" he asked during a pause in play while my health bar was regenerating after a robot punched me.

"A few, I guess." I acted like I didn't know the actual number, which was seven. Eight if you counted Zoe Mueller, who

I "went out with" for a week in fourth grade but never even spoke to.

"Would it be incredibly lame if I asked your advice on something?" His tone told me he already knew the answer to that question, but I shrugged, bracing myself.

"OK, so, Liv and I hooked up like six weeks ago," Ethan said. "But since then it's like . . . whenever we're alone . . ."

I held my breath.

". . . she doesn't really touch me," he finished. I could feel him looking at me but I didn't want to see his face. It was harder to feel good about things that way.

"At all?" I asked, hitting a button to select my next weapon.

"I mean, she'll sometimes hold my hand," he sighed. "But if I try to kiss her, she always says it's not a good time. Because we're at school. But she never wants to go anywhere that's not school. I haven't even been to her house since the party."

"Huh. Weird." I was elated and leapt off a boulder onscreen in secret celebration.

"So is that normal?" Ethan deftly leapt out from behind a rock and dropped a bomb on me.

No, I thought. "I guess it depends," I said. . . .

. . . "Yeah." Ethan got quiet for a minute, and then out of the corner of my eye I saw him drain the rest of his beer and set the bottle down. "I know . . . she'll never like me the way I like her," he finally said.

"You don't know that," I said.

Ethan paused the game and went over to the bookcase on the right of the TV. He moved some video games out of the way on the bottom shelf, opened a hidden mini fridge, and took out two more beers. I kept avoiding eye contact.

"I just wish I knew why she started it," he said, handing one to me. "I never thought she'd make a move. I figured I'd always like her, and she'd never look at me, and that it would hurt but it would be enough."

I took a slug of my beer. It tasted bitter in my throat, like stomach acid.

"But this is worse," Ethan said. "I can't tell if she's even my girlfriend, really. And I don't want to ask her because if she says no . . ." He shook his head, grimacing. "I should get a titanium exoskeleton."

"I should find a bathroom," I said, standing up.

"Around the corner." Ethan nodded in its general direction; his hands were busy resetting the game. "We can switch characters, and maybe that'll keep you alive longer."

"I don't need your pity," I said, forcing a laugh. My hand was already in my pocket, on my phone, pushing the power button.

"Speaking of which," Ethan said, "This is so pathetic, but . . . if you get the chance, will you try to find out for me?"

"Find out what?" I asked, my heart racing as I felt a series of buzzes against my leg.

Ethan didn't turn around. "What she's doing with me, I guess."

As soon as I got into the bathroom, I locked the door and stood at the sink, reading through your texts, each one making me feel more and more like a dick:

hey, where'd u go?

don't have too much fun w/o me

can u just tell me if he has a bunk bed, or a sex
doll?

I'd been as guilty of mocking Ethan as anyone, but suddenly I didn't feel like doing it anymore. Just spending a few
hours with the guy had made me feel lot sorrier for him than I
ever thought I could.

What *were* you doing with him? It was a fair question.
He was in love with you, that much was painfully obvious, so
either you were too nice to let him down, or you were screwing
with his head. Maybe both. You struck me as someone who
liked to play games and keep secrets. I liked that about you. I
never stopped to wonder why.

Pretty busy, I typed quickly. Talk later.

I turned my phone off so you couldn't distract me and went
back out to get deservedly pummeled.

Chapter Thirteen

February 25
77 days left

BY THE TIME I GOT HOME Saturday, Dad was out doing a hot-yoga singles class, which sounded gross in every possible way, and Nana and Pop-Pop were on a day trip to Connecticut. My morning at the Entskys had started with cocoa and Frank Sinatra, followed by popovers and bacon. Ethan's parents even set out little place cards at the breakfast table. It made me feel like the time I went to my girlfriend's cousin's wedding sophomore year and they made me stand in the family photos. *I shouldn't be here*, I remember thinking. *Years from now, someone will look at these and go, who the fuck was that guy?* Somehow, I think I knew I was never going to be invited back to Staten Island.

That was the one thing I managed to be psychic about. Out of everything.

On the ferry ride back, I watched Manhattan bob closer and closer, and as my face got numb my mood started to slip below freezing, too. You hadn't texted me again, and I didn't feel like talking to you. I didn't know what to say. All I knew was I still wanted you, and that it felt like shit.

I was in boxers and tube socks, watching TV on demand and eating a homemade lunch consisting of a hotdog wrapped in a corn tortilla, when the buzzer sounded. I ignored it the first time—if it was a package it could be left downstairs, and anything else I didn't want to deal with—but when it rang again a few minutes later, I begrudgingly answered.

"Hello?" I asked, with my mouth full.

"Good afternoon, Mr. Roth," Bobby, the weekend doorman, said cheerfully. "Dave's friend Libby is here."

What the fuck? I almost said out loud.

"Uh . . ." I had already picked up, but Bobby thought I was Dad. I could tell him I wasn't home. I was kind of annoyed that you'd think it was cute to show up unannounced again, or that you'd just assume I had nothing else to do. But then again, I had the house to myself. And even though I wasn't sure I felt good about what we were doing, some extremely exciting scenarios I'd been imagining would become technically possible if I just said yes. I knew in my head that given the circumstances, it would be very, very wrong to let anything happen, but my head wasn't in charge of my mouth when I said "OK" into the intercom.

"Very good," Bobby said.

I hung up and sprinted to my room to get dressed.

When I opened the door, you were already halfway out of your coat, wiping your boots on the mat.

"Is anyone home?" you asked, peering over my shoulder.

"Nope, just me."

"Damn, 'cause I came for the bagels." You smiled up at me; we were close enough to kiss.

"Why'd you really come?" It came out more blunt than I'd meant it to, and you drew back a little. I noticed your eyes were bloodshot, even though the rest of your face looked normal, extra-pretty even. It gave me a weird feeling of unease, like seeing broken windows in an otherwise perfect house.

"To hang out," you said, cocking your head playfully. "Can I come in?"

I shrugged and stepped aside. You draped your coat over a chair and walked slowly to the center of the living room, which was a mess of dirty plates and unopened mail. Dad hadn't even folded up his bed, so the couch cushions lay scattered on the floor. I realized then that whatever fantasies I'd had about you never took place amid the paisley-printed rubble of my dad's midlife crisis. The shame of you seeing it made me angry. What were you doing at my house? What were you doing with me?

"Want help cleaning up?" you asked.

"Nope." I crossed my arms over my chest.

You stared at me for a long pause, like you were trying to read me or waiting for me to talk, but I didn't want to give in either way. It couldn't have been more than ten seconds that we stood there in silence, but it felt like minutes ticked by, a weird, sexually charged high noon with balled-up socks instead of tumbleweeds.

"What's wrong?" you finally asked, narrowing your eyes. "Are you mad at me or something?"

"No," I said, my jaw getting tense.

"Okaaaaaaay," you said, pursing your lips. "So what's up?"

I shrugged. "It's kind of weird that you just dropped by again. You could have given me a heads-up."

"I'm sorry," you said, shifting uncomfortably. "I just . . . I was in the neighborhood, so . . ."

I laughed. "Come on."

"I *was*," you said. "I actually have somewhere to be, though. So if it's not a good time, I'll just be on my way." Your tone was defensive, and I was grateful. All of a sudden I was looking for a fight.

"Why are you here?" I asked. "Did you just want to see me?"

"Maybe I did," you said, crossing the room and grabbing behind me for your coat. Our bodies actually pressed together for a second, sending a dull ache of longing through my limbs. "Not anymore, though."

"Why?" I asked. "Because I didn't text you back within some allotted amount of time?"

"No," you said, struggling with your zipper. "Because you're being a jerk for no reason."

"If you wanted to find out more about Ethan, you could just ask him," I said, before I could stop myself. "Or better yet, go to his house. You're his girlfriend, right?"

You glared at me. You weren't wearing the FUCK OFF necklace, but I got the message loud and clear. "That's really none of your business."

"I think it is," I said. "Because instead of showing up at *his* house, you're at mine. And you didn't come to run lines, right?"

You stared at me wide-eyed but said nothing. Neither of us made a move for the door.

"You don't understand anything," you finally said. "I can't just . . ." You shook your head, narrowed your eyes. "It's complicated."

"Why, because of his stupid play?" I asked.

"It's not stupid to me!" you cried. "I *need* that play. I don't have an agent or a résumé or a fucking Golden Globe nomination. I'm not some diamond in the rough like Joy, and I can't write my own ticket like Ethan. I'm an aspiring actress in New York City. I might as well say I'm an ant in an ant farm."

You are special, I should have said. Instead, I laughed dismissively, like a dick.

"You can't even see what you have, can you?" you asked. "Everyone at school would kill themselves to be you. And you don't even care."

"I didn't think *you* cared," I said. "I thought you were better."

You nodded slowly, your eyes glistening somewhere between anger and tears. "I thought you were nicer," you said. I swallowed, hard.

"You should go to Staten Island," I said. "I'm not his understudy."

I felt guilty when the door slammed behind you, but not as guilty as I feel now. If I had known what you were going through, and how bad it was getting, I never would have said any of it. I never would have said anything at all. I would have opened that door and held you in my arms and never let you go.

Act Three

Liv

Chapter Fourteen

February 25
77 days left

I SHOULDN'T HAVE JUST SHOWN UP at your house, I knew that—
don't you think I knew that? I hadn't even planned to, but then
the train screeched to a stop at 86th and I was already on the
platform before I even realized I'd stood up. This time it wasn't
an accident, though—"*D, Sun, 2pm*." *God*, how high had I
been when I'd written that down? High enough to forget who
the "D" stood for—and as I climbed the stairs up to Broadway,
I just kept thinking, *maybe*. Maybe you'd be home. Maybe
you'd let me in. Maybe sitting in your room, listening to you
talk while your grandma clinked around in the kitchen would
work again, and I could leave feeling happy and hopeful and
not like I needed to get back on the train to go meet the other D,
the one who gave me that feeling in a bottle for twenty bucks.

But that had been a mistake, clearly, and so I was panick-
ing as I walked as fast as I could to the subway, my boots slip-
sliding on the black ice, my skin sweaty under my clothes, my

heart racing so fast it was hard to believe I hadn't already taken something. The night before I'd gotten drunk and stoned, which took the edge off the Ritalin, and drifted off into an easy sleep, but I'd woken up in the morning with a monster headache and I was all out of pills so I knew what I had to do if I wanted to feel normal again.

It really does go the way they say it will, a Just Say No cliché all the way. In middle school, there was this acting troupe that came to perform sometimes, a bunch of hammy college kids who did Afterschool Special–style skits about drugs and sex and all of the other things that are supposed to be scary but end up being mind-numbingly boring since they happen in middle school assemblies. A girl would be sitting on a stoop with her friends, and some popular guy—it was always the popular guy, who you could tell was a total asshole, just based on his preferred wardrobe of leather jacket and jorts—would offer her a joint and she'd be tentative but then everyone else would act like it was no big deal, and by the next scene she'd be blowing rails off the seat of someone's motorcycle, needing something, *anything*, to make her feel good.

Obviously some of the details didn't apply to me, like I would never listen to anyone wearing jorts, not even Drake, and my first joint came from my dad—well, from his sock drawer, anyway. No one was around to pressure me to light it. If anything, I became the instigator, the girl whose parents let her do whatever, who could always throw a party and who never judged. And it was just parties, for a while. I mean, I always smoked, with Jasper and by myself, but harder stuff was strictly social. I'd shroom or take ecstasy . . . I only did coke a few times, because I'd seen way too many celebrity noses cave in on themselves, and I liked mine too much to risk it. But pills were different. They were so easy, so quick—now you see it, now you don't!—and they didn't leave a mark or make my hair smell or inspire me to eat an entire can of Pringles dipped in ketchup.

Ironically I started using pills to make me feel *less* like I was dying. My mom had some Vicodin way back in the medicine cabinet from an old surgery, and the day after Jasper dumped me, when all I could do was lie motionless, crying until I couldn't breathe and then dry-heaving over the toilet, I took one just to see if it would make me feel less like the entire world was a sucking black hole—and it did. That worked for about a week, but I had to stop taking them when she noticed how empty the bottle was getting. Painkillers in general were harder to get, but I convinced my therapist to prescribe me Xanax, and to balance that out I started taking Adderall or Ritalin, or whatever smart drug I could get my psychopharmacologist to prescribe by phone when I complained that I still had trouble focusing. Those ones made me manic and wired, so I always needed booze or weed to sleep. And since Jasper was gone, I had called Dante, and he had delivered, literally.

But that kind of customer service didn't last. I'd texted him that morning and he'd said he was busy, that if I needed it so bad I could come to him, or else he'd hook me up Monday night. I ran down the subway steps two at a time. I could hear the train coming, and if I moved fast enough, I thought I could make it on before the doors closed. Maybe. *Maybe.*

He met me on 110th, at the top of the park, wearing a big puffy jacket over a hoodie and carrying a heart-shaped Russell Stover box, which was conspicuously missing its cellophane wrapper. When he saw me, he held out his arms and broke into a big grin.

"Got you something, honey," he said with a wink, holding out the box. "Sorry I'm a little late." An older couple passing by smiled at us, thinking they were witnessing a sweet moment. They didn't know he was giving me a different kind of candy.

"Clever," I said.

"Right?" Dante looked proud of himself. "Did you bring something for me?"

"Yeah, but I didn't put it in anything." I started to reach into my purse, but he stopped me.

"Yo, be discreet, please." His smile disappeared. "We're not at your house anymore. We're gonna sit on a bench and talk, and then I'm gonna hug you goodbye, and you slip it into my pocket."

I followed him to a nearby bench, where we sat side by side. He draped an arm over my shoulders. I figured it was just for show, like the candy box, but I couldn't tell, and I couldn't shove him off like I did with Ethan.

"So listen, this stuff is a little different from what I gave you last time," Dante said, squinting at a traffic cop writing a ticket across the street. "It's better, though."

"What is it?" I asked. The pills he gave me at the party had been big and white and unmarked, probably homemade. They'd felt like a mixture of molly and Percocet, turning my heart into a DJ and my brain into a swimming pool.

"Nuvigil," Dante said. "It's like a souped-up Adderall. It's for narcolepsy or some shit. It'll get you nice and buzzed, but you can get work done, too. I tried some yesterday and was mad productive. I even fixed the copy machine."

"You work? Like, in an office?"

"No, I just stand on a random corner all day whispering and handing out baggies." He rolled his eyes. "Yes, I work."

"Sorry," I mumbled.

"Anyway, it's basically a pharmaceutical-grade amphetamine. But listen, that means it's potent. You shouldn't be taking more than one a day."

"OK, doctor." I jiggled my knees, feeling the candy box rattle in my lap. It would be so easy to slip my hand inside and open the bottle, palm one pill, and pop it onto my tongue without anyone seeing. It would mean I wouldn't have to wait a single second longer to stop feeling so shitty and sad. It might even take the image of your face out of my head, when you were standing by the doorway looking at me like you could see right through me and were disgusted by what you saw.

"I'm serious, though," Dante said. "I could only get you ten, so that's got to last. The doctor out in Bayonne who hooked me up is a little jumpy about our arrangement, so until I prove I can sell it, he's squeezing them out one by one like a human Pez dispenser. Don't pop this shit like it's Advil."

"I won't," I groaned. I reached into my bag for my Tic Tacs, hoping maybe I could get a little placebo effect going. While I was in there I counted out ten twenties from my wallet and folded them into my hand. My savings account, courtesy of one commercial voice-over I'd booked junior year, was getting dangerously low. If I didn't get some means of income soon, I'd have to resort to "borrowing" mom's ATM card again.

"There are some side effects, but they're not bad," he said. "Dry mouth, nausea, dizziness . . ."

"Imminent death?" I asked with a smirk.

I was kidding, I was kidding, Jesus Christ, I was kidding.

"Stop," he said. "You'll be fine if you space them out. Now, you ready?"

I nodded.

"OK, well, see you later gorgeous," he said loudly, pulling me up and wrapping me in a bear hug that felt better than I wanted to admit. I dropped the bills into the pocket of his hoodie and slipped the fake heart into my bag.

I was only about seven blocks from Joy's place. We'd barely hung out lately—things had been tense already, and then rehearsals had consumed our lives—but I knew that if I texted her, right then, we could meet up for coffee or a movie, or sit barefoot on her couch watching some terrible rom-com on cable, eating an Entenmann's cake out of the box with plastic forks and talking shit about anyone who seemed happier than us. I needed that. But in the Joy version of my afternoon, I couldn't take the pill, and I needed that more. I just wished I didn't have to be alone.

Which made me realize, maybe I didn't have to be.

Looking back I see myself slipping, sliding, clawing at a fire escape ladder. That split-second decision was when I started to fall.

"What are you doing now?" I asked Dante. I smiled at him expectantly, trying to pretend that I liked him more. He wasn't nearly as cute as Diego, but he had a kind of gruff charm when he wasn't trying too hard.

"Just going to chill with a few friends over on the east side," he said.

"Can I come?" I asked. The question seemed to take him aback.

"Uh, you seem cool, but I don't like to socialize with customers," Dante said. He looked me up and down and smiled. "Besides, you're a little stuck up for this crowd."

"*Besa mi culo*," I said sweetly. Kiss my ass. I knew it was a gamble, but I was betting he'd laugh, and he did.

"I don't know," he sighed, rubbing his chin, which was covered in a thick growth of black stubble. "I mean, not that rolling up with a beautiful girl wouldn't make me look good, but . . ."

"I'm not really a customer, anyway," I said. "I'm your cousin's friend. I could just be your friend." I was still smiling, but I said *friend* firmly. I needed Dante to know that I wasn't interested in him that way. And besides, I was already sort of dating someone else I wasn't interested in that way.

"That's the thing, though," Dante said, frowning. "Customers aren't friends, and friends aren't customers. You pay me, you're a customer. So I don't want you coming around next week trying to get me to front you because we're buddies now."

"I won't," I promised.

"Can you be cool?" he asked.

"I'm always cool," I said. But the pulsing in my temples and the sour ache in my stomach told me otherwise. I hadn't eaten anything all day, so on our walk east we stopped at a deli,

where I got a granola bar and a Diet Coke. I had the pill in my
mouth before we were out the door, the carbonated bubbles
tickling my throat as a loud chime rang out over my head, making me feel like a boxer stepping back in the ring, getting ready
to start a new round.

It turned out that Dante's friend lived in the housing projects
just off 105th Street near the river, which made me feel uneasy
and then ashamed of feeling uneasy. After all, I wasn't supposed
to be some bougie bitch who couldn't hang. I was the cool girl
who was down for whatever, and who was about to get high.
I already felt a flutter in my veins and a cottony feeling in my
ears; I could feel it coming on, the first licks of a wave that
would eventually crash over my head, dragging me under. *Just
wait for it*, I told myself as we got buzzed in by a security guard
behind scratched, bullet-proof glass. *Any second now, it'll kick
in, and then nothing will matter.*

Dante's friend, who got introduced to me as Smoke Dog,
was tall and skinny with a deep voice and a lazy smile. The living room was lined with couches, all angled toward a big TV
where two other guys were playing some video game, the first-
person kind where you're just running around a gray waste-
land, shooting at anything that moves. The air was thick with
smoke; I saw a huge blunt propped against an ashtray on the
coffee table. Adrenaline zipped through my body; my vision
seemed to sharpen. I felt like a soda can that someone had
shaken before popping the tab.

"This is Liv," Dante said, guiding me in with his hand on
my back.

"Welcome," Smoke Dog said. "You can ditch coats any-where, but it's gonna get crazy soon, so keep whatever you need on you." I clutched my bag to my chest, my pulse beating like a bass line through the thick leather. Suddenly it felt like I needed everything. But my skin was singing and I wanted to feel light and free and so I stuck my wallet in one back pocket of my jeans, my keys in the other, and another pill in the front right pocket—just in case. Then my coat and my purse disappeared, I didn't know where, and someone was handing me a bottle and someone else was passing me the blunt and then I was gone. Just like I wanted.

Here's what I remember, spots of static through the haze: Sitting on the couch, running my nails over my wrists; laugh-ing so hard at something that I actually physically couldn't stop; having an intense conversation with a girl wearing dia-mond hoop earrings that I couldn't take my eyes off of, like a cat tracking a butterfly; leaving that pow-wow to stumble to the bathroom, where I threw up quickly while holding the door closed with my foot; walking up an endless stairwell clutching Dante's arm; standing on the roof, smoking a ciga-rette, watching the city sparkle and sway until I got pulled back, hard, and someone yelled that I was standing too close to the edge.

Somehow it had gotten dark. Time slowed down and sped up but neither it nor I could seem to stand still.

I was coming down by that point, slowly but surely, the wave retreating as the shine wore off the world. I remember staring at my phone and seeing no little number where the new messages should have been and having the brief, sudden urge to hurl it off the building, and then bursting into tears instead. Next I was tripping down the stairs and following a thumping bass line to a door and stepping inside, where I saw Smoke Dog sitting on the couch with a girl on his lap. She was facing him, kissing him, running her hands up under his shirt, and it made me want to text you, but then I remembered that you hated me and so I decided to take the second pill instead.

I traced my way back to the bathroom by holding on to the walls, and when I got inside I looked in the mirror, my face not quite in focus, like someone had dragged their thumb across and smudged it. I dug the pill out of my pocket and then dropped it by accident into the sink, and there was a brief, awful pause when I thought it had gone down the drain, and the loathing I felt for myself in that moment was so deep and piercing that I felt like turning around and going back to the roof and taking a running leap, but then I spotted it, stuck to the porcelain, damp and bitter but still intact, and that was enough.

I had just washed it down when someone started banging on the door. There was no lock and I couldn't hold it closed that time, so within a few seconds it was open and there was Dante, standing with Diego, who had the same look on his face that you'd had at your apartment that afternoon, or that Joy had had in the laundry room at the party, or that Ethan had every time I recoiled from his touch. It was a naked stare of confused disappointment. It was a deafening chorus screaming in unison, *You're not who we thought you were.*

My exit from the party was much less gracious than my entrance.

"I don't need a babysitter," I spat at Dante, who, with Diego, was physically removing me from the building.

"Keep your voice down," Dante said, as we squeezed through a cluster of people in the hallway who watched me through half-lidded eyes, laughing. "You're embarrassing me, and yourself."

"Why'd you even bring her here, man?" Diego whispered.

"I told you, she *begged* me," Dante said. Once we made it to the hallway he grabbed my arm roughly and spun me around to face him. "Listen, my supplier is here. It doesn't look good for me to be hanging around with underage bitches who can't handle their shit."

The second pill was starting to lift me up, up, up by that point, so the words barely registered. "I'm sorry," I said, blinking into the fluorescent lights. My coat and bag had magically reappeared, and Diego was helping me put them on.

"You can find a way to make it up to me," Dante said.

"She doesn't owe you anything, man," Diego said. "If anything, this is your fault. Come on, Liv." We were halfway down the stairs when Dante called after us.

"*No me jodas.*" Don't fuck with me.

Diego winced, but we kept going.

"Sorry I don't have money for a cab," he said once we got back out onto the street.

"I don't care!" I said, and I didn't. The air felt sharp against my face, in a good way, like pins and needles, a rush of blood into an empty limb. The street lamps had just turned on. They looked like stars caught in fishing nets. "I can get home," I said, the words slurring together. If he had let me, I probably would have walked the whole way.

"No, I'm coming with you," Diego said. "You look . . . tired."

I didn't feel tired, not in my brain, anyway, but my legs were getting heavy, so I leaned on him while we walked the four long blocks over to 5th Avenue and then five blocks north to the train. I concentrated on the sound of my heels clacking on the concrete, trying to keep time with my thundering heart.

I threw up again at the mouth of the subway, into a garbage can. I couldn't tell if the pill came out. Maybe Dante had been right—maybe one was enough. I felt shaky and sick.

"You won't tell Joy, will you?" I asked, when Diego emerged from the nearby convenience store with napkins and Gatorade. He guided me over to the same bench that Dante and I had sat on hours earlier—it seemed like a lifetime ago—and helped me wipe my face.

"No," he said. "Not yet."

"Is that a threat?" I flopped back against the bench closed my eyes, feeling the street tilt. He held the bottle up to my lips. Fruit punch. I made a gagging noise.

"No," he said again. "I don't know. I just know she's worr— she thinks about you. Misses you or something."

"Fuck her," I groaned. "I mean, I'm sorry, I know you're in love with her, but fuck her. If she misses me so much why doesn't she fucking text me?" Diego got quiet for a long time after that.

"Does she know?" he finally asked.

"About me or you?"

"Me."

"No," I said. "She doesn't notice anything that's not part of perfect Joyland."

He laughed.

"Well, I won't tell if you won't tell," I said, slumping against him. The words came out in a slush, linked like a daisy chain.

"Let's get you home," he said.

I slept fitfully through the train ride—the pill must have come up, either that or it was a pretty shitty drug for narcolepsy—and the next thing I knew Diego was more or less carrying me through the lobby of my building, past Hector, and into the elevator. He couldn't hold me up and root through my bag for keys, so he knocked, and Mom answered the door in silk pajamas, holding a glass of wine.

"It's only 9:30," she said, with a little smile. "I didn't expect to see you until tomorrow."

"Surprise!" I said, still clutching Diego for support. My eyelids felt so heavy, I could barely keep them open.

We walked—well, he walked—into the living room, where Dad was sitting on the couch. There were takeout boxes on the coffee table and an old movie was playing on the TV.

"*We go back a long way,*" some guy on screen was saying. "*And I'm not gonna piss that away because you're higher than a kite.*" I started giggling.

"Honey," Dad said, frowning, "I think you should go to bed."

"Sleep it off, baby," Mom agreed, giving me a swift, dry kiss on the cheek. "There's aspirin in the cabinet. Diego, are you"—my eyes were just slits by then but I could hear the raised eyebrow in the tone of her voice—"staying over?"

"No, I'm just dropping her off," Diego said, ushering me down the hallway to my room, basically lifting me by the armpits while my toes brushed the carpet runner.

"Thank you for that," I heard Mom call after us. "I'm glad she has good friends to look out for her."

I can look out for myself, I thought, the words dragging through my brain, heavy as bricks. I believed it. I thought I was holding it together, when really I was falling fast.

Which wouldn't have been so bad if I hadn't taken everyone else down with me.

Everything that happened next, it was all my fault.

Don't you think I know that?

There's no drug strong enough to ever let me forget.

Chapter Fifteen

March
Two months left

IT DIDN'T TAKE LONG for Nuvigil to become my new best friend. It made my skin tingle, took a hundred pounds off my brain and another five off my body because I was too busy to eat but never too busy to drink, gallons and gallons of water, like a camel, or bottles of soda that fired like Pop Rocks on my desert of a tongue. At the beginning it kept me high for ten hours at a time, but the best kind of high, the kind that dulls the pain and heightens the senses at the same time. I could memorize the entire *Boroughed Trouble* script in an afternoon, or write a paper on the Harlem Renaissance that actually sounded good because I'd stayed up till four reading the books and writing feverish notes in the margins instead of googling the Wikipedia entries an hour beforehand like usual.

But it was hard to come down from, and I couldn't sleep unless I took a few Ambien or smoked a few bowls, sometimes both, washed down with at least two glasses of wine from the stash in the pantry, the good stuff that tasted like velvet and left a purple ring on my lips. And then I'd wake up feeling like shit run over by a dump truck, so I had to take a pill as soon as I got up, and then it all started again. Pretty soon I was up to one and a half a day, then two, going through them twice as fast as Dr. Dante recommended, but that was the thing with medicine: when it wore off you had to take more, otherwise it stopped working.

I needed it to work, because Showcase was looming, getting bigger and bigger in the distance like a wave crashing into shore, and I had to be better than I'd ever been, with a director who never gave me notes because he was too busy trying to make out with me, and a costar who all of a sudden hated being in the same room as me. Which kind of affected our chemistry.

"WHAT HAPPENED?" Ethan yelled one day when we did a run-through for our faculty supervisor, Mr. Francisco. "This scene was *perfect* last week!"

I couldn't remember when last week was, or what we had done differently, but apparently it was important because Ethan shut his script with a thud and ran his hands through his hair, his eyes popping out behind his glasses like he was a NASA engineer watching a space shuttle explode. I glared at him and chewed the inside of my cheeks. This terrible thing had happened where just looking at him had started to repulse me, so I was being a giant bitch pretty much all the time, and I was actually even better at being a bitch on Nuvigil since I was so focused.

"You look and sound exactly like Charlie Brown right now," I said under my breath.

"Bill," he said, turning to Mr. Francisco, which was exactly the kind of thing Ethan did on purpose to make people not like him, calling teachers by their first names. "I promise, it's not usually like this."

"What is it usually like, then?" Mr. Francisco asked. He had snow-white hair and a face dotted with broken blood vessels. Gin blossoms, people called them. I wondered if Mr. Francisco was a boozehound, or if he'd done so much acid in the 60s that his brain looked like a big gray honeycomb. (Joy would sometimes comment, out of nowhere, that MDMA took "ice cream scoops" out of the frontal lobe, or that the DEA listed Adderall in the same class as heroin and coke. I'm pretty sure eighth-grade health class scared her straight forever.)

"Let's just take it from the top," Ethan said, sitting back down in his seat looking sweaty and mad. "Scene one, Viola's entrance. If we can't get this one right, people, then I don't know what we're doing here."

"I don't know what *I'm* doing here," you said under your breath.

I'd almost forgotten you were there because I was trying so hard to forget you just weren't talking to me. But I looked straight at you and smiled to pretend it was a joke, so that Ethan wouldn't flip out. You looked disgusted. I wanted another pill.

"Places!" Ethan barked and walked off stage while you assumed a crouched position front and center, building your bridge. *Or burning it*, I thought miserably. One thing Nuvigil couldn't seem to do was take my mind off you. But I guess if anyone ever marketed a drug that made you forget a crush, no one would even go outside anymore, we'd all just lie in bed overdosing.

I watched the muscles in your back move under your shirt as you pantomimed hammering, desire bubbling up from beneath the restless relay race of electrodes in my brain trying to keep me steady.

"And . . . action!" Ethan called.

"It's not a film set," Mr. Francisco sighed.

I took a deep breath and tried to get into character. I was totally off-book, but as exhausted as I was from so little sleep and food it was really hard to commit to being a suicidal Polish garment worker whose mother had just died of tuberculosis. Still, I tried to channel how I'd felt leaving, humiliated, from your apartment building—that need to just be anywhere else, and fast.

I ran toward you, trying to arrange my features in a way that looked like I was "making a choice" about how to enter the scene instead of just moving from one place to another. You saw me and leapt up. Rodolpho was supposed to be shocked, but you just looked bored. At least we were both phoning it in.

I stopped short and turned around.

"Wait, wait!" you called. "Who are you? What are you doing here?"

I looked back over my shoulder. Maybe I was hearing things, but I could swear that the line hadn't always sounded so accusatory. *Why are you here? Did you just want to see me?* Then it dawned on me: we'd already done the scene at your apartment.

"Nothing," I said, suddenly much more defensive than Viola was supposed to be. *Maybe I did. But not anymore.* "I was just leaving. I lost my way."

"It's the middle of the night," you said. "This bridge isn't finished."

"Cut!" Ethan yelled. "You're not supposed to be pissed that she's there. You work the night shift with a bunch of old dudes who don't talk to you—this is a beautiful woman your age. You want to keep her there forever, not scare her off."

"Right," you said, looking down at the stage.

"And Liv, you look like you don't know where you're going. Do you know where you're going?"

"To jump off a bridge," I said, crossing my arms over my chest, feeling the faint but manic *thumpthumpthumpthumpthump* that had become my heart. In the theater's state-of-the-art acoustics, I wondered if everyone could hear it.

"Exactly," Ethan sighed, "so that should be the only thing motivating you in this scene. You are *determined* to jump off that bridge and you're not going to let some handsome stranger you just met get in your way."

"Got it."

"Do you?" Ethan narrowed his eyes, tapping his pen on his knee. "Do you get it? Because there's a difference between being determined and being on speed." He pushed up his glasses. "You look like the Roadrunner."

Icy fear shot through my veins. How could he know? No one knew, that was the magic. Not that my parents even cared that I drank their wine or smoked pot in my room, but I was careful. I only drank from open bottles. I left my windows cracked and lit lavender-scented candles. I kept my weed folded up in a maxi pad at the bottom of a box of super-plus tampons. I took fucking photos and put everything back, and I never got caught, I was *careful.*

I was trying to think of something to come back with, some explanation or defense, when Ethan just laughed and said, "Stop drinking so much diet soda, that stuff'll kill you."

The relief hit so quick it made me nauseated.

When I came back from the bathroom, you and Ethan were alone on stage. You both looked miserable, like you were waiting for Godot but with period cramps.

"Well," Ethan shouted when he saw me, pacing back and forth across the "bridge" that was marked on the floor with three pieces of gaff tape, "Mr. Francisco thinks we're not ready to go up in a month. He told me I should consider recasting."

"What?!" The pill hadn't even dropped into my stomach and I felt a rush of vertigo. I knew if one of us got recast it would be me. You were a name people recognized. They didn't know everything you'd told me in confidence, how you'd never even wanted to act, how your mom had pushed you into it, or how the *Saving Nathan* shoot ended up being so stressful that by the end of filming your parents were sleeping in separate rooms. They didn't know and you wouldn't tell them, so it would be me on the chopping block. Showcase could come and go and everyone else would get handshakes and business cards from agents and casting directors and I would get some terrible gap-year job folding palazzo pants at Forever 21. Even worse, Showcase was a half course credit. Without it, I wouldn't even graduate.

"Don't worry, I'm not doing it," Ethan said, walking over and putting his hand on my back. It wouldn't have been so bad except he kept moving his fingers around like he was trying to give me the world's tiniest massage. "He's a bloviating hack, but he made some good points. I mean, Jesus. I should at least have cast some understudies."

You and I looked up at each other at the same time. *You're not his understudy*, I wanted to scream. *Don't you see? He's yours.*

"Whatever," you said, stretching your arms over your head.

"Glad to see you care so much," Ethan snapped. He stopped pacing and put his hands on his hips. "Listen, your performances make or break this play. Two weeks ago you were on point. I need you back there. I don't care what it takes."

I glanced over at you, but you were staring pointedly at the empty front row. I wondered if it had been the same for both of us, before: the secret thrill of seeing a text come in, the delicious possibility of an innocent sentence ended with a semicolon followed by a right parenthesis. What would it take for us to get back there? I already knew the answer; he was still drawing circles on my spine.

"We only have a couple weeks before spring break," Ethan sighed, and I let myself float out of the conversation, into ten days of possibility I'd forgotten were getting so close. Just remembering they existed made my heart stop sputtering like an outboard motor for a second. Over spring break I could sleep all day. I could stop making myself stay up and just chill, reset, start to fix things.

"I wish there was some way for me to get out of going to Florida with my parents, but it's my cousin's wedding, so I'm screwed," Ethan continued, somehow managing to make a tropical vacation in the dead of winter sound like a punishment. "I thought we were in a good place, but obviously we're not. So we'll need to amp up our rehearsals for now."

"Come on," you said, finally breaking your silence. "That's crazy. We're both already off-book. We've got the blocking down. Once we decide what we—what our characters want . . ." You looked at me, and for the first time in days you didn't look angry. "It'll all fall into place," you finished.

"What they want?" Ethan asked, finally moving his hand from my back to gesture theatrically at you. "What do you mean, *what they want*? I think it's pretty clear what they want."

"To jump off the bridge," I said, biting my lip. The second pill was finally starting its magic; the filter on the room changed.

"*No,*" Ethan said. "I mean, yes, that's what they do, or try to do, but it's not what they *want*. What they want is to be seen, and heard, and connected with." He walked over to me and took my hand, lifted it to his mouth, and kissed it gently. It was actually sweet, and caught me off guard. It didn't make me cringe. It reminded me of little Ethan Entsky from my ninth grade diction class, with the voice that hadn't fully changed and would crack at inopportune moments.

"What they want," Ethan said, looking at me earnestly, "is each other."

"Right," I said, running my dry tongue across the roof of my mouth. I didn't know what to do. I didn't want Ethan, but I didn't want to hurt him, either, or ruin the play he'd worked so hard on . . . for me. He'd done it for me, I knew that—everyone did. All that time I'd been throwing it in his face, when I should have been thanking him. Some people got liquid courage, but in that moment I had 150 milligrams of clarity.

I couldn't choose you. That wasn't an option—too much was at stake, we were already in too deep. In five weeks, when the curtain fell and it was all over, I could tell you how your smile made my knees shake, how I'd secretly stolen the drama cast list from the bulletin board, folded it up and stuck it in my purse just to be able to file it away in a closet shoebox with all of my old birthday cards and passed notes and love letters, because I knew someday I would look back at our names side by side and say, *that was the beginning.* In five weeks I could tell you everything. I just had to hold on until then.

"So when do you want to—" I dropped Ethan's hand and turned to ask you about your schedule, but all I saw was the curtain swaying from your stage-left exit.

I didn't know how much I'd hurt you then. I didn't know how much more damage I'd do before I was finished.

All I knew was that you were already gone.

Chapter Sixteen

March
Two months left

MARCH WAS A RABBIT HOLE. I have memories of places without knowing exactly how I got there, or why. One Saturday I even ended up at a *Law & Order* open casting call in some depressing midtown office. I read for a valedictorian who was getting cyber-bullied, but my hands were shaking so hard I couldn't read the sides and they told me to go get some water but instead I took two muscle relaxers and walked over to Bryant Park and fell asleep on the grass.

At school I started avoiding everyone, hanging out on the squares with the art kids at lunch, chain-smoking and watching Jasper hold court with his stupid tongue-pierced, ombré-haired groupies and shivering in my coat even as the temperature climbed into the sixties week by week. I was always cold, and when I made a fist you could see the grooves in the bones under my skin, like a Día de los Muertos figurine. My parents kept asking me if I was OK and I would tell them it was just stress. I stayed in my room most of the time and pretended to be working but instead I was hunched over my desk with a CVS pill crusher, grinding up the Nuvigil and Adderall and whatever else I could find to experiment with and sucking them through a plastic straw because they weren't working anymore. Nothing was working, everyone had a different reason to hate me, and no one cared where I was, so I could do anything. So much for my septum.

At some point my ritual stopped making me better and started making me worse, but it was way too late to stop, so I just kept marching, going through the motions at rehearsals and nodding at any criticisms like I knew just how to fix it, even though the words had lost all meaning. I was treating the lines like they were just a very long password spelled out phonetically, and if I said them in the right order and at the right volume I'd be set free for the night. If Showcase still scared me during those lost weeks I don't remember it, but I don't think I had the capacity to be scared anymore. I barely felt anything, which was the whole point.

I went uptown on the weekends, saying I was going to Joy's but ending up at one of Dante's friends' instead, repeats of Smoke Dog's party only without me crying or throwing up, because I'd developed a tolerance and because Dante told me he'd ban me if I ever "acted like a basic high school bitch" again. I'm pretty sure I texted you from some of those parties, but in the mornings I'd just delete everything, as if erasing the messages could take them back. For all I knew you'd blocked me. You never responded, and I burned with shame every single time.

One night on the way home, I took something palmed to me by Dante's friend "T"—that he whispered was some homemade brew of heroin and speed. My heart started skipping beats when I was by myself in an empty subway car, and I got dizzy and slid off the bench onto the grimy floor next to an empty Cup Noodles. I don't know how long I was lying there, but I woke up to an old Chinese woman standing over me yelling something I couldn't understand, so I got up and staggered off the train and realized I was in Brooklyn. I walked home, I guess—somehow I was in my bed the next morning, feeling like someone drilled a hole in my skull and put a brick on my chest. I stayed home "sick" for a few days and slept, but the sleeping wasn't enough, my brain wouldn't start without jumper cables, and so I gave in and got out my straw and when I took the first sniff my brain caught on fire and I actually screamed. But then after a minute it started to feel better, even good, almost, so I told my mom I'd seen a roach and kept the door shut.

Ethan came by after school to check on me. He brought me flowers and soup and ran his fingers through my hair, and for the first time ever I didn't want him to stop touching me, so I pulled him down and kissed him with my eyes closed so I could pretend he was you. After a minute, though, he pulled back and looked at me with that hungry, glassy-eyed look that boys get and said, "Why can't we do this all the time?" And when I said I didn't know, he asked me if he was my boyfriend, and I shook my head, not sure if my chin was moving up and down or side to side.

I did manage to hang with Joy once, on a weekend when she wasn't rehearsing. I invited her over to make cookies from a roll of premade dough and watch DVR'd episodes of *I Survived*, a creepy budget reality show about people who should pretty much be dead, but weren't. (Back then I think I thought it made me feel better about my own situation—like, at least I hadn't been stabbed a million times in a home invasion and wrapped in a carpet—but now I think I watched it because I wanted to see life from the other side.) Right before she came over, though, I was running around the house checking everything to make sure it looked normal, layering sweaters to hide my skinny arms, and blinking back tears of Visine to get the pink tint out of my eyes. I was setting up for my supposed best friend the way I usually set up for a party, scrambling to hide everything that mattered.

We said all the things that girls always say when there's tension that nobody wants to address—*I miss you!* (a veiled accusation); *How ARE you?* (cheerful, but with a sad smile that lets her know she doesn't text enough); *Life's just been craaaaazy lately!* (with a shrug that translates to "You would know what I'm talking about if you'd been there."). If someone else had been eavesdropping it would have sounded seminormal, but it wasn't. I wish I had just told her what was going on, but I couldn't risk making her even more upset with me. So instead I freaked out after she left and went to Dante's. He had friends over and acted like I was crazy for showing up, which reminded me of you, and made me sad all over again. (You talked to me only if it was scripted. One night, after rehearsal, I'd caught up with you at the corner of Broadway but when I touched your arm, you shook you head and said, "Sorry, I just can't do this.")

You can't tell Diego I see you, I begged Dante. *You can't tell him I come up here.*

"What's in it for me?" Dante asked with a slow smile, and before I knew what was happening I walked out with a deal and three bottles of pills that I paid for by taking out a cash advance on my dad's AmEx at a bodega ATM. One bottle was for me, and the others were for me to "distribute."

I guess you could say I'd found my motivation.

I guess you could say I was making a choice.

Chapter Seventeen

Mid-April
Less than a month left

THE FRIDAY BEFORE SPRING BREAK Ethan left school early to catch his flight to Key West, leaving you and me with strict instructions to rehearse every day while he was gone. That seemed at least like a legitimate reason to talk to you without having you avoid me, but when I found you at the fountain during lunch and asked you when you were free you made a face and said, "I don't think we need to. It's going to suck anyway."

It was warm and bright and perfect that day, like a Woody Allen movie. My head was refreshingly clear since I'd added an online Klonopin prescription into my regimen, and I was suddenly the most popular girl in school again, thanks to my al fresco lunchtime sales calls. I didn't know if it was the promise of spring or the promise of being alone with you, but for the first time in a long time, I wasn't cold.

"What, the play?" I asked.

"Everything," you said. You looked at me for a few seconds,

longer than we'd held eye contact in months, and I felt my breath hitch.

I miss you, I wanted to say. Instead I said, "We should at least try."

You looked pained. "I don't think that's a good idea."

"It's not my idea, it's Ethan's *command*," I said, raising my arm in a salute. The corners of your lips twitched and when I raised an eyebrow you finally gave me a begrudging half-smile.

"I guess I can do tonight," you said. "But after that, no promises."

"Promises are overrated," I said.

After my midday Nuvigil (I was up to three a day and had to borrow from my inventory so that Dante wouldn't know how much I was using, but all I had to do to even out the till was up my prices—it was so easy, as long as I took enough pills to stay on top of it), I stalked the dance studios, trying to find the room where Joy was rehearsing. I missed her so much it actually hurt sometimes, like the bruises I seemed to wake up with every day despite having no memory of falling down. And Ethan being gone felt like a trap opening; kissing him back in January had been the mistake that set everything in motion, and since he was always around, it was always hanging over every interaction. But maybe, I thought, just *maybe*, now that I had some breathing room I could get Joy alone and try to explain things—maybe not everything, but some things. Maybe she would understand, and maybe things could go back to the way they were. Maybe. *Maybe.*

I finally saw her through one of the doors, framed in a

small window webbed with cracks: Joy, Diego, the piano guy, and that asshole dance teacher with the raisin face. I couldn't hear the music very well, but Diego was standing in the center of the floor, turning to watch Joy with a dreamy smile as she twirled around him. Then he came up and put his arms gently on her waist, beaming as he lifted her off the floor, her long legs extended in an effortless-looking jeté. (At least, I think it was a jeté, Joy had explained all of the terms to me during a sleepover freshman year while we got wired on orange Crush and laughed hysterically through the movie *Center Stage*, but I was constantly confusing them.)

I couldn't hear the music, but I didn't have to. They were perfect together. It made me weirdly sad to watch. Diego could look at Joy that way because she wasn't pretending to date anyone, let alone the third person in the room. And Joy could look at him that way if she wanted to, but she didn't because she was stubborn or blind or both. Diligent, hardworking Joy, so focused and responsible that she brought flash cards to the temple to memorize during my bat mitzvah, since we had a French quiz the next day. "That girl has her eyes on the prize," my dad had said. But watching her dance, I wondered if she knew there was more than one kind of prize, and that sometimes you didn't have to keep your eyes on them for them to come to you.

Diego stood to the side while Joy crossed the floor in a series of turns en pointe. She started out fine, but after a second she suddenly faltered, stepping down quickly onto the other foot and screwing up her mouth in pain. My heart started racing; I had my hand on the knob and had almost opened the door before I remembered I wasn't supposed to be there. Luckily, Diego rushed to help her. I turned quickly and pressed my back against the wall outside the studio, letting my bag slide to the floor. Being high and jittery and lonely with no place to go wasn't fun, but I had at least another hour to kill before the rehearsal that you had finally agreed to at five o'clock.

A few minutes later, the door opened, and Ms. Bitchface stepped out halfway, pointing one ballet-slipper-clad toe into the hallway.

"I'm concerned, Joy," she said. "I want you icing, heating, compressing, and elevating over break. And I'm going to have Lolly come in once we're back to learn your part, just in case." She rapped on the doorframe with a bony fist. "We can't be too careful."

"What the fuck?" I said out loud, before I could catch myself.

"Hello, Ms. Gerstein," she said coolly, turning to me with a sour smirk. "Practicing your diction, I see."

"Liv?" Joy called from inside. The teacher took off down the hall and I caught the door before it swung shut. Joy was sitting against the far wall of the studio, unlacing her pointe shoes, and Diego was standing with his hands on his hips and his sweaty hair plastered to his face, looking uneasy.

"I'm sorry," I said, clenching and unclenching my fists behind my back. Lunch had consisted of four cigarettes, half an apple, and two Diet Cokes, and I was getting lightheaded and twitchy.

"You shouldn't be." Diego shook his head angrily. "You don't get someone to perform by psyching them out and threatening them."

"It works on me," Joy sighed.

"She knows, that's why she does it," Diego said. He wiped his face with the bottom of his tank top, exposing a lean, flat six-pack. Joy didn't even glance up. "At least we don't have to see her for ten days, right?"

"Yup, it's a nice, relaxing stay of execution," Joy said. She bent her bare right foot over her left knee and started massaging the ankle, wincing with each push.

"Are you OK?" I asked. She and Diego exchanged a look before she shrugged and quickly switched feet.

"Just tired," she said. "I'll be fine." She looked up at me and frowned. "Are *you* OK? . . ."

"Just stressed," I said. "The usual." It was weird to feel so uncomfortable with someone I'd loved so long that I'd stenciled her name onto the lower half of my bunk bed. I tried to remind myself that the room had already been tense before I walked in.

"Yeah, tell me about it." Joy pulled on some socks. "Do you need to vent?" She said it in a monotone that made it clear that wasn't what *she* wanted to do, but it was enough of an effort for me after weeks and weeks of nothing.

"Can I buy you an early dinner?" I asked. I'd taken out money in the middle of the night to pay Dante for my next order, but I wasn't seeing him until Saturday, and besides, I'd taken out extra to give myself a cushion.

"You sure?" Joy asked. She looked over at Diego for permission, which stung a little—I guess they must have had a routine going, packing up and taking the subway together—but I couldn't really be mad. I used to look forward all day to those ten minutes with you.

"After the next couple weeks, you'll be sick of my face," Diego laughed, picking up his duffel. "Get out while you can."

"Yeah," I said. "Let's get out of here."

I had one pill left until I got home. I could almost feel it bouncing around inside my purse like a pea under a princess's mattress. I wanted to see Joy, I was aching to be in a room alone with you, but if I'm being honest I was just as excited to take that fucking pill, to plot when and where and how I would take it. That was how I planned my days. That had been all that was keeping me going.

Get out while you can.

I didn't even hear the words.

Sitting across from Joy in a diner booth felt almost normal, although conversation tripped and stalled at first, both of us staring at the menu like it was a script we couldn't find our lines on.

"What are you getting?" she asked.

"I don't know . . . cereal, maybe? I'm not really hungry."

"You should eat more. You look too skinny," Joy said bluntly. "And I don't mean that as a messed-up compliment."

I raised my eyebrows. "*Okaaay*. I won't thank you, then."

The waiter came and took our order. Joy got a turkey wrap, and I asked for a veggie burger deluxe I didn't even want. I gulped down my water and chewed on the straw.

"I'm sorry," she said, once he'd left. "I'm not trying to be a bitch. I'm just freaking out right now."

"It's OK," I said. "Me, too. I thought second-semester senior year was supposed to be like a big chill orgy. What happened?"

Joy laughed. "Right? The pressure is so crazy right now that if I didn't have Diego there most days, I legitimately think I would have punched Adair."

"Too bad she's not busy sleeping off a hangover like Mr. Francisco," I said. "Although the one time he showed up to a run-through he suggested Ethan recast me."

"What?" Joy looked honestly shocked, and I loved her for it.

"Yup. He's probably right, though. It's such a weird vibe, the play's going to suck unless . . ." I paused, unsure of how to finish the sentence. Luckily, or unluckily, maybe, one thing about Nuvigil was that it was great at filling awkward silences with words.

"I'm really sorry about stealing Dave at the party," I blurted, clasping my hands together, digging the nails of one into the palm of the other methodically as I spoke. "I mean, nothing ever happened, but you were right. I liked him—I still like him—and I should have just said that. I don't know why I tried to act like I didn't care. I think I just didn't want him to know I was just like everyone else, you know?"

"Whoa," Joy said. "Slow down." She pressed her lips together and took a deep breath. "You can't own a person, so you can't steal a person. He was never mine." She looked straight at me then. "But if you had just been honest with me, I would have had your back," she said. "Instead I felt like you made it a competition or something."

I looked down at my hands. I'd broken the skin. "I can't compete with you," I said. "Trust me, I'm a hot mess." A lump surfaced unexpectedly in my throat, and I gulped water to keep it down.

"Hey, what's wrong?" Joy asked. "*Olivia*," she said—which she never said, which is how I knew it was really showing. "What is going on with you?"

"I'll tell you if you tell me," I said, hedging. I already knew it was a lie, because at that moment I honestly thought that if I told Joy the truth, everything would fall apart. Because back then, on the other side, "falling apart" just meant that everyone would know how far gone I was, and that people would be mad at me and I would have to drop out and go to some rehab facility where I'd sweat and heave and feel like shit for a week. *That* seemed like the worst possible thing in the world. I was so fucking selfish.

I'll tell you if you tell me. One step up from *Secrets, secrets are no fun, secrets, secrets hurt someone.*

"Something's the matter with my ankle," Joy said, looking into her water glass as she stirred and stirred, watching the ice cubes melt down to nothing. "Only Diego knows. So please don't say anything."

Diego knew all of our secrets, apparently.

"What is it?" I asked, before the waiter came with our food, and we did that thing of suddenly pretending we were deaf-mutes while he set down the plates and arranged the silverware.

When we were alone again, Joy shrugged and picked up a pickle. "I don't know, I haven't been to a doctor."

"Why not?" A huge platter sat in front of me, my burger sitting on a lettuce raft in a sea of golden fries, but I was craving something much smaller and less filling.

"I can't go without my parents finding out," Joy said. "And if they found out they'd tell me to stop dancing on it."

"Maybe you should." I ran my dry tongue over my teeth. My ears popped.

Joy pressed her lips together and took a deep breath. "This is my one shot," she said, her face tense just like I'd seen it through the glass panel on the studio door. "No offense, but I'm not gonna have a gap year to figure it out. You know my mom and dad. If I don't get recruited by a company, the deal's off. It's over."

We ate in silence for a minute. I took a tiny bite of my veggie burger and tasted wet cardboard.

"So," I finally said. "What happens if it gets worse?"

"I don't know." Joy frowned. "I'm just trying to make it through the next couple weeks." She reached across the table to steal a fry and shot me an embarrassed smile. "Actually, I've been spending some lunch periods icing it in the handicapped stall of the fourth floor bathroom."

So Joy had a lunchtime bathroom habit, too. "You could have told me," I said.

She shook her head emphatically. "I don't need anyone else worrying about me. Diego's bad enough. He's only helping me because he knows I would dance on it anyway and he wants to be there to make sure I don't do anything stupid."

"I don't think that's why," I said. The summer between ninth and tenth grades was when Kyle first started buying me forties from the corner store with his fake ID, saying he knew I would drink anyway and he wanted to make sure I was being responsible. It turned out he just wanted to try to kiss me in the hallway near the garbage disposal. When I didn't let him and he kept buying, I felt more powerful than I knew what to do with.

"OK, so now you know my drama," Joy said, chewing. "So what's yours? You seem really upset."

"Nope, just melodrama," I sighed, relieved I had been smart enough to hold off confessing. "I'm just in such an awkward position. Stuck between a rock and a hard place, et cetera."

"Between an Ethan and a Dave place?" Joy quipped.

"Pretty much." I could feel my brain start to decelerate, the whirring and clicking getting slower, like a train approaching a station. I started to worry if I would need more before I got home, especially if my rehearsal with you went well and we decided to hang out afterward, which I knew was a long shot, maybe *the* longest shot, but still a shot I wanted to take. I wondered when Dante got off work, if he could meet me halfway. If I could find a good moment to excuse myself, I could text him and take my next dose at the same time. Two birds, one bathroom. I laughed, and Joy looked at me funny.

"Don't take this wrong," she said, "but to me, yours has an easy solution. Just let Ethan down gently."

"It's not, though," I said. I thought about Ethan's lips, and how nice they felt—but only when I was imagining he wasn't attached to them.

"I know," Joy said. But I could tell she didn't.

"And I know you think a gap year is some kind of vacation," I continued, working myself up, "but I kind of wish my parents cared more about what I do. Because if I don't start getting auditions, I'll just be the girl who lives at home and goes nowhere." I pushed my fries around fussily on my plate. "I'll be the girl who peaks in high school."

"Uh-uh," Joy said. "That won't happen. Besides, I don't think you can peak when you're a hot mess, right?"

I laughed and launched a fry across the table. "Shut up."

"Then again, Dave peaked early, too, so maybe you two are destined," she said. I didn't want to laugh—you were so insecure about that, and you'd confided in me—but Joy broke first and started giggling, and I was so relieved at the break in tension that I started too, loud enough to get a shush from an old lady in the next booth.

"*Aaaaanyway*," Joy said, in an exaggerated whisper, "it's not like I have time for anything besides rehearsals and home-work right now. I'm glad I don't have anyone making me crazy. Besides you, obviously."

I smiled, but I wanted to tell Joy that she was wrong, and that she didn't know what she was missing. I wanted to tell her that you were the only thing about the past few months of my life that felt real, and that I'd been spending every single day for two months chasing the electric feeling that had sparked when we first met. I wanted to tell her that someone like that makes everything easier, makes everything seem *more* possible, not less.

But I didn't end up telling her any of that, because while I was staring off into space thinking about you, I looked up and saw the clock behind the counter.

The moment I first realized I was in love with you? That was also the moment I realized I'd stood you up.

Chapter Eighteen

Mid-April
Less than a month left

WHEN I GOT TO THE REHEARSAL ROOM, you were packing up your stuff. The sun was almost gone, and the sky through the windows was orange-gray like a coal on fire from the inside. You had your back to me, but I saw you flinch when I opened the door.

"I'm really sorry," I said. The last pill bobbed bitterly in my throat; I'd panicked and swallowed it dry on the way over. I plunged my arm into my bag, hoping to find some half-empty bottle I could use to wash it down.

"You're unbelievable," you said, not moving.

"I said I'm sorry." My fingers closed around a plastic cap and I pulled out a days-old water, gratefully chugging the last inch that was left. That felt better. "I ran into Joy," I explained. "I lost track of time. I'm ready now."

"The funny thing," you said, finally turning to face me, "is that when you say you'll be someplace you lose track of time, but when you're not supposed to be there, you just magically appear. You're never ready at the right time." Your eyes flashed with anger. I could tell you wanted me to apologize, but not just for running late. Couldn't you see how complicated it all was? You couldn't own a person, Joy had said, and it was true. So why did you and Ethan both insist on acting like I had to belong to you?

"That's not fair," I said.

"This was a bad idea." You picked up your coat. "I'm over it. I'm just gonna tell Ethan to find someone else."

"*Seriously?*"

"Better than this." You shrugged your bag onto your shoulder.

"Wow. Well, way to quit." I tried to keep my voice steady, even though the prospect of facing rehearsals without you—of facing anything without you—made me feel like crying.

"I think it's for the best," you said.

"Really?" It was hard to hide my disappointment, but I didn't care anymore. "For someone so worried about the future, you give up on good things pretty quickly."

You laughed bitterly. "I don't think I would describe this as a good thing."

"It could be."

"Look, what's the best-case scenario?" you asked. "We do this, and it doesn't suck, and then it's over, right?"

"That's better than not trying." I tossed my bag against the wall, where it landed with a dull thud.

"So what?" you asked, shaking your head. "You just want to run lines now? For real?" I opened my mouth and then shut it again. I forgot we were talking, in theory at least, about the play.

The sky was dark; in the time it had taken us to fight, the sun had beat a hasty retreat below the Hudson. If you left, I knew I would have nowhere to go but uptown on the 1 to the top of the park, where I would meet Dante so I could lose track of time, on purpose. Just like that Sunday when I'd walked off the subway without meaning to, I felt a powerful pull to derail. Maybe, if I could just get you to stay for a little while, you would change your mind. Maybe then we could both change course.

"Yeah," I said.

You let out a deep sigh but pulled off your bag and hung it on a chair. "Fine. Five minutes. Where should we start?"

"I don't know," I said. "I guess . . . at the beginning."

"On a night like this, you can see the whole city," you said.

We were standing a safe distance apart, ignoring the blocking and just saying the words, facing forward, as if we were doing a staged reading in a black box theater. When we'd started it hadn't been good, exactly, but some of the venom had dripped away, slowly, and once we we'd gotten about halfway through—five minutes had become ten had become fifteen—we'd found a flow. We weren't sparking, but we weren't sparring, either. We were just voices rising and falling on the right beats, building a rhythm. Telling a story.

"Sometimes," I said, "I wish I couldn't see it at all. I long for the mountains back home." Normally at that part I was supposed to be sitting next to you, leaning into your shoulder, and holding your hand. I knew we would skip the stage directions like we always did, and fly past the kiss without even discussing it, but still, it was getting close. I glanced over at you, expecting you to stop any second, roll your eyes, and tell me it was time for you to go. But you were just staring out at nothing, your focus somewhere far away.

"How can you say that?" you asked. "It's so much better here. There's so much . . . opportunity."

"Sewing underclothing in a stifling factory until my fingers bleed doesn't seem much like opportunity," I said, trying to slow myself down—learning my lines high had been efficient, but they'd imprinted in a speedy rush that wanted to come out all at once. "The conditions were better traveling steerage." My fingers twitched at my sides. I needed to do something with my body soon or else I felt like I would explode.

"That can't be true," you said. "Besides—" You were supposed to gesture out at the imaginary cityscape in front of us, the metaphorical future ahead, but instead you turned and looked at me. "This is just the beginning," you said. "You speak as if this is the end."

"Maybe I wish it was."

I closed my eyes and tried to breathe. My mind was racing and it was hard to stand still. But closing them only made the room tilt. Joy had been right again; I should have eaten more at dinner. I needed to hold on to something. I just wanted to feel grounded.

"I just want to feel something," I said, gesturing wildly with my arms to release the pent-up energy. (Mom used to call it "shaking the sillies out." We had a whole dance we'd do.) "I want to feel something other than homesickness."

(It was Viola talking, but I was homesick, too, wasn't I? Only not for some country across the ocean, but for my own apartment, where I used to feel so safe. When did that stop? How could I get back?)

"I want to know something other than sadness," I said, my chest starting to tighten. "I want to see something besides my mother's face as she—" *Answers the door and doesn't even seem to notice how fucked up I am.* "As she . . ."

"Liv?" You were looking at me again, concerned this time.

"Sorry. Where was I?

"I want to see something besides my mother's face." You paused, a flicker of annoyance registering in your tensed jaw. "I thought you were off-book."

"I am, I am. Right. OK. I want to see something other than my mother's face as she lay dying," I said, the words tumbling out too fast again. "I want to touch something—" You. I wanted to run across the room and touch *you*, hold your hand, lean on your shoulder, raise my fingers up to your chin and pull you down toward me and kiss you, breathe you in. "—other than a sewing needle," I finished, feeling my face flush.

"I think we can stop," you said.

"No! I want to keep going." This time my voice came out louder than I'd meant it to, almost a shout. You took a step back.

"OK, you seem weird . . . I don't think you should . . ."

"Just let me finish!" I cried, my eyes suddenly filling with tears. "I want to finish my monologue!"

I'm not sure what made me break—why that moment was the tipping point when I'd been teetering on the edge for months—but something just swelled up inside, so fast I barely saw before it broke the surface. I was scared (my first thought, a whisper in the dark: *Did I take too much?*) and deeply, deeply sad—and embarrassed, a little—but mostly, against all odds, I was grateful. Because finally, even if Ethan didn't, *I* understood what Viola was feeling on that bridge, and why she had run there. For the first time, maybe in my whole life, I could say lines and actually mean them.

"I want to feel something more powerful than I am," I said, my breath coming in gasps, the tears blurring my vision. I was glad I couldn't see you. "I want to feel the current dragging me under. I want to feel something that makes me know I was alive once. I just want—" My voice broke then, because I couldn't stand it anymore, how true it was, and I didn't care anymore who knew.

"I just want to feel something *real.*"

My hands flew to my face and then I was sobbing, big wracking gasps that rolled in waves down my body, pulling me toward the floor, where I would have gone if you hadn't stopped me, wrapping your arms around me, squeezing like a tourniquet with your face bowed into my hair, whispering, "*I'm sorry. I'm sorry.*"

And then I was leaning into your shoulder, and then I was looking into your eyes, and I don't think I pulled you and I don't think you pulled me, but something pulled us together, because then we were kissing, stumbling, until my back found the wall and your hands found my face, my neck, my breasts, my waist.

I tasted the salt of my tears on your tongue and arched toward you, my fingers slipping under your shirt, splaying open on the taut, warm skin of your stomach. It was breathless and sudden, like a fall in the seconds before you hit the ground. I remember the urgency of it more than anything. It felt like if we stopped, we might die.

It felt like our time had run out before it started.

Intermission

Joy

Chapter Nineteen

April 16
27 days left

"HAPPY BIRTHDAY, BABY!"

Mom beamed at me from across the table, her face partially obscured by a candle sticking out of a wedge of tiramisu. We were at V&T Pizza—my favorite restaurant since I was old enough to behave well enough to be taken out to eat—and the whole Sunday dinner-rush crowd was singing to me as I held my breath and pinched my face in my best impression of a smile. I didn't want to seem surly or ungrateful, but I hated being serenaded, which my parents knew but were willfully, gleefully ignoring. Eighteen was special, they insisted. Adulthood was something to celebrate.

I might have been in a more celebratory mood if the fourth chair at our table hadn't been empty. It had been sort of last-minute, sure, but Liv could have at least texted me back. Our impromptu dinner date on Friday had gone pretty well—aside from her throwing down a fistful of twenties and running out before the check arrived—so when I messaged her later that night to ask if she would come out for my birthday (no official party this year, not that she'd offered to throw me one and not that I would have wanted her to after the last party at her apartment), I thought she'd say yes. Or, at least, I thought she'd say *something*. But two more texts and not so much as a flimsy excuse accompanied by a frowny emoji shedding a single tear, so apparently we were back to not really talking.

"Come on, honey," Dad said. "Quit stalling and blow out the damn thing before you set the tablecloth on fire!" My eyes snapped back into focus just in time to see the tiramisu listing to one side as the candle started melting the chocolate powder on top. I blew it out in a quick, perfunctory burst, and everyone clapped.

"So, what did you wish for?" Mom asked, propping her chin up with her fingertips, her hands pressed together in prayer position. It was the stance she took whenever she expected a thoughtful answer, but I wasn't in the mood. Underneath the tablecloth, under my jeans, I could feel my ankle pulsing angrily against the layers of Ace bandages, which had stopped working weeks back. I was in trouble and I knew it. Walking without limping took more effort than performing on stage ever had.

"What do you think?" I asked, digging into the dessert with my fork, instantly turning the artful layers of sponge cake and mascarpone into an amorphous mush. As I raised it to my mouth, I could see my parents exchange a look, like, *here we go again*, which is exactly what *I* was thinking. Because, seriously, what did they expect me to say? That I suddenly wanted to become a dance professor instead of actually dancing? That

I'd fallen and hit my head during a leap and woken up with a passion for microbiology? Or maybe I should have just made like a Miss America contestant and asked for world peace.

"You know we're excited about your performance . . ." Dad started unconvincingly, looking at Mom in a way that made me realize they'd probably planned this out; they each had lines and he was telling her to wait for her cue.

"Great!" I said brightly, taking another bite. In fact, I pulled the plate all the way over from the center of the table. If I was going to have to sit through a birthday lecture, then they weren't getting one goddamn bite of my birthday tiramisu.

". . . but we want you to be prepared for every outcome," he went on.

"It's very likely," Mom jumped in, "that even if you win an apprenticeship, it will be hard to move up the ranks in a company. It's extremely competitive. I've been looking at the statistics."

"I know the numbers," I said. I fought the urge to roll my eyes and instead stared down at the wobbly mess on my plate, imagining Miss Adair watching the scene unfold with an I-told-you-so smirk. *You need to trim down before May.* I lay down my fork and swallowed, suddenly feeling uncomfortably full.

"We just want to make sure you consider all of your options," Dad said. "You're eighteen now, which means that you get to make your own decisions about your future . . ."

"And we just want to make sure they're the *right* ones," Mom said.

I wanted to tell them that I was making decisions already.

That I didn't need their permission anymore, and that I didn't want their advice. The thought gave me a buoy of self-confidence.

"You guys know that someday, when I'm giving my press conference like Misty, and we're all sitting on some pristine white couch with our shoes off in a spread in *People* magazine, you're going to have to pretend you believed in me the whole time, right?" I smiled to pretend it was a joke.

"Baby, we *do* believe in you," Mom said, looking a little hurt. "We don't believe in *them*."

"We just want you to be happy," Dad jumped in, balling up his fists on the checkered tablecloth. "Not struggling every day to prove yourself and fit into a world that doesn't want you!"

"It's all right, Stuart," Mom said, laying a hand on top of his arm. "We can save this for another time." But I was already getting fired up. I'd inherited my father's freight train temper; once you stoked the coals, we could run all night.

"But nothing would ever change if people never broke boundaries," I said, struggling not to raise my voice. "You're always saying that. So how can it be different when it comes to me?"

"Well . . . it isn't," Mom said, "but—"

"Yes it is!" Dad was clearly going off-script. "Because you're our daughter and we raised you to make change in the world, yes, but how about working for social justice? How about education reform, how about the wage gap, how about the White House?" He tossed his napkin across his empty dessert plate.

"I *will* change the world," I heard myself say, my voice emotionless and steady. "And I'll do it in pointe shoes, and they won't see me coming." They exchanged another look, but this one was more resigned.

"Why don't we change topics to something less contentious," Mom said. "Did you see the *Times* Style section today? Apparently 'mom jeans' are hot now."

"Keep the faith," I muttered, as I felt my phone buzz in the pocket of my coat hanging over my chair. I looked over at Dad, raising my eyebrows like a temporary white flag in order to ask permission to check it. Normally, in our family, devices at the table were met with as much hostility as wanting to pursue your performing arts dream instead of go to a four-year college. But that night, he nodded.

"Go ahead, it's probably one of your friends, wishing you a happy birthday," he said. But all of my friends had already texted me, with one unsurprising exception, who had probably dropped her phone into a gallon of Amaghetto that she was still sleeping off.

I slipped my phone out and saw an e-mail notification. It was a Save the Date from the Entskys, to a party in honor of *Boroughed Trouble* that would be held the weekend after Showcase at their house in Staten Island. *Poor Ethan*, I thought. I'd have to go, just to make up for all the other times I blew him off. Maybe I could even convince you to come with me, make a day of it. Sort of like a—well, not like a date, that would be so weird . . . but something. Something that gave me a tingle of anticipation that I tried to ignore.

Somewhere along the line, after weeks and weeks of lifts and turns, I'd lost my inhibitions about touching you. And I was thinking about you when I got home, something I never used to do. *A pas de deux is a dialogue of love*, I thought suddenly. Nureyev had said that, hadn't he? Mr. Dyshlenko was only slightly less poetic. Just that week, he'd compared us to IKEA furniture: "If the pieces do not fit together, the whole thing is shit and needs to be returned!"

Luckily, we fit together perfectly. We always had.

"All right, what are you grinning about?" Mom asked.

"*Nothing*," I groaned. But just as I was putting my phone back in my pocket it buzzed again.

did you make your wish yet?

I bit my lip to keep from smiling, glancing down at the extinguished candle lying on my plate.

I'd always made the same wish, year after year, since I was six. There was no point; I'd never wanted anything else.

But something told me that was starting to change.

Chapter Twenty

April 18 (second day of Spring Break)
25 days left

BECOMING A LEGAL ADULT didn't mean much. OK, I could vote. I could buy cigarettes, if I smoked, which I didn't. I could get married (ha). But I was still living at home, still annoyed by my parents, who clearly had no intention, despite their delusions, of letting me make my own decisions anytime soon.

Nope, it didn't change anything in an immediate sense—except for one thing. If you were eighteen, you could make your own doctor's appointments.

"I've never seen this grade of sprain in a professional track dancer," the orthopedist murmured, pressing his thick fingers into the flesh of my ankle. He was short and bald and had a diamond ear stud. The photos on the wall were all of him posing with minor celebrities. But having the nickname "Dr. Dance" didn't make him a miracle worker, like I'd hoped. "I'm giving you ninety-nine out of a hundred odds," he grumbled, while I gritted my teeth and focused on an autographed photo of the Knicks City Dancers. They were all performing hip-hop moves in high-heeled sneaker boots, meanwhile I couldn't stay up balancing on my own damn toes. Ninety-nine out of 100 seemed a lot better than 1 in 1,086, but it wasn't, not when the odds were tearing a ligament completely in half.

"My performance is next month," I said. "After that I can stay off it."

"Joy," Dr. Pashkin said sternly, "if you dance on this injury you might not dance, period. I'm amazed you can even walk, let alone go en pointe. Your ankle is *grossly* unstable."

"But the swelling's going down," I said, trying to sound positive even though I wasn't sure. "I've been icing it," I added.

"A severe sprain doesn't always swell that much, especially when it's a high sprain like yours," he said. "The syndesmosis ligaments"—he drew a short line with his thumb along the top outside of my ankle—"take a long time to heal, and with a tear like this, I'd want you off of it for at least eight weeks." He looked at me and raised his bushy white eyebrows. "*Minimum*."

"I can't," I said. "You don't know—this is my only chance."

Dr. Pashkin sighed. "Look, I know you kids don't want to wait for anything," he said impatiently, scribbling something on a notepad. "This recital probably feels like the most important thing in the world. But I promise you, someday you'll look back and realize life wasn't moving as fast as you thought."

He was wrong. It was moving faster. We didn't have eight weeks. We barely had three. But I didn't know that then. I tuned out his blithe condescension, said a curt thank-you, let him fit me for an air cast and then tore it off in the elevator as I left that fancy high-rise office, running on pure, stubborn pride, thinking about how I was going to prove him and everybody else wrong. As the tears sprung to my eyes with each excruciating step, I just kept picturing you and Lolly, dancing *our* pas de deux while I sat with everyone else in the safe, anonymous dark. It seemed so wrong on so many levels.

I wasn't going to let it happen.

You must have read it all on my face, because as soon as I stepped into the dance hallway, you pulled me into Studio 2, before Mr. Dyshlenko could see me from the main stage door.

"What's wrong?" you asked, helping me onto the piano bench. Some sheet music was open on a stand a few feet away—the finale from *Swan Lake*. As if I needed another bad omen.

"He wouldn't give me an out," I said. You were the only person who knew I had gone to see a doctor. In fact, you'd come to school the week before with a list of the five top-rated specialists in Manhattan who took my insurance.

"What do you mean?"

I took a deep breath, trying to keep my face calm. *Make it look easy, Joy. Make it look . . .* joy*ful.* "He said I shouldn't dance on it, period. He wanted to put me in an air cast and order an MRI. He said, and I quote, that I'm 'on borrowed time.'"

"That sounds like the title of Ethan's next play," you said, attempting a grim smile.

"Yup." I looked down at my feet.

"So what are you going to do?" You shook your head. "That's a stupid question, huh?"

"If I tape it tight and warm it up enough, it doesn't hurt

right away," I said. "It's worse when I'm *not* dancing. And I
don't want to be dramatic; I mean, there are people who have
broken bones in the middle of a ballet and still finished. This is
just a sprain."

"Adrenaline is a crazy drug," you said. "But you can't tape
it for the show. And if I let you fall I'd never forgive myself."

"So what, you want me to pull out of the Showcase?" I
asked.

"I didn't say that."

I crossed my arms defiantly. "Well, what, then?"

"I just don't want you to get hurt."

"I don't want to get hurt, either. But if I stop now, they
won't even put me in the corps. I'll be sitting in the audience,
watching you . . . and *her*." This time my mental image was
even clearer: Lolly and her smug smile and her stupid fan. Your
hands on her little twig waist. I leapt up and shrugged off my
coat. "I'm not about to throw away my shot. Not while I'm still
standing, anyway."

"Slow down, Hamilton," you laughed. "You still have to be
careful. They're watching you. Well, Adair is. Dyshlenko would
probably slow-clap you for snapping an Achilles in the name
of passion."

It's my syndesmosis, I almost said, but then you put your
hands on my hips and my breath caught in my throat.

I wondered if you could tell that I sometimes thought about
kissing you. That was a new thing, just a week or two old. It
had started during a rehearsal, the day we'd practiced the adagio. Specifically, this one part of the adagio that was sort of like
a slightly more chaste version of the scene in *Dirty Dancing*

when Johnny comes up behind Baby and runs his fingers down her arm. You had just spun me in a pirouette, and your right arm encircled my waist and pulled me into you, so close I could feel your breath hot on my neck. Then I leaned right and turned my face toward yours before breaking away, and in that split second when our eyes locked, something happened. I forgot we were in a fluorescent-lit studio with Ms. Adair and Mr. Stratechuck six feet away, because it felt like we were alone somewhere in the dark, about to do something we couldn't take back. I forgot you were the gangly boy I met when I was fourteen, because I could feel the stubble on your chin grazing my upturned cheek, and the muscles in your arms flexing against me, and suddenly I was acutely aware of parts of you I'd never thought much about before, separated from me only by a few thin layers of fabric. I got so flustered I botched a simple chassé, and Ms. Adair told us to take five. I'd gone straight to the bathroom to splash some cold water on my face and some sense into my head, and by the time I got back you had been you again, mostly. But I couldn't shake that moment.

"Loosen up," you said, shaking me gently, and I snapped back to reality.

"Look, if you move your hips too far left, you'll throw your whole balance off. We've got to practice having you lean on me without *looking* like you're leaning."

"So, what?" I asked, "We're going to be doing our own rehearsals outside of rehearsal?"

"Unless you've got something better to do." You moved behind me, repositioning your hands gently on my waist and shifting me over, lifting me ever so slightly.

"No," I laughed. "I just don't know how you're going to manage to spot me from halfway across the room. You can't hold me up the whole time."

"I mean . . ." You clasped my hand and guided me to put more of my weight into your palm. I could feel your pulse racing under the skin. "Basilio is in love with Kitri, right, so he'd want to touch her all the time anyway."

"I guess you'll just have to pretend to love me, then," I said, feeling suddenly unsteady in a way that had nothing to do with my feet.

"I guess so," you said softly.

After rehearsal, you surprised me with a belated birthday cake—Entenmann's marshmallow-iced devil's food, my favorite—and we took it to the fountain with two plastic forks just as the sun started to dip down below the skyline. I propped my leg up across your lap.

"This is very high-low culture right here," I said, licking crumbs off my fingertips while looking up at the twinkling lights of Avery Fisher Hall. The New York City Ballet spring season was about to begin, and a big banner promoting *A Midsummer Night's Dream* had replaced *Sleeping Beauty* on the front of the building. Tourists enjoying the first breath of warmth after the bitter winter were wandering around with their jackets draped over their arms.

"What, you and me?" you asked jokingly, scooping up nearly half the cake in one bite. You swallowed and grinned, a blob of white frosting resting perfectly in the center of your top lip, that part that people call the Cupid's Bow, because God forbid you should ever kiss someone without thinking about a little, naked cherub sniper. I reached up and wiped it off with my thumb, and your smile faltered for a second.

In every dance movie ever made—and I knew because I'd seen them all at least ten times—the two leads fall in love. That is just a fact of life, like the nitrogen cycle, or that one person who always leans on the pole in a crowded subway car. I wondered if it was because dancing was so physical. If forcing yourself to smile could create happiness, like Ms. Adair claimed, then maybe repeatedly pressing your body against someone else's could create desire. It seemed logical, but also incredibly inconvenient. What if the person you were dancing with was someone you hated? Or, worse—what if they were one of your best friends?

"What are you thinking about?" you asked. You took another forkful of cake and marched it playfully toward my mouth, but I shook my head. I was already riding a sugar high, if my hammering pulse was any indication.

"College-acceptance letters," I said quickly. "They should be coming in a few weeks."

"Right." You put the fork down and I instantly felt a pang of guilt. I should have said something else, something that didn't exclude you. My parents were snobs, but I didn't want to be.

"It's boring," I said, trying to backtrack. "I'm not even going, so it's pointless."

"No, it's not. It's smart to have a backup plan."

"It's *depressing* to have a backup plan."

You laughed. "See, you're being pessimistic. My mom once

told me that if you want something bad enough, it becomes a part of you, whether you get it or not."

I raised my eyebrows. "You believe that?"

"Actually, I think she was just trying to make me feel better about what Dante wrote on my dance bag," you said. "But it sounds true."

"Then I'm already a prima ballerina."

"The best." You grinned.

"And you're already in your spotlight?" I took another bite of cake and clutched my coat around me. The wind was picking up.

"Nah." You smiled. "I'm just waiting for my cue to join you onstage."

You and me. It was all clicking into place like a line of dominoes falling, so fast not even my thundering heart could keep pace. It was terrifying. "What, you followed me?" I asked, trying to act like I didn't notice your hand, which had casually dropped onto my leg.

"Rode your coattails is more accurate, but yeah." Neither of us said anything for a minute. Over on Broadway, cabs flashed by in the dim light, leaving a flurry of staccato honks in their wake.

What are you *thinking?* I wanted to ask, but I was too afraid to say the words. Besides, I'd been burned before with that move. Once, Caleb had been staring off dreamily after we made out, and I'd posed that question, expecting something romantic, and he'd just turned to me and said, "I love dogs." So even though everything was telling me that something important was happening—I almost couldn't look at you, I was so afraid of the charge humming between us—I couldn't *completely* rule out the possibility that your mind was actually on the cocker spaniel being walked around the corner of 66th Street.

"I was thinking," you finally said, as if reading my mind. "I want to . . . um, you know . . . go do something sometime. With you." Your kept your eyes, which were barely visible under a tousle of disheveled curls, locked on the ground. "Not just eat a box of cake."

"I like boxed cake." It was my clumsy attempt at flirting. It felt like the time I'd gone to Paris with my family after taking two years of French, and then promptly told the hotel concierge, *Je suis anglaise.* I am English. I'd gotten my own country wrong on the first try.

"You know what I mean," you said. You smiled nervously, finally looking up at me. I'd never seen you so unsure of yourself. "I want to take you out. On a . . ." *date,* I thought, my stomach churning wildly ". . . n adventure," you said.

"An adventure," I parroted.

"A date-y adventure."

"Oh," I said. I got a rush of adrenaline like the first time I'd gone up en pointe. Just one little muscle shift and then, suddenly, a whole different world. "Um. Well. Yeah. I mean, how could I say no?"

"Yeah?" Your face lit up. "OK. All right. I'll start planning, then."

"Something non-weight-bearing," I said quickly, not sure how to fill the new, uncertain space between us. "I need to be elevated."

You smiled slowly. "Not a problem."

"I guess—" I cleared my throat, moved my leg. "I guess we should probably get going?"

You shot me a dose of my own premium side-eye. "But I haven't sung you 'Happy Birthday' yet."

"You know what, that's OK. Really. You don't have to—"

But I was too late; you were already singing, adorably off-key and so loud that everyone around us turned to look. For some reason, though, your serenade didn't make me cringe like the one I'd endured just forty-eight hours earlier at V&T.

I sat and watched you quietly, warmth spreading through my aching body like someone had snuck in and lit a lantern deep inside.

Chapter Twenty-One

April 21 (fifth day of Spring Break)
22 days left

"NO! DIEGO, your face should be just under her crotch," Mr. Dyshlenko shouted, in his deep, gravelly accent.

I was hovering over you in a frozen arabesque, trembling a little, for more reasons than one. Your left hand was on the underside of my left thigh, and your right hand was wedged just over my right hip bone. It was the first time we were practicing our press lift, the culmination to a week of firsts: the first time we rehearsed our choreography on the main stage, with its state-of-the-art lights and dizzying, panoramic view of eight hundred tiered seats. The first time I got off the subway with my heart in my throat at the thought of seeing you. The first time we greeted each other without a "Hey," or a "What's up," but instead with a series of shy yet irrepressible smiles. The first time our dancing felt like flirting, or like practice for something else, some more intimate choreography that I hadn't learned yet. And, of course, the first time your face was any-where near my crotch. I tried in vain to stare stoically into the middle distance.

"The leg should be right in front of your face," Mr. Dyshlenko continued, motioning with his arms while I held my position suspended in midair. The lift reminded me of the séances Liv used to spearhead at our childhood sleepovers—one of us would lie down and the others would kneel around her, two fingers wedged between body and carpet, whispering, *light as a feather, stiff as a board.* The incantation had never made any of us levitate, but it was, as it turned out, a pretty good mantra for ballet. The only difference was that this was a hell of lot more uncomfortable.

"Yeah, get behind the leg. No one wants to see you," I joked. Even though it wasn't easy holding an arabesque for that long, I was downright giddy to be off my feet. My ankle was a fireball of pain every time I put my weight on it. In particular, there was a manège of piqué pirouettes that was brutal. Luckily, most of the rest of my solo choreography was on the backburner until after break, when Ms. Adair would coach me one-on-one.

"Everyone will want to see him," Mr. Dyshlenko said, giving me some strong Russian side-eye. "But, yes, for now, Diego, your job is to showcase her." He motioned for you to put me down, and I could feel your muscles shake as you lowered me inch by inch, taking care to rest me gently on the box of my right shoe while still supporting me more than you needed to.

"For *you*, Joy, the important thing to remember is that while he is holding you, you don't just relax," Mr. D continued while we shook out our limbs. "You are being displayed like a fine jewel, so you've got to give him something to work with. The dance hinges on *your* strength and ability. So while he technically carries your weight, he is only as strong as you are."

I gave you a look like, *Sucks for you.*

You shook your head and winked. *You got this.*

We practiced the lift a few more times, which meant more manèges of piqué pirouettes. They were supposed to be quick and light—I was basically running away from you as you followed me across the stage, playing the charming suitor—but it was hard to relax my face when every second en pointe felt like torture.

"Watch your form, Joy, your ankle is sickling!" Mr. Dyshlenko called as I stepped woodenly out of my last turn. "Are you seeing Sylvia?" Sylvia was our department physical therapist, and I knew she'd helped plenty of Janus students through sprains and other injuries. But Sylvia also had the ear of Ms. Adair, and if Dr. Pashkin was right, there was no *way* I was letting her examine me.

"I'll make an appointment," I lied.

When he asked us to start from the beginning I almost wept, but at least that was a partnered section, and you stayed right behind me, keeping my weight off my bad ankle so discreetly that Mr. Dyshlenko couldn't tell you were helping me. It left me shaking, and I still can't tell you if it was fear, gratitude, or something else entirely.

"This dance, it is lust, it is love, it is *passion*!" Mr. Dyshlenko cried. "And Joy, while your line needs work, the fire in your

expression is perfect, don't change it, OK?" I nodded, despite
the fact that I hadn't even been thinking about my face.

"Are you free tomorrow?" you whispered, setting me down
again as Mr. Dyshlenko went backstage to make a phone call.

"Maybe." I lowered myself down to the floor, grateful for
the chance to rest. "Why?"

You sat next to me, dangling your legs over the stage.
"'Cause I thought of the perfect outing," you grinned. "It has
all the elements you need: rest, ice, compression, and elevation."

"Please tell me we're watching *Step Up* and eating Klondike
Bars?"

"That can be the next date," you laughed. "Trust me, this
is better."

"The next date?" I raised my eyebrows. "We haven't even
been on one."

"Yeah, well, I'm making up for lost time." You leaned
toward me, and for a split second I couldn't feel my ankle at
all, or any part of my body, because all of a sudden we were
right there in the spotlight, alone onstage, and we were close
enough to—

"You want to try it one-handed?" Mr. Dyshlenko boomed.
You leapt up while I tried to catch my breath. The whole week
had me in a tailspin. You were different, we were different, the
game had been changed, and no amount of cold water on my
face was ever going to make things go back to normal.

Mr. D showed us how to approach the more advanced,
dangerous lift, which began like the two-handed version but
then had you quickly letting go of my arabesque leg, and me

leaning forward so that my leg dipped into a penché above my head. The first time we tried, we lost our balance and I toppled into Mr. D's outstretched arms.

"I'm so sorry," you said, shaking out your left arm.

"It's not easy. You have to really hold your position, Joy, otherwise the whole thing will fall apart," Mr. Dyshlenko instructed, lifting me up gently to demonstrate. Even though he must have been fifty, he felt like a redwood, and suddenly I was weightless. "You see?" he asked, as you looked up at me from what felt like miles away. "You hold on, hold on, and then— quickly! Before you even think about it!—let go." I felt myself swaying a little, but I kept my eyes on you. We were always being told to pick a focal point, something steady that we could return to again and again, that would keep us balanced.

That was you. It had always been you.

"Trust in her," Mr. Dyshlenko said, looking up at me. "And she will trust in you. Feel that risk of falling and accept it, but do not give in."

As he righted me and set me back down, I looked at you expectantly.

"Want to risk it?" I asked.

"Say the word," you said. "I'm ready when you are."

You picked me up after breakfast on Saturday, revealing that despite its many confusions, the absolute best thing about going on a first date with someone who had been placed firmly in the friend zone was that your parents didn't notice the shift.

"Have fun with Diego," Mom said without looking up from her newspaper.

"Tell that boy to cut his hair," Dad called.

I took the elevator down, trying not to think about how I looked, or more specifically how hard I'd worked on looking like I wasn't thinking about how I looked. I had my hair pulled up in a high puff—my go-to style, nothing fancy—and was wearing my glasses, just in case. Below the neck, I had on jeans and sneakers (and, under my jacket, a gray sweatshirt I'd cut so it fell off the shoulder like the one Jennifer Beals wears on the poster for *Flashdance*). So far, so normal. But I'd also stolen into Mom's makeup drawer and dusted something called Candlelight Glow highlighting powder onto my cheekbones, rubbing some on my eyelids, too, for good measure. That was new. I turned my head side to side, peering up into the tiny, triangular elevator mirror to see if I looked even the slightest bit more luminous. Given that the mirror looked to have been installed in the 1890s, it was hard to say.

You were waiting out on the sidewalk, hiding something behind your back. *Don't be flowers*, I thought, cringing a little, ungratefully, at the thought of having to hold them on the subway, or explain them to my parents. But it wasn't flowers.

"Your chariot awaits," you laughed, whipping out a pair of janky crutches. "They were my abuela's."

"Doesn't she need them, though?"

"Nah, she's in a wheelchair now."

You helped slip them under my arms and watched as I lurched and heaved myself over to the crosswalk. The crutches were a few inches too short, and the rubber was nearly worn off the bottoms, so they clanked a little on the pavement, but other than that, if I kept my left leg bent, they worked perfectly.

"I know it's not exactly flowers," you said, holding my arm as a bus careened past. "But this is your rest. This way you can stay off your bad foot."

"Thanks," I said, feeling foolish for rubbing all that fake glow on my face when you'd managed to give me the real deal in less than five minutes. Sure, hand-me-down walking aides from a disabled grandma wasn't the usual way of sweeping someone off their feet, but I decided that it definitely passed anyway, on a technicality.

"So where are we going?" I asked as we shoved ourselves onto a crowded downtown 1 train.

"She will trust in you," you said teasingly, in a bad impression of Mr. Dyshlenko's thick Russian baritone that came out sounding more like Yoda.

At Times Square, you squeezed my hand, and you must have seen the look of horror on my face—crossing 42nd Street on the first nice spring weekend of the year was definitely what Dante's inferno was originally based on, I was pretty sure—because you laughed. "Don't worry, we're just switching to the Q." The station turned out to be just as crazy, though, with huge groups of tourists and school kids lumbering through in seas of matching T-shirts, getting in the way of the fast-walking native New Yorkers, who bobbed and weaved around elbows and suitcases like weary-looking ninjas. At one particularly tricky intersection, where a team of break dancers was performing for a semicircle of onlookers, I got hip-checked so many times that you actually picked me up and carried me piggyback, holding the crutches out in front of you like a divining rod.

"This is practice," you explained, as I wrapped my arms around your neck. "The one-handed commuter clusterfuck lift."

"Criminally underused by Balanchine," I said.

"See? I'm bringing ballet to the people." You grinned.

We took the Q all the way downtown and into Brooklyn, until it snaked around Prospect Park and rose up out of the tunnels, hurtling along the elevated track, past Midwood and Sheepshead Bay. As most of the city receded behind us, I pulled out my phone.

"When should I tell my mom I'll be home?" I asked, pretending to start a text.

"I don't know. When's the latest they'll let you stay out?"

"I don't know, that depends on what we're doing." You raised your eyebrows and I felt my cheeks redden. "Not like—I just meant, where we're going."

"All the way," you said.

My neck got hot. "What do you mean?"

"The last stop. Coney Island." You paused, pulled back, and smiled suspiciously. "Why, what did you think I meant?"

"Nothing. I've just . . . never been to the last stop before." That was a lie; my dad used to take me to Cyclones games and I'd even gone to the Mermaid Parade once, with Liv and her mom, when I was eleven, before my parents had realized—because I had diligently reported back—that some of the mermaids went topless as part of their costumes. But I couldn't admit to you that all I could think about as the pale blue sky flashed by in the windows was when it would happen. We'd been flirting all week, getting used to our new, different chemistry like cautious kids doing a science project, curious about the results but too afraid to mix anything that might blow up in our faces. But the tension kept on building, and it couldn't hold forever. Sooner or later one of us was going to have to cross a line that would make it impossible to pretend that we were still just friends. The prospect was both thrilling and completely terrifying. I couldn't stop looking at your lips.

"You've *never* gone to Coney Island?" I watched them say, incredulously.

I shrugged. "New York City's a big place."

"Oh, man," you laughed, clapping your hands together. "I can't wait. This is gonna be the best."

It already is, I felt like saying.

Our first stop was Nathan's Famous Hot Dogs on the board-walk, where you made a big show of buying two hot dogs twice the length of their buns, plus curly fries and giant sodas that dripped condensation onto the table.

"A good, greasy meal is the foundation of the true Coney Island experience," you explained, brandishing the squirt-top ketchup like a paintbrush. "If you don't feel at least a little sick on the rides, you're doing it wrong."

"Rides?" I shook my head, swallowing my curly fry half-chewed. "Uh-uh. Who said anything about rides?"

You looked at me like I was crazy. "C'mon," you said. "We have to ride the rides. At least the Cyclone. That's the whole point."

"When I was—" I was about to tell you that when I was eight, I'd ridden the Cyclone and busted my nose on the safety bar (because I'd been hiding my face in my lap out of sheer terror, and the G-force during the descent had jerked my head upward). But then I remembered that as far as you were concerned I hadn't been to Coney Island. "When I was a kid I had a bad roller-coaster experience," I said, guiltily grabbing another fry.

"Then let me"—you took an enormous bite of your hot dog and grinned at me through bun-filled chipmunk cheeks— "replace it with a *good* experience."

"On that rickety-ass thing?" I laughed.

"It's only ninety years old. Besides, you can't really talk, gimpy." You gave me a look like, *It's on,* and it was a battle not to smile.

"I'll *think* about it," I said.

"That's the elevation portion of the day," you said. "It's the most important part of the healing process. We can't skip it."

"Mmmm hmmm." I gestured to our fast food feast. "And what's this supposed to be?"

You picked up your soda and shook it. "Ice, ice, baby."

I raised an eyebrow. "Flimsy, but I'll allow it." We toasted and knocked back the rest of our drinks. "What about compression?" I asked.

"Wait and see. That's the next stop."

"We going back to Times Square?" I laughed.

You smiled in a way that made my stomach flip. The ice joke had been lame, but at least we had heat covered.

"You'll see," you said.

The wind coming off the ocean was freezing, so we darted down the boardwalk, past an old man sitting on a folding chair under a beach umbrella, holding a boombox that was blaring "La Bamba." You pulled me into a brightly lit arcade and led me by the hand to an old-fashioned photobooth.

"Compression," you announced proudly, opening the curtain. I slipped off my glasses and leaned Abuela's crutches against the outside of the booth. Once we squeezed in, not knowing what to do, I perched awkwardly on your lap. I tried to make myself light and dainty by keeping as much weight as I could on my feet, like I was doing a static squat.

"OK, what faces are we making?" I asked as you fed three crumpled bills into the machine. "Silly or serious?"

"Let's alternate," you said, resting your hands on my hips.

The first pose was silly; I crossed my eyes and made a fish face. For the next one, we tried to look tough, all cocked eyebrows and mafioso sneers. On the third one, you tickled my ribs, so I was frozen mid-laugh, my face contorted in giggles while I tried to swat you at the same time. Once you stopped, I turned to tell you off but we were so close our noses brushed and I could feel your body tense under mine. So in the last split second before the flash went off, I whipped my face forward. When the photos came out a few minutes later, the last frame was just me looking nervous and blank-faced while you stared meaningfully into my ear.

"We definitely nailed it," you said, tucking the strip into your pocket.

I put off the Cyclone as long as possible, but by the late afternoon we'd eaten enough popcorn and churros to fuel a small circus, and I was getting tired of swinging up and down the boardwalk on the crutches. After our tenth game of Skee-Ball, I could tell your heart was someplace else, so I screwed up my courage and lied and told you I was ready.

"One ride," I said.

"Seriously?" You picked me up and spun me around, and when we stopped, our bodies pressed against each other for just a few extra seconds too long. I tilted my face up and thought, dizzily, *this is it.*

But it wasn't; you broke away and handed our prize tickets to a couple of little kids playing a basketball free-throw game nearby.

"Let's go," you said. "The line is probably insane."

The old man with the boombox was still in his spot under the beach umbrella, and as we walked by he started playing Whitney Houston's "I Wanna Dance with Somebody." I stopped cold. People like to talk about things being "their jam," but most of the time they're just posturing or trying to sound cool. But that song . . . that song was what I'd listened to in my room growing up, when I'd practiced my first "routines." My mom had it in a box of cassette tapes she'd kept from high school, and I'd always loved the way Whitney looked on the cover, lifting up the bottom of her tank top with her hair all big and unkempt like she gave zero shits. That song was my *jam.*

"What?" you asked, smirking at me. "You look like you're about to toss those crutches in the air like Tiny Tim and bust out the Running Man."

"Shut up!" I said. "This is my favorite song."

You just smiled and shook your head. "Of course it is."

Half an hour later we were still in line, waiting under the

shuddering support beams of the behemoth roller coaster, watching its little cars clatter and clack up and down a track that still looked to me, ten years later, like it had been built out of popsicle sticks by kindergartners as a joke.

"I can tell you're freaking," you said, laying a gentle hand on my back. "You're making that mad face."

"I don't like heights," I muttered, in between deep breaths.

"You were fine yesterday with the presage lift."

"Yeah, well—that was because of you."

You wrapped your arms around me from behind, resting your chin on my head. "Good thing I'm here now, too, right?" you asked, and I could feel the vibration of your voice in my whole body. "But if you're really that scared"—you squeezed me gently—"we don't have to."

I leaned back against your chest and thought about suggesting that we elevate on the much tamer Wonder Wheel instead, but then the ride was slowing to a stop and the last group was stumbling out, and all of a sudden I was handing your abuela's crutches to the bored-and-or-stoned-looking operator, and then we were in. It was too late to change my mind.

"You OK?" you asked, trying but failing to hold my left hand, which was gripping the safety bar like a vise.

"Don't ask," I said as the ride lurched into motion. Immediately, we were inching up a steep incline that would send us careening down an 85-foot drop at a 58-degree angle. A sign at the top read, STAY SEATED! DO NOT STAND UP! For anyone with a death wish, I guess.

"It will be fine," you said, adopting your Mr. Dyshlenko voice again. "You just have to hold on, hold on"—you gripped the bar, making a grim, nervous face—"and let go!" You threw your arms up like you were doing the wave at a ball game.

"I'm not doing that," I said, closing my eyes, wincing, waiting for the drop.

"Come on," you whispered. "Just look. It's amazing, you'll see."

I shook my head and squeezed my eyelids shut even tighter. "That's easy for you to say. Nothing scares you."

"That's not true."

The car was slowing down, gravity pulling us back. We were almost there. I could barely get the words out. "Name . . . one . . . thing."

There was a pause, and then you said, "Kissing you."

"What?" Without meaning to, I let go of the bar and opened my eyes, just in time to see the world drop away. You grabbed my hand, and then we were in free fall.

Afterward, once I'd regained the use of my legs and vocal chords, I pulled you onto a bench and made you tell me again.

"It scares me, too," I said. We were holding hands, smiling shyly at each other, and then at the ground. I traced the life line curving across your palm with tip of my finger.

"So, what, then?" you asked.

"Well . . ." I turned my face up to yours. "You know what those motivational posters say: Do something that scares you, every day."

You grinned, pulling me closer. "Just once a day?" you asked.

"I don't know," I said, pushing the hair out of your eyes. "I think we can get away with more. I mean, we *are* making up for lost time."

"How much—" you started to say, but then you shut up, because I took your face in my hands and pulled it onto mine.

We made up for lost time on that bench, warm, slow, intoxicating kisses that—once we got past the first, tentative, trembling ones—swelled like waves in no hurry to make it to shore. Later, we made up for lost time on the Wonder Wheel, our little boxcar swinging back and forth a hundred feet off the ground while we swayed together, our breath quickening, completely ignoring the view of the sun setting over the city. We somehow lost the crutches, but neither of us cared. More than a few times, I was overcome: my desire felt feverish, too big for my body. It escaped through my throat in halting sighs. I never wanted it to end.

I didn't want to get on the train to go home. I still wish we hadn't. Sometimes I like to pretend we're still up there on the ferris wheel, suspended someplace between heaven and Earth, preserved in a perfect moment in time when everything seemed like it was going to be all right.

That was the first day I knew I loved you, Diego.

There won't be a last.

Chapter Twenty-Two

April 24–29 (last week of Spring Break)
14 days left

LIFE DOESN'T HAPPEN IN MONTAGE, with newspapers spinning, or calendar pages falling off one by one. Dance sure as hell doesn't happen in montage, although I'd be the first to admit that it looks good on screen to see beautiful people go from lead-footed to flawless in the span of two minutes. But that second week with you—after you dropped me off on my corner, pressing me up against the graffiti-covered lamppost I'd Sharpied my name onto in fifth grade, and whispered, "Promise this will still be real tomorrow?"—felt like a flip book of best moments, lived in real time.

There was Monday: Coming up out of the subway into one of those impossibly beautiful Manhattan spring mornings, like God had Gershwin on surround sound, still tasting you on my lips, my whole body humming as I took the stairs two at a time, barely feeling my feet (you were right: adrenaline *is* a crazy drug). We flew across that stage, nailed the lift, and could barely keep our hands off each other, which Mr. Dyshlenko and the pianist pretended not to notice. "I will tell Sofia she has nothing to worry about," he said with a wry smile.

After rehearsal, we got lunch and walked to Central Park West, up to Sheep Meadow, where we lay for hours in various states of entanglement. With your head resting on my stomach, gazing up at a cloudless sky, you rewrote history, telling me everything you'd thought but hadn't said for the past four years. I was especially shocked by the fact that Caleb—who you'd been so nice to—had inspired various revenge fantasies in which you unleashed some crazy capoeira on him in the orchestra pit.

"Maybe you should double major in drama," I teased.

"What, you weren't jealous?"

"Of your lady friends?" I thought for a minute. You flirted with so many people, I never really knew who you were just talking to and who you were actually *talking to*. "No."

"Not even a little?" You sounded disappointed, and I wondered if I should tell you that whenever Liv or Ethan would start telling me about one of your hookups, I would stop them and change the subject. Liv always thought I was being a prude, and Ethan acted pissed, like I was robbing him of a valuable storytelling opportunity, but really I just never wanted to think about you, like that, with anyone.

"I mean, I guess I'm glad you never had anything serious." I ran my fingers through your hair. "That would have been weird."

"Actually," you said, "I did have something kind of for real with—"

A stab of envy tore through my gut. "I don't want to know!" I cried.

"I knew it!" You sat up and grinned, then leaned down and kissed me. "Don't worry," you whispered, your lips still grazing mine, your thick lashes fluttering against my cheek, "I was just waiting for you."

There was Tuesday: sitting in the locker room with ice on my ankle and heat everywhere else, as you gently explored the territory under my thin cotton tank, your mouth on my neck. Things were moving fast, but then again we weren't exactly starting from the beginning; it felt all of a sudden like we'd been dating for years and had only just realized we were allowed to touch.

On the uptown train ride I asked you, vaguely, if you'd ever had sex. I didn't really get the words out, but you could tell where I was going and saved me from having to get too detailed about the most intimate act two humans could share while we were squished next to an enormous sleeping construction worker.

"A few times," you said. "I'm sorry I didn't wait. I didn't know if—"

"No, I'm relieved," I said, leaning over to whisper the next part: "One of us should know what we're doing." Your ears turned red.

"Girl," you murmured, "Stop it. You're going to kill me."

We had dinner at your house, crowded around the tiny dining table with your mom and little brothers, eating pork and plantains while the Yankees game played on the radio. "I've given up," your mom laughed. "I've surrendered to chaos!" But

I loved how noisy and homey it felt, and how playful and loving the fighting was (except for Miggy and Emilio, who seemed
resolved to do each other serious bodily harm through a series
of post-meal couch-wrestling matches). In my family, I was
used to silence, passive-aggressiveness, or the classical station
on NPR. Deep belly laughter was not a Rogers-Wilson house-
hold specialty.

There was no chance I'd be staying over—a triple threat of
Catholicism, a shared bedroom, and my parents' curfew policy
made that abundantly clear—but your mom pulled me aside
before I left, both to send me home with extra food and to tell
me how happy she was about us.

"This just fills my heart," she said. When she smiled, she
looked like you—or, maybe, you looked like her—all dimples
and bright, dancing chestnut-colored eyes. "Between my job
and his rehearsals I barely see him, and it's hard not to worry.
But now that he has you . . ." She laughed and waved at her
face, blinking back tears. "You lift him up, that's all."

"Actually," you said, coming up and giving her a half sincere,
half *shut up now* hug, "I lift *her* up. If we're being technical."

"We're not," I said dryly, and your mom burst out laughing.

"Don't let this one go," she told you.

"I wasn't planning on it," you said, just as Emilio beaned
you in the face with a throw pillow.

And then there was Wednesday: Mr. D emailed us to say that he
was sick, but you quickly texted that we should rehearse anyway,
since we had security clearance to be at school and the whole
stage to ourselves, so I dragged myself out of bed (oh, who am

I kidding, I leapt. *Leapt!* Despite the lightning rod of pain in my leg), showered, and threw on my warm-up clothes, skipping coffee since I was already running strong on what felt like a battalion of butterflies madly flapping their wings inside my chest.

The first clue that something was up was Coach, who greeted me at the back entrance with a big smile and an envelope.

"I always told you," he said. "I said from the beginning, Joy, you need to give this boy a chance. Can't you see he loves you?"

"I don't remember it exactly like that," I laughed. "I remember it more like you wandering the halls, awkwardly forcing people into pretend arranged marriages."

"You are welcome," he said with an affectionate wink, handing me the note.

STEP UP . . . to your locker, it read in your small, slanted printing. *(But actually take the elevator so you don't break your foot)*.

Inside the elevator, stuck to the second-floor button, was a Post-it that read, *You give me SATURDAY NIGHT FEVER (without the depressing ending)*. I grinned stupidly at it as the doors closed.

Sticking out of the side of my locker was a second envelope. *There's some GREASE waiting for you in Studio 2, HONEY.* On the floor, you'd laid out a little picnic blanket with a bacon, egg, and cheese sandwich, coffee, and another note: *SAVE THE LAST DANCE for me. I'll be waiting CENTER STAGE.*

I couldn't wait. I grabbed the food and made a beeline for the auditorium as fast as I could, swinging open the heavy door and practically spilling the coffee in my excitement to see you. But no one was there.

"Hello?" I called as I made my way down the aisle. The stage lights were on, but I didn't see any evidence of you—no dance bag, no jacket. But as I got closer, I saw that there was something out of place. Sitting on the edge of the stage, surrounded by the little pieces of gaffe tape Ethan used to mark the blocking for his play . . . was a boombox.

MAKE YOUR MOVE, read a Post-it taped to the play button.

I looked around, peering into the wings with a smile so wide my cheeks hurt. "OK!" I yelled. "I'm about to press play, so you'd better be ready with your *Magic Mike* striptease! If I don't hear Ginuwine, I'm walking out!" I set down the coffee and tossed my bag onto a front-row seat. Then I followed instructions.

The sound that filled the auditorium nearly made me weep. I would have known those bouncy beats and claps anywhere. I'd probably listened to them a hundred times, over and over, as I'd twirled around on my rug in stocking feet, my face stoic with focus, imagining I was a *very* serious prima ballerina who just happened to prefer late-80s pop hits to Tchaikovsky.

By the time Whitney unleashed the effervescent "Whoooo!" that started the music in earnest, you appeared, in a black tank top and dance pants, taking a graceful leap that ended with you sliding across the stage toward me on your knees. You got up grinning and shimmying your hips, beckoning me with one finger. When you started mouthing the words, I threw my head back and laughed.

"What?" you asked, lifting me up onstage and guiding me into a penchée. "You're not the only one with a mom who hoards her golden oldies." I spun around and kissed you, but you broke away after a few seconds.

"Later," you laughed, "This is a rehearsal."

You meant it. We basically ran through the entire pas de deux, modifying the ankle-busting moves and adjusting the pacing slightly for the pulse-pounding beats of 1987's #4 Billboard Hot 100 hit. It was exhilarating, all that childhood nostalgia crashing up against the first blush of love in some kind of retro, high-impact cardio fever dream.

"Think we should tell Adair to change the music?" you asked when it was over, catching your breath long enough to deliver a slow, knee-weakening kiss.

"Oh, yeah," I said. "She'll definitely go for it."

"This dance, it is love! It is passion! It is synthesizers!" you joked.

"It is lust," I said, before I could help myself. We looked at each other for one electric minute, and then you asked, "Are your parents home?"

They weren't, but a thick envelope from Barnard was, propped up under the narrow row of mailboxes it was too wide to fit in.

"That's good news, right?" you asked, reacting to my crest-fallen face.

"It's good news for my dad," I said. "It might be good news for me if I wanted to go."

"That's the thing," you said, kissing my neck, "You don't have to. The great thing about life is that you get to choose what you want to do."

"Not for us," I said, squirming out of your grasp. I was

more upset than I wanted you to know. I could already hear the
dinner table conversation, packed with tense buzzwords like
opportunity and *privilege*. I could practically feel the weight
of my father's elbows on the table as he gesticulated, trying to
make me see how foolish I was for taking a chance over a guar-
antee. "We don't get to choose a ballet company, they have to
choose *us*." I swallowed hard, reluctantly picking up the envelope. "What if no one chooses me?"

"I choose you," you said.

"You know what I mean." I pressed the elevator button. It
was stopped, indefinitely it seemed, on the fourth floor—one
more thing that felt close enough to touch but just out of reach.

"I do know, but listen—" You spun me around and made
me look at you. "You can't worry so much about the future. It's
coming, it's gonna happen, and it'll be beautiful and terrible but
everything will be OK."

"Beautiful and terrible, huh?" I smiled, impressed with your
off-the-cuff poetry. "What makes you say that?"

"It's from a page on my mom's 365 Quotes of Faith calendar," you admitted sheepishly.

"Huh." I pressed the button again; this time the doors
sprang open. "That where you get all your pickup lines?"

"Not all of them. The Book of Job is pretty dark, makes for
awkward sexting."

I shot you a particularly charged side-eye, and you laughed.

"Hey," you said, "I'm kidding, but I know this is serious for
you, so if you want me to go . . ."

"No." I looked up at your face, marveling for the hun-
dredth time in days how I could have looked at it for so many

years and not felt the spine-tingling tremor of longing I was feeling just then. I pulled you in and kissed you as the elevator made its slow ascent, lingering on every floor like it had a mad crush. You finally pulled back, your eyes warm and dark, searching.

"You sure?" you asked.

I nodded, still holding you, dizzy from adrenaline. "I need the distraction."

When the elevator doors dinged opened again, I led you inside my apartment and tossed the thick Barnard envelope on the dining room table, unopened.

"Are you sure?" you asked again as we paused outside my bedroom door. A breeze was coming in through the open window, and the chimes I'd hung out on the fire escape crashed together, releasing a tumble of notes that washed over me like a sweet fever—like your touch on my skin.

I nodded and kissed you, first on the mouth and then on each cheekbone, each eyelid, the side of your neck, your Adam's apple. I heard your breath catch in your throat, felt your heart as I traced my fingers down your chest.

We were standing on one side of a door, and I think we both knew that once we stepped through, there was no going back.

I pressed into you and felt your arms encircle me, lifting me ever so slightly just like you did onstage. All that time you'd been literally sweeping me off my feet, and it had taken me so long to feel it that it was almost too much—a dam breaking deep inside, pulling me under, leaving me breathless.

I love you, I almost said, but the words felt too new on my tongue, green like unripened fruit.

So instead I whispered, "I need you," which was just as true. . . .

The only thing missing from that week was Liv. I was bursting to tell her what was happening. She'd spent so many years trying to force me to fall in love—wrong-headedly, of course, but kind of sweetly, in her way—and I finally understood why. It felt like she'd been speaking another language since we turned fourteen, and I'd suddenly become fluent overnight. I couldn't wait to practice.

I told my parents—not everything, don't worry, I wasn't trying to kill anyone—but it wasn't the same. They were cautiously happy for me (they'd always liked you) but kept interjecting my lovestruck babbling, saying things like, "How will you find time for him with your ballet schedule and all your finals?" and "You know, it's highly unlikely you two will end up in the same place next year."

What I needed was someone who would shriek when I told them, who would breathlessly ask me what it was like, and how I felt, and what *exactly* had happened and in what order, spare *no* details. I needed someone I could confess to, and whose job it was to tolerate long, rambling monologues about infinitesimal gestures and glances and what they might mean, while prophesizing wildly with me about the future. I needed my best friend.

But she was gone. Every text I sent went unanswered—even my shameless attempts to drop hints that that I had big, big news—and when I finally called her, her voicemail box was full. On Friday I caved, and asked you to ask Dave to find out if he'd seen her, just to make sure she was OK. When you reported back that she was alive and in the city and "just flaky, like she is," I'd stopped feeling worried and started feeling hurt. How many times had I patiently listened while Liv talked about a crush, or "educated" me about sex, or painstakingly analyzed a boyfriend's motives? You were my first real boyfriend, my first real anything, and she didn't even know. She didn't seem to care.

"I just thought she'd be excited," I said. That was Saturday. We were waiting in line at the movies. I was in excruciating pain by then; I'd been so caught up in you that I'd been careless. I had to wear the air cast Dr. Pashkin had given me just to be able to walk, and I couldn't take a step without feeling a tingle of paranoia that someone would see me, and that I'd lose everything. (That was when I thought "everything" meant the chance to dance in Showcase.) At least you kept me distracted. You liked to joke that I probably needed to spend more time lying down.

I'd been talking to you a lot about how I wanted to talk to Liv *about* you, which was what happened when the best friend was taken out of the equation: a crazy-making feedback loop of misplaced angst.

"She'd probably be *too* excited, actually," I went on. "She'd try to micromanage everything and I would hate it after about five seconds. But I just want her to know about us for some reason."

"To make it real?" you asked.

"Nah." I leaned into you playfully. "It's gotten pretty real already. Maybe it's just a girl thing."

You smiled. "I tell people about you."

"Oh, yeah? Who?"

"Theo and Dominic," you said. "Abuela, obviously, although she can't really hear so she thinks I'm dating a guy named Joe."

"Stop it," I laughed, burying my nose in your shirt.

"And I told Roth, too."

"Do you think he told Liv?" I blurted before I could think of a way to ask it less blatantly. You'd been patient, but I could tell that my endless speculation about Liv wasn't exactly your favorite conversation topic.

"I don't know." You shrugged. "I don't know how much they hang, just that they're rehearsing." You wrapped an arm around me. "And you know what rehearsing can do to people."

"Ha," I said, as if saying a syllable of laughter out loud could make it seem funny. Liv and Dave hooking up wouldn't have surprised me. But if it was true—if *that* was why she'd gone so AWOL—then it was even worse. Because she hadn't told me. She hadn't even gotten in touch to share her *own* drama, which she had always done, without fail, even when I didn't have time to listen.

It would mean Liv wasn't just being flaky, she was done with me.

are we still friends? Y/N, I typed quickly as we made our way into the theater. It was an infantile tactic, but I was done playing the responsible one.

The next morning, I got my answer: A single thumbs-up emoji. No explanation, no apology, no acknowledgment of all the other messages. A thumbs. Fucking. Up.

good to know, I wrote, and then deleted the thread—which had been a one-sided parade of blue bubbles, anyway.

That was Sunday, one week to the day after I'd woken up after my date with you, tingling with excitement, feeling like the sun was rising over the earth from inside my body. In just a week, I'd gained my first real boyfriend and lost my first real friend.

Life doesn't happen in montage, but sometimes it feels that way. A bud can blossom overnight; a fracture can break just as fast. I don't believe anything happens for a reason anymore, but I have learned one thing about fate:

It's got a hair trigger.

Act Four

Ethan

Chapter Twenty-Three

April 30
13 days left

THE MOST PATHETIC THING, the thing that makes me cringe now, is how hard I tried. And the biggest punch line is that I didn't try hard at anything until I met you.

My parents never expected much—apparently my conception itself was such a miracle that just the fact of my being was enough for them—and in elementary and middle school, teachers always seemed to sense that they should call as little attention to me as possible, since I got enough shit for being so tiny and shy, with the kind of cartoon carrot-red hair that earned me nicknames like Ginger Ale, Gingerbread, and Ginger Rogers. The last one was especially insulting, since I knew there was no way those thick-necked third-grade mouth-breathers even knew who she was, but I also knew that admitting I watched old MGM musicals with my geriatric dad would only add to the ridicule, so I kept my mouth shut and my head down, writing revenge scenes in the back pages of my notebooks. I always liked making up dialogue; it came naturally to me, telling people what to say, controlling the words. Bending it to my whims.

But you were impossible to direct off-stage. The whole time in Key West, I kept trying to come up with something that would make you do what I wanted you to do in real life, i.e., kissing me more than once every six weeks; not acting like everything about me annoyed the living shit out of you. While my parents sipped their frozen cocktails at the bar, I composed saccharine sonnets about the sunsets, and how they reminded me of your eyes. At poolside bingo, I used the resort's Wi-Fi to look up Spanish endearments on my phone. I bought one of those grains of rice with your name on it. During my cousin Candy's rehearsal dinner, I got drunk and poured my heart out with my thumbs, typing a string of texts under the tablecloth that thankfully didn't send because of Verizon's piss-poor roaming. At night I lay awake imagining your unexpected change of heart in my absence, casting you in a silent movie full of loneliness and regret and lots of Holden Caulfield–esque navel-gazing at the Central Park duck pond, culminating in a string of lusty messages I'd get as soon as we touched down at JFK:

> i miss you.
>
> i'm sorry i've been so distant.
>
> i'm going crazy here.
>
> come back.

come over.

i need you.

i want you.

I replayed our sporadic, frustratingly PG-rated love scenes over and over, writing and rewriting the surrounding scenes. What had I done right in those moments to make you like me? And what had I done wrong to fuck it up?

I wish I could say I maintained even one iota of cool and waited to text you until I got home, but we hadn't even taxied all the way to the terminal.

hey killer, need to catch up on what i missed while
i was poolside in kw. buy u dinner?

Fucking idiot. That was my inner voice talking, the one my child psychologist had (patronizingly and not particularly creatively, I thought) called Angry Ethan, but which I called the Director. It wasn't a multiple personality, so I wasn't crazy or anything. I had just gone through a rough patch in middle school that had included a lot of depression and crying and what I later learned was called "passive ideation," like fantasizing about being run down by a semi truck, or shot with a stray bullet meant for someone else—the classic innocent bystander. Also, my mom had found a draft I'd written of a thoroughly mediocre, amateur-hour play called *The Big Sleep*, about a kid trying to plan his suicide (it was supposed to be a black comedy, because all he does is plan, he never actually does anything, get it?), and so the therapist had been called and meds had been prescribed, and it all worked out and I was fine. Except for the Director, who still excoriated me on the regular. But I had gotten used to it, and besides, he was usually right.

Leave her alone! She's not into you. You're just embarrassing yourself at this point. Take your sad grain of rice and your awful poetry and go shove them in a drawer along with your blue balls.

But then three little dots appeared in a bubble on my screen. You were typing. They kept vanishing and then popping back up again, suggesting that you were revising the message, putting some thought into it. And then it occurred to me that a constantly disappearing ellipsis was exactly what you were, in general, in my life, and that I needed to use that metaphor in the next thing I wrote that wasn't set before the dawn of cellular technology.

kk, when/where?

I must have made some kind of noise, some gasp of shocked elation, because my dad clapped his book shut and peered over at me.

"What is happening in the world?" he asked, like I would use my first minute of Internet connectivity to check the news.

"Nothing," I mumbled. "I'm just texting with Liv."

"I remember those days," he said dreamily, with a humiliatingly conspicuous wink. It was hard to believe my dad, with his thick gut and the forest of gray hair covering every inch of his body except for half his head, had ever been considered a playboy, but part of the reason he didn't settle down until he was in his mid-fifties was that he had been what people called "a confirmed bachelor"—before it was code for gay.

"She wants me to take her to dinner," I said, puffing my chest out a little, even though moving at all still hurt a little because of my sunburn.

"Absence makes the heart grow fonder, eh?" He smiled and settled back into his seat, presumably thinking of the mountains of eager young women he'd gone through in his early years, as a dashing Russian immigrant with his own air conditioning repair shop in Queens.

Too bad he got such a cowardly, sensitive little virgin for a son.

Even before I met you, on my first day at Janus, I could tell I was out of my league. The only reason I'd even started acting in the first place was because I was small enough that I could still play all the little kid parts in community theater productions while being able to memorize lines and say them without crying. After the whole *Big Sleep* debacle, I begged my parents to let me go to high school off-island, with kids who didn't know anything about me. I was gunning for LaGuardia, so when I got into Janus it was a total shock. It was true that I'd auditioned with the monologue from *Saving Nathan*, the depressing one Roth did right before he flatlined. I'd poured everything into it, all of the confusion and sadness and anger, all of the darkest parts of my tortured pubescent brain. "Your son is the most naturalistic actor I've ever seen," Ms. Hagen had written in a personal note to my mother along with my acceptance offer. What she didn't realize was that I had only been naturalistic because I was pretending I was dying. It was the one and only method trick I had.

I stared at my phone screen, trying to come up with something that would impress you, and simultaneously hating myself for even trying. You'd always tolerated me—maybe even liked me sometimes—but I'd known what I was getting into from day one. You were beautiful, cool, and instantly popular, my ticket to social acceptance and access. It took me awhile to figure out what I could offer you in return, but once it became apparent to everyone that my Janus audition had been a fluke, I saw a niche with my name on it. I could write for you, make you my muse. You might never want me, but I could make you need me.

Or think you did, anyway.

"Wow, this is fancy."

You handed your chicly oversized army jacket to the maître d', who looked down at your outfit—motorcycle boots, leggings, and an asymmetrical gray sweatshirt emblazoned with the neon pink letters LOL JK—with weary trepidation. I'd chosen an old-school New York steakhouse famous for its romantic atmosphere and celebrity clientele, not realizing there was also a dress code. I shifted uncomfortably in my too-large brown suit jacket, which had been forced on me at the door, after an ID check had confirmed that yes, I *was* the Mr. Entsky with the 6:30 reservation and the credit card authorization from his daddy on file. At least I'd gotten there before you, so you didn't witness that part.

Asshole, the Director sneered. *Now she thinks you're stuck up and the restaurant thinks you're a low-class spoiled brat.*

"It's classic," I said. "You look gorgeous, by the way." I took your hand and started to lift it to my lips—so far, that move had been the only one I'd managed to pull off—but you pulled it back and crossed your arms over your chest.

"I'm underdressed," you said, with a self-conscious half-laugh.

They didn't bother giving us a wine menu, so we ordered Cokes—one regular, one diet—and sat on opposite sides of a round booth, examining the thick, leather-bound menus. I kept trying to catch your eye, but you hardly looked up. I could feel your boot tapping incessantly against the table leg, making my silverware jiggle on the maroon silk napkin. It made me nervous.

"I, uh, got you something," I said, taking the little vial with the rice grain out of my shirt pocket. It felt so stupid and insignificant as I pushed it across the table, like giving someone a paper clip or a stray button, but you actually looked touched when you saw what it was.

"I used to want one of these so bad!" you cried. "Well, that and getting shells braided into my hair." You examined the gift in the palm of your hand and looked at me guiltily. "I didn't get you anything."

"You didn't go anywhere," I said. "Plus, your presence is present enough." I tried to soften the corny line—which I'd basically stolen from my mom, who always told me not to get her anything for Mother's Day because *I* was the gift—with a wink. You opened your mouth and then closed it again.

"You look like you got . . . some color," you finally said, squinting.

A waiter came to take our order. I asked for a porterhouse, you asked for a mixed-green salad. You insisted you weren't hungry, which was kind of inconvenient considering we were out to dinner.

"Don't be the starving actress, that's such a cliché!" I joked, but you got quiet for a while after that, so I guess I hit a nerve. At the table next to us, one elderly man was telling another elderly man about his nephew's prostate cancer.

"So," I finally said, "when are we going to talk about the elephant in the room?"

"Huh?" Your eyes flitted up, widening briefly, before returning to your lap. "What do you mean?"

"*The play*. I didn't hear anything from you or Roth over break. So did you make it work, or am I going to have to redo the whole thing as a black-box monologue?"

The truth was, even though I wanted badly for it not to suck, I had the least at stake of all of us when it came to Showcase. I'd already gotten into the dramatic writing program at Tisch, anyway, so all I really needed at that point was the credit. The fact that you and Roth had been acting like it was a production of *Who's Afraid of Virginia Woolf?* since the beginning of March was bizarre and disappointing, but I'd made my peace with it. That night I was more interested in what your motivations were in real life. And big surprise, even when you were right in front of me, I still wasn't sure. What *had* you been doing for the past two weeks? I wondered. You looked flushed but drawn, your eyes bright and bloodshot. Only you could manage to fade and glow at the same time.

"We rehearsed," you said vaguely.

"What," I pressed, "like . . . once?"

You shrugged, but your boot kept tapping, and my silverware kept jiggling. "Once was enough," you said. "We fixed it."

"Care to elaborate?"

"We just . . ." You weren't looking at your lap, I realized. You were looking at something under the table, next to your leg. Your phone, probably. ". . . worked out the kinks," you finished.

She'd rather be anywhere but here. You thought you could buy her attention with an expensive dinner? LOL, buddy. J fucking K.

"Oh, well . . . good!" I said cheerfully, trying to change my approach. "I can't wait to see it."

Your eyes darted up from wherever they'd been, and I saw what looked like a flash of pity.

"What *were* you doing, if you weren't rehearsing?" I asked before I could stop myself.

"Hanging with Joy, mostly." You reached into your bag and I heard the telltale sound of Tic Tacs rattling. "When she wasn't with Diego, anyway." You popped one into your mouth and raised your eyebrows. "They finally hooked up."

"Good for them." My voice was dry ice; it was hard to work up much enthusiasm for someone like Diego Ortega, hardly an antihero with his curls and dimples and muscles, who had girls swooning left and right without even trying. And besides, I doubted Diego and Joy were spending their night having a wooden, awkward conversation over a stuffy early-bird dinner. They were probably alone somewhere, all over each other, the way you're *supposed* to be when you finally hook up with the person you've always wanted.

Only she's never wanted you. An important difference.

"Here we are." The waiter reappeared with our food, making a big show of setting down the plates and grinding fresh pepper onto your architectural pile of $16 lettuce.

"Are you sure you don't want some steak?" I asked. You looked like you could use some, but I couldn't think of a way to say it that wouldn't sound insulting or like I was trying to hit on you.

"Nope." You poked at your salad, your eyes still dropping down to some unseen distraction every thirty seconds. Your right hand disappeared under the tablecloth.

"Hey, are you—um, I mean, do you need to make a call or something?"

You froze for a second but then flashed a quick, apologetic smile. "Just texting Joy. She's new to this, so . . . you know."

Actually, I didn't, and I think you knew that, too. "Well," I said, "Maybe it could wait until after." I could hear my own voice, whiny and high-pitched, like I was one of those sixteenth-century Italian singers who got their nuts cut off so their voices wouldn't change. No wonder you weren't jumping my bones. But then again, I'd always looked and sounded like me, and you'd kissed me anyway. So—what, then? I couldn't ask you *why* you'd done it without sounding like a complete idiot, but it was all I could think about. Your lips on my neck, your tongue in my mouth, like I was having some surreal, waking wet dream in front of the whole school. The only reason I hadn't given up yet was the chance it might happen again.

"I'm going to the bathroom," you announced.

"Have fun," I said. Like an asshole.

You'd only been gone for about ten seconds when I realized I could look at your phone. I had a sudden, paranoid need to know if you'd really been texting Joy about Diego, or about how stupid and lame I was. If you'd really been texting Joy at all. Luckily I could scoot around the booth without drawing too much attention to myself. I moved a foot closer to your side and then reached my arm around. Your bag was so big, it was easy to grab one of the handles and pull it closer to me.

In the dim, "romantic" lighting I'd been so excited about, it was hard to see much, but since 95 percent of your purse's contents seemed to be bottles and tissues, it didn't take too long to find the flat planes of your iPhone. The screen was locked on a picture of Madonna from the 90s, when she was in her lackluster Marilyn phase. I tried your birthday and then, in a fit of desperate delusion, the keypad numbers that spelled out my own name, but I didn't want to have the phone lock you out and reveal my trespassing, so I quickly threw it back in. I couldn't stop, though. I waded my fingers through the detritus of your private life, feeling for a clue that would tell me something that might complete the ellipsis and put me out of my misery. Keys, Tic Tacs, coins, wallet, something long and crinkly that turned out to be a tampon . . . finally, I stumbled on a bumpy foreign object. Glancing over the banquette to make sure you weren't coming back, I pulled it out.

It was a little fabric zipper pouch—screen-printed with big

yellow letters that spelled out WHAAM!—and inside was a small Ziploc bag. It was cloudy with chalky dust, but in the bottom corner there were a few visible chunks of white pills, a clear plastic cylinder that looked like some kind of salt shaker or something, and a rolled-up dollar bill. I stared at it for a few seconds.

What in the actual fuck?!

That was something you would have said. I was even thinking in your voice. But if I loved you that much, if I was so completely obsessed with everything about you, wouldn't I have noticed that you were on what looked like pretty hard drugs? I sat there motionless, tingling with adrenaline.

At least it's not another dude.

I hated myself for it, but there it was.

Or maybe she had to get high to want to touch you in the first place.

You had definitely been blitzed at the party, that was never up for debate. But the rest of the time—I wracked my brain, trying to separate out the hours and hours we'd spent together since then, but there was no incident that I could remember, no red flag marking the dividing line between "before" and "after." You'd been sort of erratic and mean, but that wasn't totally abnormal. You'd also devolved into a mediocre actress, but maybe the WHAAM! explained it.

That's when I heard a door swing open and realized I was still holding the pouch. As fast as I could, I zipped it shut, stuffed it back into your bag, and pushed my way back to my spot in the booth. I made it just in time to see your head bob into view.

"Sorry I kept you waiting," you said.

I forced a smile. "I'll always wait for you," I said.

I walked you home, despite your protestations that it was close and still light outside. I decided that if you blew me off three times I would stop trying—obviously in most situations no means no and there's no gray area, but I was trying to be gentlemanly, and I was worried about you after my discovery at the restaurant, and besides, you didn't know that the Staten Island ferry left every thirty minutes, so you believed me when I claimed I was stuck until eight—but on the third ask you just kind of shrugged and took out your phone, so I fell into step with you on 9th Avenue, trying to keep up, so that people would think we were at least friends, if not together.

We'd used to be friends without having to try so hard. Freshman year, during *Godspell* rehearsals, you'd seemed to think I was cute, treating me in a slightly condescending but affectionate way, like I was your adorable sidekick, or some talking Pixar animal (apparently Joy never really played that role the way you wanted). You would call me Jesus, but pronounced the Spanish way, and ruffle my hair, making all the pretty, strong-chinned drama boys *wish* they were Ginger Rogers, just to get that kind of attention. But your love, such as it was, was conditional on remaining nonthreatening. Once I started to get ambitious, when I realized I could stop pretending to be able to act and write my way into a new major instead, that was when we started clashing. The tension only made me want you more, although the one time I made the mistake of talking to my mom about it, she told me there was no such thing as a "love-hate" relationship.

"If there's any hate, then it's not really love, is it?" she'd said, like she knew what she was talking about. Apparently she never watched TV.

After five blocks of monk-like silence, we got to your building, a 60s monolith of butter-colored brick and a big plate glass entryway. It was a balmy night, so the door was propped open, and the elderly doorman smiled at us from his chair just inside.

"Miss Liv!" he called out. "*No puedo seguir el ritmo de todos sus novios.*" He chuckled and waved at me. It was the first good response I'd gotten since the rice grain. If your doorman remembered who I was, then you must have at least mentioned me. Then I wasn't completely delusional.

"Ignore him," you mumbled, looking tense.

"So, see you tomorrow, I guess—"

"I had a nice time," you said brusquely.

"—unless you want me to . . ." I shifted from foot to foot, tried on a smile. "I could come up and . . ."

And what, moron? Make awkward small talk with her parents? Stage an intervention? Or do you think if you manage to get her alone and stand in the right light, she'll suddenly realize her animal desire and drag you into bed?

"Actually, I'm pretty tired." In the harsh lobby lights, your pupils were comically dilated. I wondered what you were on, and how I'd never noticed it before.

"Right," I said.

"But thank you for dinner." You leaned forward and braced

yourself on my shoulders, delivering a dry peck on my cheek. It felt like some cigar-smoking mogul stamping a letter in a black and white movie while cackling maniacally. VOID. REJECTED.

I stuffed my hands in my pockets and watched you walk to the elevator, jamming the button impatiently, digging in your bag for something you'd never, in all the years I'd known you, seemed to find. Only maybe you had found it, and maybe I finally knew what it was.

Once the doors had closed and you were gone, I stood there for another minute, wondering what I was supposed to do. A good boyfriend, a stand-up guy, would probably tell you he knew, and that he was worried about you, and that you needed to stop. But I was more of a stand-down kind of guy, and I was pretty sure I wasn't your boyfriend, either.

"Hey, man, everything OK?" the doorman finally asked, noticing my impression of a sad statue.

"Yeah, sorry." I moved to leave but then stopped short. I had to say something. Even if it wasn't directly to you. "Has she . . . um, has *she* been OK?" I asked.

"Oh, yeah, she's tough," he said with a dismissive wave. "She takes care of herself." He smiled. "And besides, Miss Liv's got lots of friends. Someone's been here all week. They barely left."

"Joy?" I asked hopefully. "Black girl, like my height?" He narrowed his eyes, and I tried to backtrack. "I mean, like African American . . . woman?"

"Nah, I know Miss Joy," the doorman said. "I don't know the new one. They never stop to talk to me. He's—"

He.

My face must have changed, because he stopped short. "You know what, I can't really keep track," he laughed. "She's always making new friends."

"Right," I said hollowly.

It could be her dealer! my brain practically screamed, as if that would be good news. If you were using so much that you saw your dealer every day, then you were really in trouble.

"What did he look like?" I asked.

"I—you know, I didn't get a good look, man," he said. "So many people coming and going." But his expression had changed; there was pity in his eyes. And there it was. The boom I'd been waiting for. The remote detonation I hadn't seen coming.

There was someone else. The radio silence over break, the texting under the table—it all made sense. Listen, I wasn't stupid; I knew you never loved me. What hurt was that "*he*," whoever he was, had weaseled his way into your life—maybe even into your bed—in a matter of days when I had put in so much time already. I was the only one who had always been there for you. I was the only one who really knew you.

Or was I?

It's trite to say you broke my heart, so instead I'll say you broke my brain.

Because the thing of it was, if I did know you better than anyone, how could I have missed two such glaring omissions from your biography? My love wasn't of the oblivious greeting card variety that everyone else seemed so blindly happy to practice; I'd always thought I saw you for exactly who you were—smart and funny and gorgeous, sure, but also manipulative, self-interested, insecure, and a little devious, which frankly made you all the more glorious in my eyes.

I walked back down Charles Street toward the subway station in total shock, not so much at the evening's revelations as at what they seemed to imply.

Either I'd never really known you or I'd never really loved you.

I didn't know which was worse.

Chapter Twenty-Four

First week of May
12 days left

JEALOUSY WAS A MISERABLE SICKNESS, but I'd lived with it for so long I barely noticed its symptoms anymore. There was no way for me to soothe the painful cognitive dissonance that came from the realization that I didn't know you as well as I thought, or from loving you desperately despite having been so betrayed, so instead I spent all my free time the first week after spring break trying to find a better target for my hatred: *him*.

I scoured the Internet for clues, but you were one of those people who mostly ghosted on social media, not posting for weeks at a time. The same could not be said, sadly, for your hipster douchebag of an ex-boyfriend, Jasper Davenport, who seemed to think the world needed to see every kindergarten-level collage he made with "found" pieces of trash (the skateboard he'd recently découpaged with stale Twinkies and empty condom wrappers was especially poignant). But based on his artful, shadow-drenched selfies, Jasper looked to be shacked up with a dark-eyed sophomore vocal major, so that was a dead end. None of your exes' feeds made any mention of you. I even tried to find Diego's cousin, but I couldn't remember his name, and besides, I figured, drug dealers probably didn't have Tumblr accounts.

I knew Joy would tell on me if I pumped her for information, and that Diego was just Joy once removed, but in a moment of panic I did text Roth after a few beers in my basement late one night to find out if he knew what you'd been up to over break. I didn't relish giving him another glimpse inside my ever-increasing emasculation (**Would you ask her what she wants with me?** Jesus, that was sad, no wonder no one ever came to my house), but I also didn't have much of a choice. It was either trust him, or fly blind.

Sorry man, just saw her at rehearsals, he wrote back, so I got drunk and worked some more on my new play, a monologue about a World War II soldier cuckolded by his wife back home.

At school it was hard to keep a straight face. The anger and mortification just kept growing. I blamed myself, obviously, and your doorman and the lucky, probably brain-dead male model idiot you'd been taking upstairs and every single person I ran into, especially the couples, rubbing their happiness in everyone's faces, the Diegos and Joys of the world getting exactly what they wanted. And then, of course, there was you.

Being high didn't excuse what you'd done to me. The more I thought about it, the more I was sure about that, at least.

The saving grace of tech week was that it consumed me by necessity even more than you consumed me by choice. I spent most

of my time in the darkened theater with our technical director, Chris, a recent college grad whose sole role on the faculty
was to do the technical jobs all of the actors felt were beneath
them. Over the next few days I also started a little experiment
in which I stopped talking to you unless you directly asked me
a question. We could do a whole run-through and I might say
nothing. It was fun to watch the insecurity take hold as I gave
Roth notes and completely ignored you. I wanted to make you
crave my attention, and the only way I could force you to realize you needed it was to take it away.

I was relieved at first that whatever you two had done
over break, however infrequently, seemed to have worked.
The energy was back, the dialogue wasn't as rushed, and your
chemistry was believable again—onstage, at least. The weird
thing was that when you *weren't* saying lines, you still seemed
to be avoiding each other. At the end of rehearsal, you'd leave
not only at separate times, but through separate exits. Without
the hostility that had plagued the weeks before break, the dis-
connect seemed out of place, like overacting for an audience of
one. In retrospect, that was my first real clue.

My second came courtesy of Diego, who I ran into in the
costume shop, getting fitted for a bolero.

"Looking fancy, dude," I said, scanning the racks for the
post-Victorian work clothes the costumer, Ms. Gaspard, had
been tailoring for our dress rehearsal.

"Feeling pretty fancy," he grinned.

"Don't move your arms, honey," Ms. Gaspard mumbled
through a mouthful of pins.

"So how's it coming together?" I didn't care, really—dance

was never my thing, and I got bored watching anything with no dialogue—but in order to pump him for information, I had to go through the motions of social graces.

"Amazing," he said. "Although I guess I can't speak for Joy, since she's working twice as hard as me."

"Is it different now that you two are . . ." I let my ellipsis do the talking, and Diego blushed.

"Yeah," he said. "I mean, no, but—it's just better, you know? Everything's better." He smiled, like he couldn't believe his luck, and I focused hard on making my face look normal, forcing the bitterness down.

"I've seen this happen so many times," Ms. Gaspard said, placing her final pin in Diego's velvet lapel. "Get kids together, rehearsing nonstop . . . something always clicks."

"Not for everyone," I said. "I almost had to recast, but luckily my leads got back on track."

"Well, there's an exception to every rule." Ms. Gaspard turned Diego so that he could admire himself in the full-length mirror, and then busied herself getting my costumes off the rack. "But when it's there, anyone can see it. You can fake a lot of things, but you can't fake chemistry."

I bristled. Your chemistry with Roth had been natural—that was partially why I cast him, even though he was way too classically handsome for the gangly, nondescript Rodolpho I had envisioned when I wrote the play. I hadn't been worried because I thought you were mine then—and also because by the end of February you two had been constantly sniping at each other. It was only since I'd gotten back that things had shifted. Anything that had happened would have happened while I was gone.

Someone's been here all week. They barely left. A stomach-turning casting choice for your "new friend" snaked its way into my brain with a venomous hiss.

He wouldn't, I thought. It's so sad and telling how I never doubted that *you* would. But not him. He was my friend.

"Can we, uh, get some more soot on this?" I asked, inspecting the vintage cap Roth would be wearing. I faced the mirror and put it on, turning my head slowly while keeping my eyes in the same spot.

If you narrow your focus enough, you stop using your peripheral vision, the Director whispered. *You start to miss things.*

"Looks pretty dirty to me," Ms. Gaspard laughed. It took me a second to remember we were talking about the hat.

"He" couldn't be Roth. He was the reason I had gotten into Janus in the first place. Without Dave Roth, one could argue, I never even would have met you.

Then again, without me, you never would have met each other.

No one could argue with that.

Chapter Twenty-Five

May 8
5 days left

"HEY, HANDSOME."

The Monday before Showcase, you sat down next to me at the fountain, flashing a smile on the small section of your face that was still visible underneath your huge sunglasses, and I quietly seethed. Mom had been wrong. It was Shakespeare who's been right. Like Romeo said, love could easily spring from hate. Or, as it so happened, vice versa.

"Hey, yourself," I said, avoiding eye contact. You'd blown off school on Friday, which meant we'd had to reschedule our cue-to-cue, which meant that Roth had disappeared, too, and neither of you responded to messages over the weekend. I didn't have any real proof yet, but it certainly wasn't for lack of trying. I'd been leaving you guys alone in the theater as much as possible, taking prolonged coffee breaks, making an excuse to drag Chris with me, and then bursting back in when (I hoped) you least expected it. But so far, I hadn't walked in

YOU IN FIVE ACTS

on anything worse than you blasting Justin Bieber. The hardest piece of evidence I had to go on was that Roth had texted the word *rehearsals*, plural, when I'd asked him about break. You'd been very clear at dinner that there had been only one. But I couldn't confront you with that. I'd look like a complete paranoid asshole.

Diego and Joy were slowly making their way across the square, apparently late because they had to stop every two seconds to kiss or whisper something to each other. I'd only witnessed them as a couple for a week and I was already sick of it.

"What's up, E?" Diego said, sitting down and pulling Joy onto his lap. She winced slightly, which made me darkly happy. "Missing the beach yet?"

"No," I deadpanned.

"You ready for the Showcase Showdown?" Joy asked.

"Wait, did you just drop a *Price Is Right* reference?" Diego beamed at her in mock horror. "That's it, we're done."

"Where's Roth?" I asked, ignoring them, scanning the plaza. You two kept "coincidentally" missing each other, swapping places like you were pulling some kind of Clark Kent outfit change.

"I think he might have Career Management," you said, examining your tray of deli sushi. Career Management was the Janus version of a guidance counselor. Seeing as it was a private appointment instead of a class, I found it hard to believe you would know he was there if you two weren't at least talking.

"Well, we need to go over the schedule," I said. "I haven't been able to get in touch with either of you."

"Uh, you see me every day," you laughed.

And you don't see me at all, I thought, seething. *You think you can just humiliate me and I'll lie down and take it.*

"Showing up is half the battle," Joy said, looking pointedly at you.

"Shouldn't you be in a better mood, man?" Diego asked, popping open a bag of Cheetos. "I mean, your part is basically done, right?"

I glared at him. Performers always thought it was all about them—*they* were the ones onstage, *they* were getting the attention (and, most importantly, the applause, which they needed like oxygen). They never seemed to think about the fact that someone else was *really* doing all the work. They were like puppets, deluded into thinking they were moving and talking on their own.

"Hardly," I said. "It's tech week, which means endless sound and lighting fixes, sets and costumes, the cue-to-cue, and then a dress rehearsal. I'll be living and breathing this thing until curtain."

"I hear you," Joy said. "I feel like a broken wind-up toy, just going and going and going." She turned to Diego and frowned. "Adair put me through hell this morning. I basically got a full physical." They exchanged a few concerned whispers.

"Secrets, secrets are no fun," you started to sing, but then Joy shot you a death stare and you shut up.

"Your schedule is cleared this week, right?" I asked. You nodded, tapping on your phone.

"Because I need your full . . . commitment," I said, savoring the irony of the last word.

"What else would I be doing?" you asked, still not really

paying attention. I don't know what bothered me more, the fact that you were hiding something, or the fact that you were such a shitty actress that you couldn't even be bothered to do a good job of it.

"I don't know, you seem pretty busy lately," Joy said. The words were acid-tinged and made me reconsider Joy's potential value. You sniffed and rubbed your nose with your wrist. I was about to make a loaded comment about seasonal allergies when Roth finally showed up.

"Hey, sorry I'm late." He walked over with his thumbs hooked into his pockets, hunching his shoulders, his eyes darting from your face to mine. "I was in Career Management." I raised my eyebrows; you two were syncing your alibis.

"Cool story, bro," I said. "What did Ms. Lopez have to say?"

"Just that I have no career," Roth said with a self-deprecating smile. "It was a short meeting."

"The casting directors will be knocking down your door come Monday," Diego said. "Right, E?"

"We'll see," I said, frowning out at the sea of tourists with their selfie sticks. "We still have a lot of work to do."

"It'll come together," you said, looking at either me or Dave—with your sunglasses on, it was impossible to tell where your eyes were. "It always does."

"That's a pretty confident statement coming from someone who can barely make it to school," I snapped.

Everyone fell silent for a minute or two, but I had the distinct, paranoid feeling of messages being exchanged silently across the transom, beyond my peripheral vision.

"Trouble in paradise?" Diego finally laughed, but no one

joined him. Anyone could see what a joke we were. Everyone had seen it, months ago—except for me.

"All right," you sighed. "I think that's my cue to go to the ladies' room." You picked up your bag and sauntered off, and Roth took your seat, fidgeting with the straps on his messenger bag.

"You know, I think she's actually trying pretty hard," he said. "I mean, it's getting better, right?"

I looked at him and frowned. "Depends on where you're sitting," I said.

"I don't know." He shrugged. "Except for the obvious, I think we've got it down."

"The obvious?"

"Yeah, I mean, the part we're leaving to performance. The, uh, spur-of-the-moment choice." He laughed uncomfortably, and I realized he meant the kiss. We'd skipped over it so many times I didn't even read the stage directions anymore. I'd forgotten it was even there. Sitting right in front of me.

I'd tried everything to get you to crack . . . except for the obvious.

We did the cue-to-cue the next day. Since the main stage would host four different short plays in a row for Drama Showcase, the set had to be easy to load in and break down. My solution, a minimalist, single steel beam (made of spray-painted foam blocks—for once, the visual arts stoners had come in handy) that stretched from wing to wing, needed intricate lighting design to avoid looking as cheap as it was. So in addition to

Chris, I had a junior tech geek named Faiqa up in the booth, adjusting the levels.

True to form, you and Roth arrived through doors on opposite ends of the theater, avoiding eye contact.

"There are my star-crossed lovers!" I cried, just to see if you would look at each other before looking at me.

"Looks great, man," Roth said, keeping his eyes on the stage.

"Yeah, great," you parroted, with unconvincing enthusiasm.

"Great!" I said. "We're going to make this quick and dirty." I opened my script, which I'd marked up in advance with the cues. "If all goes well, it will be very . . . illuminating."

"Good one," Faiqa said through her headset from the booth.

"Places!" I yelled.

I called the cues while you and Roth moved from mark to mark onstage, saying one-off lines to show Faiqa where you'd be standing when she changed the lighting. Per my instructions, she made it dark and moody, with a film noir spot in the center and colored gels to create a dark, midnight blue cast on the background, which would slowly fade to an early morning orange by the end of the play. There wasn't much for you two to do—while I worked on finessing each cue with the tech team, you stood like bored mannequins. I was the only one who knew there was a surprise coming.

"OK, this is cue ten," I said to the room at large, when the moment finally arrived. "This is the kiss after Viola says, 'I just want to feel something real.' Page seventeen."

You and Dave, who were already sitting side by side on

one of the blocks center stage, staring intently at the ground, didn't move.

"OK, so they're in the same place as cue nine, so I'll just—" Faiqa said as she lowered the spotlight and brought up a backlight that cast you in hazy silhouette.

"I'd like to actually see it," I said. "Their faces will be turned to the side, so I want to see what that looks like."

You and Dave turned to face each other.

"Now say the line," I called.

"I just want to feel something . . . *real*," you said, substituting volume for emotion.

"Do it with your hand on his face. Faiqa needs to see it."

"Actually, I don't," she said through the headset, but I ignored her.

You reached a hand up to Dave's temple and brushed some hair off of his forehead. I saw the corners of his mouth twitch up.

"OK, now say it again . . ." I said, trying not to clench my teeth.

"I just want to feel something . . . *real*," you repeated, gazing up at him.

". . . and now kiss."

"What?" Your eyes darted nervously over to me. "I thought that was supposed to be improvised."

"I changed my mind," I said. "I need to make sure it's believable."

Dave shifted uncomfortably. "Won't it be more believable if it's a first kiss?" he asked.

"It would be more believable if you were actually a teen-aged welder, but we're letting that slide."

"Right. I just—" he looked at you helplessly. "Um."

"Well, I'm glad we're running it now if it's such a struggle," I said, feeling bile rise in my throat. Your pathetic protestations sealed the deal. I hadn't been completely convinced my hunch was right until that moment.

That's what you get for casting such a matinee idol in the part you wrote for yourself, dipshit.

It was true—I'd originally written *Boroughed Trouble* as a way to make sure I got to kiss you before graduation, and to show the VIPs in the audience that I was a triple-threat writer/actor/director. I was planning to play Rodolpho myself, after holding a casting call just for show. But then you'd kissed me, and everything changed. I'd let my guard down, just in time for Dave Roth to enter on cue.

"I think what Dave and I both feel," you said, a segue that spiked my heart rate on its own, "is that it would be more . . . *powerful* for it to happen during the performance."

"Well, I'm the director and I disagree."

"It just feels weird, since—" Dave started, but I cut him off.

"We're not together," I said. "I'm not an idiot, and it means nothing to me, so just kiss her!" Through my headset I could hear Faiqa and Chris breathing, but I didn't care anymore. *Let them watch*, I thought.

You and Dave looked at each other for a long minute filled with tense hesitation before finally, awkwardly, leaning in to peck each other quickly on the lips. It was the kind of kiss two fifth graders might do on a dare. It was even more damning than your previous refusals.

"Once more, with feeling!" I yelled.

I saw you shake your head at Dave, and then hunch over a little bit. It was only once you looked back at me that I noticed the tears glistening in your eyes.

"What are you doing, man?" Dave asked, looking pained—probably because he couldn't comfort you without blowing your carefully orchestrated cover of ambivalence.

"I'm just giving you both what you want," I snapped.

"I don't know what you're talking about," he said, with a straight face. No wonder he didn't win that Golden Globe. "Don't punish her, OK? She didn't do anything wrong."

"You wouldn't call messing around behind my back doing something wrong?" My voice, high and trembling, was magnified by the Janus Academy Theater's truly cutting-edge acoustics. That was when the house lights came up, and I heard Faiqa whisper to Chris, "*Let's get out of here.*"

"What was I supposed to do?" you cried, wiping your eyes and leaping to your feet. "I was drunk, and I made a mistake, and you acted like you owned me." Dave stood up and put a hand on your back. You turned to him, folding into his arms, nestling your face in his neck. My brain buzzed with a furious static.

What was she supposed to DO? Just tell you, and not be such a manipulative bitch. For once, the Director was on my side.

"So it's true," I said, stating the obvious, just in case anyone had missed it.

"We didn't mean for it to happen." That was Dave, bravely playing the Good Guy.

"Now, that's just bad dialogue," I laughed. "Good thing

you're not a writer. Although I guess it's actually kind of a shame, considering the state of your acting career."

Dave looked like I'd hit him in the face. It was almost as good as actually hitting him in the face.

"Stop it!" you said angrily. "You can't control this, and I know it kills you. But I'm sorry, you can't just make someone love you, don't you understand that by now?"

Surprise, surprise. Another defense straight from the soap opera cutting room floor. But that one hit me in the gut. Because what you were saying, without saying it, was that you weren't just hooking up with Dave Roth. You were telling me you loved him, when I'd loved you, *worshipped* you, for years. All that time you'd barely acknowledged me . . . and all he'd had to do was show up. My grand plan to show you how I felt about you had pushed you right into Dave's arms instead.

Despair started to dampen the anger, and I had the sudden, humiliating urge to cry. Luckily, that was when I remembered that I had the power to hurt you even more publicly than you'd hurt me. That was when I realized I could show you a thing or two about choices, and their consequences.

"Kill the lights," I shouted into my headset. "Kill the set, kill the play, kill everything."

Kill yourself, a familiar old voice suggested helpfully, as I stormed out of the auditorium.

Chapter Twenty-Six

May 9
4 days left

UNFORTUNATELY, I'm not the one who died. I didn't go jump off the Queensboro Bridge to complete some sad, artistic circle-jerk with myself. I could have—I'd be lying if I said the thought didn't cross my mind, complete with a final, fuck-you text to you and Dave. But I didn't want to kill myself so much as I wanted to kill any evidence that I had ever made myself so vulnerable to you. Or that you had subsequently stomped all over my insides.

"I'm pulling the play," I announced breathlessly to Ms. Hagen. I'd literally run from the theater and caught her just as she was closing up her office for the night. She already had a coat on and was tying a scarf around her neck.

"Ethan," she sighed. She had a flapper-style bob of stark white hair and a fine-boned patrician face that perfectly matched her status as a cultural grande dame. At that moment it was frowning wearily. "We cannot pull the play."

"But it's my work," I said, clutching the back of her leather guest chair. I could tell I was visibly sweating. "I already copyrighted it with Writer's Guild East. So you need my permission to put it on."

"That is technically true," she said, fixing me with a cold stare. "However it's also true that you currently need it to graduate. So we may be at an impasse." She had no idea that she was playing right into my hand.

"Oh," I said, trying to look deflated. It wasn't too much of a stretch, based on the events of the last hour. "That does put me in a difficult situation, I guess."

"How so?"

"Well, I was hoping not to have to tell you this, but one of my actors . . ." I swallowed, feigning nervousness so that I could draw it out and enjoy the schadenfreude. ". . . has a drug problem," I finished.

That finally made Ms. Hagen sit down.

"That's a very serious allegation," she said, raising her eyebrows and folding her hands on her wide mahogany desk. "Are you certain you want to make it, now of all times?"

"What do you mean?"

"I mean," she said, enunciating each word in her low, lilting German-accented English, "that we have a zero-tolerance policy when it comes to drugs at Janus Academy. Once a report has been made, the student in question is subject to a search, and if any illegal substances are found, the student in question is subject to suspension, with the possibility of expulsion. That suspension is *immediate*, which means that if you report this to me *today*, and your actor is found in possession of illegal drugs, then your play cannot go on." She blinked and smiled tightly. "However, if you report this to me on Monday morning, *after* the play . . ." She raised her hands in a what-can-I do? gesture, letting the rest of the sentence float unsaid in the air between us. "I just wouldn't want you to lose your spot at Tisch over someone else's poor judgment," she added.

I was way ahead of her; I knew that if I sabotaged Showcase entirely, I would just be committing a different type of suicide. I didn't want to blow everything to smithereens. I just wanted to take out two specific targets.

"Believe me, I don't, either," I said. "But she's barely lucid. I can't put her onstage. I don't think I have a choice."

Ms. Hagen took a deep breath. "She. All right. So I assume we're talking about Olivia."

I nodded, as if it pained me to give you up. (It did pain me to give you up, by the way. Letting go of the image I had of you, of the pedestal I'd built brick by brick for you, and the hope I had for us, was agony.)

"I'll need you to write and sign a statement detailing exactly what you know or suspect," she said. "Tomorrow I'll meet with the dean, and assuming he wants to proceed, security guards will search her locker, and then we'll detain her and search her person pending the results of the locker." She reached under her desk and pulled out a legal pad, which she pushed across to me along with a heavy fountain pen. "I should tell you," Ms. Hagen added, "She's entitled to know who reported her. This isn't anonymous."

"That's OK," I said. "I don't care if she hates me. I just want her to get help." The first part was a given—you already hated me, I'd made sure of that. The second part was sort of true. I did want you to get help, but only after everyone at school knew why you needed it.

"If evidence of drug abuse is uncovered, we do work with families on finding treatment centers."

"Great," I said. I was already writing.

"You know—" She put a hand on mine, halting me mid-word; the pen scratched across the paper in a jagged line. "It occurs to me that this doesn't have to end your play. Couldn't you find an understudy?"

"Everyone else is already cast in something," I said. "Besides, there's no way anyone could learn so much dialogue and blocking in two days." I paused, preparing to deliver the masterstroke. "But there is another play I wrote. It's a black box–style monologue, really easy to set up. And I know it by heart."

Ms. Hagen frowned. "I'd have to vet it before approving it," she said.

"Of course."

"And that's bad news for David Roth. He won't graduate either without the credit."

I shrugged, finished my statement, pushed it across the desk, and went back into the empty theater. The house lights were still on, and my bridge to nowhere filled the stage, looking more fake than I'd ever noticed before. Just like you, I remember thinking.

It was all so stupid. I know that now, OK? But at the time, there didn't seem like anything worse. I had basically forgotten about the drugs at that point. Substances could kill your body, but they couldn't break your heart. What you'd done to me was the depths of human misery as far as I was concerned. All I wanted was to hurt you back.

I didn't mean to set the final act in motion. I didn't mean to get anyone killed.

Act Five

Diego

Chapter Twenty-Seven

May 10
3 days left

I'VE FELT THE WORLD slow down three times. One was the first day I stepped on a stage. For me, ballet was athletic, just another sport with less padding, same as what I did on the courts every weekend with the guys from my neighborhood, even if they gave me never-ending shit for the tights—which, I mean, come on. Dancers wore tights and lifted up beautiful girls, eye-to-crotch level, and that was "gay." Wrestlers wore tights and pressed their faces in one another's nuts, but that was legit. Okay.

Anyway, most of the time dancing felt like hard work, all coiled muscles and springing steps and torque and sweat and effort, but once my feet left the ground? Man, it was like I was flying. Everything got still and soft for a second, just a second, but it was enough to hook me. It was a breath before I came back down to Earth. It was the only time the clock stopped. The second thing that made it happen was kissing you.

"I can't believe it's almost over."

We were lying on a blanket in Fort Tryon Park, looking out at the silhouette of the George Washington Bridge as the sky lit up neon behind it. You sighed and splayed on your back, stretching your arms and legs out like a kid making a snow angel. "I can't even imagine what it's gonna feel like, after. Can you?"

I shook my head. I really couldn't picture it. In my mind, after the curtain call, everything just fell off a cliff into nothing, like a drawing that wasn't finished. It was like I knew.

I ran my thumb from your chin up to your temple, drawing it across your hairline to the other side.

"You'll go back to the doctor," I said, leaning in to kiss you upside-down. "You'll stay off that ankle. I'll carry you if I have to."

You smiled with your eyes closed. "I bet you would. The one-handed commuter clusterfuck rides again."

"I'm serious, though." I lay next to you, propping myself up on an elbow. "You can't play around."

"I know that." You rolled over and looked at me like Mr. T pitying his last fool. "I'm *not* playing. Which is why I'm still dancing." Your eyes softened. "I just have to make it three more days. And then . ." You let the sentence trail off, knowing neither of us could finish it.

I know I always talked about luck and fate and not thinking about tomorrow, but of course that was bullshit. Everyone who talks that kind of game is just talking to keep the panic at bay. I mean, look, I knew I was good, but professional ballet was one of the most competitive fields in the world, and my heartwarming barrio-to-Balanchine story would only take me so far. Even if I got invited to apprentice for a company, I would be competing for a contract against guys with more than a decade of training, guys who lived and breathed ballet, who were also the best in their (much better) academies. If I didn't get a paying dance gig soon—like end-of-summer soon—I'd be cutting keys at my uncle's hardware store. That wouldn't even get me my own place, let alone the cash to keep taking classes.

"You know what's weird?" You shifted to rest your head on my chest. "Wanting something for so long you don't even know if you could handle getting it."

"What do you mean?" I murmured into your hair.

"Like, I've wanted to dance since before I even had memories," you said. "I don't know how to function without that being the driving force behind everything. If I actually made it, I honestly don't know what I'd do."

"Tough life," I teased, and you swatted at me.

"Come on, don't act like you don't know. When people tell you you can't do something, don't you just *live* to prove them wrong?"

"Not really," I said. "I don't care what anybody thinks, I just want to get out. You know those people who want to go to Mars and never come back? That's what this is, for me. A one-way ticket."

"Huh." You looked up at the sky for a minute. "You better let me visit."

I kissed you again. "You'll be there, too."

"You really think we'll end up in the same place?"

I leaned back. The sky was fading to purple, and I could even see a few stars through the haze. "Why not?" I said.

"What do you think the chances are of us getting into the same company?" you asked. "One in a thousand?"

"They can't be *that* low."

"You'd be surprised." You sat up and turned to me, pulling your legs up against your chest. "We'll have to go wherever there's work. We don't get to choose." I flashed back to you in the lobby of your building, when you'd gotten your acceptance letter. The day we'd gone upstairs and—"It's not funny," you said softly, and I realized I was smiling.

"Sorry," I said, trying to banish the impure thoughts. "I know. But we'll see. I mean, there's no point in future-tripping when we don't even know what's going to happen."

"You're not worried?" You raised an eyebrow. "Not even about me?"

"No," I lied.

"OK, fine." You draped your arms around my shoulders and nuzzled your face into my neck. *I want to live here forever*, I thought. I still do. "I still just want to fast-forward to Sunday morning," you whispered as your lips brushed my ear. All the blood left my brain.

"Me too." I smiled, pulling you down to the blanket. The world slowed.

I didn't know yet there wouldn't be a Sunday morning.

Chapter Twenty-Eight

May 11
Two days left

"*ARE YOU READY?*" You rose up en pointe to brush my hair out of my eyes, and I instinctively grabbed your waist, lifting you to relieve the pressure on your ankle.

"It's OK, I'm on my left," you said, taking my hands away and lowering back down. "Besides, only forty-eight hours. Then it can fall off." You were trying to keep it light but I could see you grimacing in pain; you always looked so mad when you got nervous. You glanced out at the stage, where Mr. Dyshlenko and Ms. Adair were still arguing over one of the set pieces, a cardboard cactus that looked a little too . . . anatomical from some angles.

"It will look *more* phallic in silhouette, not less!" Ms. Adair was shouting. It was only noon—way too early to hear that shit from anyone, let alone a teacher.

I shook my head, trying not to smile, but then I looked at you and lost the battle. You were wearing your tailor-fit Kitri dress for the dress rehearsal, a fiery red flamenco number that Ms. Gaspard had reinforced with a tight, plunging black leotard top that left very little to the imagination. Not that I had to imagine anymore.

"Don't stroke out on me, Basilio," you joked, threading your fingers through mine. "Forget my foot, you've got my *life* in your hands with that lift, boy."

"I got you," I said earnestly. I meant it every way there was to mean it.

The dress rehearsal went OK. I wish I could say we tore it up, the way we had over break with Mr. D, but with Ms. Adair standing at the front of the stage and Lolly literally waiting in the wings, there was tension that was hard to ignore. It was the feeling of someone waiting for us to make a mistake. I knew if the screw-up was on me, it didn't matter . . . but Adair was watching you like she was looking for a fight. So we were both too careful; we danced like we were afraid to let go.

"It's feeling a little stiff," Ms. Adair said once we hit our final fish dive. "It feels like you're holding back, Joy. Could I see it with Lolly, just for comparison?"

"What?" you said. I set you back upright and you put your hands on your hips, still catching your breath. In the bright stage lights, I could see the beads of sweat on your temples, straining inward as your brow furrowed. "No, really; I'm fine. I can do it again."

"She hasn't run the whole thing yet," Ms. Adair said evenly. "It's a practical matter, not a personal one."

You stood there for a minute, sucking in your cheeks like

you were debating whether to fight her on it, before turning and walking off backstage. You went slowly, but there was no mistaking the way your left hip jutted out, the way your right foot dragged. I pressed my lips together and closed my eyes, sending up a quick prayer. *Please, God, just let her last through tomorrow night.* I wasn't an altar boy or anything—me and God were casual acquaintances at best—but I figured it couldn't hurt. It just had to hold long enough so that everyone who mattered could see what I saw every day—how there was no one else who even came close to you.

After I went through the motions with Lolly, Ms. Adair dismissed her and then rushed Mr. D off to one of the studios so they could "confer privately."

"Not personal, my ass," you said, wincing and propping your leg up on my lap while I hung my feet over the lip of the stage. "I don't know why she didn't just cast Lolly in the first place."

"Uh, maybe because you practically did a mic drop at the audition. No one could have voted you down."

"She did."

"Yeah, well, she's wrong."

You sighed. "You wanna tell her, or should I?"

"I'm serious," I said. "Some people are on the wrong side of history. There are the real obvious, crazy racists, who want to build a wall between us and Mexico, and then there are the people so scared and lazy they'll defend the rules set up by the old-school bigots because that's how it's always been done." I turned up my nose and adopted my best Ms. Adair voice. "Ballerinas are supposed to be white swans," I drawled.

You smirked. "And even the black swan gets played by Natalie Portman, so I'm screwed either way."

"That's not what I'm saying. I meant—"

"I know what you meant," you said. "And thank you." You tipped your face up and I leaned down to kiss you, my heart racing a mile a minute the same way it had on the Cyclone. It still didn't feel real.

"You're blowing up," you murmured after a minute, pulling back.

"Huh?"

"Your phone." You pointed to my bag, which was vibrating crazily.

"Oh. Sorry." My heart kept going, but for a different reason. I didn't get many texts during the day, but unless I was in dance class I always kept my phone on, because if anyone would need to reach me, it would be Mom. And it would be because he'd shown up again.

My dad had been gone for nearly eight years, but gone like a bottle cap slipped down a subway grate is gone—still there, just hidden close by, buried in some filth no one wants to think about. When he lived with us, he drank and yelled, didn't hit much, but only because his coordination was bad after a case of Presidente. Finally she kicked him out and changed the locks, and after a few days of pleas and threats, he went on a bender and disappeared for months. Eventually we found out he'd moved in with my uncle a few blocks away. He refused to sign divorce papers but still came around, either in a stupor or an angry rage. He'd gotten Mom fired from two different clinics already. Mostly, though, apparently not remembering that most people had jobs, he'd come over to bang on the door of an empty apartment in the middle of the day, and our elderly neighbors would call Mom on her cell to complain about the noise.

My hand closed on my phone and I steeled myself for the semiannual routine: Leave school, call my uncle Luis—my mom's brother—and meet him at top of the stairs at 103rd, northeast corner. Luis owned a hardware store, so he'd bring hammers, and we'd climb all seven flights through the back of the building, ambushing dad from behind and telling him to leave so we wouldn't have to call the cops, which was basically a joke since the cops would probably arrest all three of us if they ever showed. The last time it had happened, over the summer, Dad had stared at me, watery-eyed, for a minute, and just when I thought he was going to show some kind of remorse he just grunted, "Which one are you?" Which pretty much summed up our relationship.

I took a deep breath and looked at the screen.

I CANNOT BELIEVE YOU

Relief: it wasn't from Mom. Less relief: It was an all-caps rant from Liv.

WHAT IN THE ACTUAL FUCK, DIEGO???????

I drew back. What the hell was she talking about? "What?" you asked. "Who is it?"

MY LIFE IS RUINED. HOW COULD YOU DO THIS???

what are you smoking? I typed. It was kind of a low blow, but also a legit question. I hadn't confronted Liv about her partying since the night I dragged her home wasted from Dante's friend's place. And even then I hadn't really pressed her on it.

FUUUUUUUCK.YOUUUUUUUU, came the reply. **COME MEET ME NOW OR I'LL TELL JOY YOU MADE A MOVE ON ME I SWEAR TO FUCKING GOD**

"What?" you asked again.

"Uh, nothing," I said, quickly clicking my screen dark, trying not to show my fear. "Family stuff." What had happened to her? What had *I* done? My mouth was bone dry.

"You wanna talk about it?"

"Not really."

You looked hurt, and I was trying to think of a better story when Ms. Adair came back into the auditorium alone.

"Joy, you can go get changed," she called as she made her way down the long aisle. "I need to speak to Diego for a few minutes."

"Great," you muttered under your breath.

"Don't worry," I said. "I'll tell you everything." A new text buzzed against my fist, reminding me what a lie that was.

Once Adair and I were alone, she crossed her arms and looked at me expectantly.

"Phone away," she said, arching an eyebrow.

"Yes, ma'am." I tossed it back in my bag and clasped my hands in front of me like a kindergartner, pushing Liv out of my mind. It's too bad I was so good at doing that.

"Diego," she began, "I know you're in an awkward position here, since you and Joy are—" she smiled, but it wasn't kind "—*close*, but I need you to be honest with me. You know what happens up there tomorrow night determines your future, too, and you need a partner who makes you the best you can be, without a handicap dragging you down. So tell me. Truthfully. *Selfishly*. Can she dance it?"

I think I can admit now—and I hope you'll forgive me— that I had a moment of pause. Not just because I knew Adair wanted me to look like I was thinking it over, either, but because I *really* needed to think it over. Of course you could dance it, and kick the shit out of it, I knew that. But I couldn't fight the nagging feeling that maybe you shouldn't. If something happened to you, I'd never forgive myself. And unlike me, you had a whole other life waiting for you, a big, thick envelope of a life just sitting there, begging to be opened. If I'd had that, I wasn't sure I'd still be dancing like my life depended on it.

So there was a second of hesitation. But I didn't let it show.

"Yes," I said, looking Ms. Adair straight in the eyes. "She can do it."

She pursed her lips. "All right, I'll take your word for it. I just want to avoid the kind of disaster going on with the drama performance."

"What?" I asked, my heart racing. I'd seen Dave just the other day, and things seemed to be going fine. Better than fine, even. He'd looked happier than I'd seen him. He even beat my ass at layups.

"You don't know?" she asked, smiling slowly. "They found illegal prescription drugs in Olivia Gerstein's locker this morning. She's been suspended indefinitely."

I bounced restlessly as I rode uptown on the 2, leaning on the door, my body trying to keep rhythm with the movement of the train. Liv was waiting for me on the same bench we'd sat on all those weeks before by the entrance to the 110th Street station at the top of Central Park. I didn't need to ask why she was so far from home—I knew why she was up there.

I couldn't believe Dante. We'd grown up like brothers, until my dad left and factions formed. But apparently none of that mattered. I still had the slingshot he'd given me on my seventh birthday, and he still had me in his pocket, without me even knowing. He'd wanted me to deal to Janus kids for years, calling me a pussy when I said no, not caring that it could ruin my life, leave me without a high school diploma, rotting in jail or even worse. With Liv, he'd found a loophole. I should have stopped it before it started, but I never really tried.

At the party, the night everything started to derail if you turn back the clock second by second—which is all I do, I'm living in rewind—Dante had swung an arm around my neck as I watched you walk away, teasing, "Yo, you gonna close the deal on that later, or what?" That really was all I had been thinking about—getting you alone, telling you how I felt, finally making my move. I was too tipsy and heartsick to care that much about what Liv did behind closed doors. She'd made a reckless choice, Dante had closed a deal, but it was my fault, really, and I was furious.

I wasn't the only one.

"You fucking asshole!" Liv cried when I crossed the street to where she was sitting. She leapt up and ran at me, and I had to think fast, basically pick her up and spin her just to keep her from scratching my face. Her eyes were bloodshot, her nostrils red and raw. Liv was a beautiful girl, but she'd lost at least ten pounds, and her face looked winter-gray even in the blinding sun.

She looks like a junkie. I couldn't stop the thought.

"Whoa, whoa, whoa, it wasn't me," I said, grabbing her by both arms to keep her still while she wriggled and grunted. "I didn't do anything, I didn't tell anyone, so would you calm the fuck down, please?" A passing mother with a toddler in a stroller crossed the street to avoid us. I didn't even want to think about what we looked like.

Liv glared up at me. "No one else knew!" she shouted.

"Someone must have," I said, struggling to hold her as her eyes darted back and forth from my face to some unseen points behind me. She looked scared and paranoid. I loosened my grip a little. "Because I am telling you, I didn't say a word."

Her face went slack and I led her over to the bench, putting my hand on her back as she cried in deep, wracking sobs.

"Why is this happening to me?" she wailed, wiping her snotty nose with one arm. Her boots clicked manically on the pavement; her knees jiggled.

"I don't know," I said. "Because life sucks sometimes. But it can stop now."

"Yeah, well. Everything stops now." She looked up at the tree over our heads, a petrified tangle of dead branches, the only one on the whole block that hadn't bloomed. "No more school," she murmured. "No more acting. No more parties. No more life."

"What did your parents say?" I asked.

"Well, they were 'shocked.' And 'incredibly disappointed.'" She laughed bitterly. "But they didn't make me go home."

"Well, I'm telling you then," I said. "Go home. Don't do"—Liv glared at me, and I could tell I was losing ground—"whatever you were gonna do up here."

"Fuck you," she snapped. "I can take care of myself."

"You sure?"

Liv looked down at the ground and shook her head, sticking her tongue in her cheek, running it over the front of her teeth. "I don't need this," she finally said, jumping up and swinging her bag over one shoulder. I stood up, too, trying to block her way, but she shoved past me. "Why should I even believe you?" she yelled, spinning around. "You probably did tell them. I bet Joy just loves that her goody-goody boyfriend is swooping in to save me from myself."

"Joy doesn't know," I said angrily.

"Wow." Liv sniffed, wiped her nose again. "Then she's even more oblivious than I thought."

"That's not fair. She's been trying to talk to you for months and you've been too"—*fucked up*—"busy to notice."

"She wants to talk about *you*," Liv said. "She doesn't care about me anymore."

"That's not true," I said, trying to soften my voice. "We can't be here for you if you don't let us. Look, maybe you could take some time off, focus on auditions, being with Dave—that's what you want, right?" I took a step forward, with my palms out. *Hands up, don't shoot.* "I know he wants you. He's crazy about you."

"Oh yeah?" Liv's face crumpled, and her eyes filled with tears. "Well, he hasn't texted me once today, so . . ." She shrugged as the first tear spilled its way down her cheek. "I guess I have nothing left to lose." She spun around and stormed off, east, along Central Park North, but when I started after her she screamed, "DON'T FOLLOW ME!" which caught the attention of a burly cop leaving a deli across the street. He stared at me, one hand on his coffee, one hand on his belt, and I stopped cold, raising my hands for the second time in sixty seconds.

Luckily, after a beat he just waved me away, and I all but ran back to the subway, every step pounding in my chest like a drumroll leading up to some ominous climax waiting in the wings.

You found out about Liv at school, along with everyone else. You wept on my shoulder in the corner of the auditorium that afternoon, called yourself a bad friend, blamed yourself for not seeing it. I just held you and swallowed my guilt while you texted and called her, poring over her photos, searching for clues.

That's kind of what this feels like, you know? Like putting together a puzzle, examining every piece, and trying to find another way—any other way—it could all fit together.

Dante came over for dinner, unannounced, which was the only way he ever showed up—it must have run on that side of the family. Even with hurricanes you usually got a warning.

From the minute he walked in, I could tell he had an agenda. He was watching me out of the corner of his eye the whole time we ate. I wondered if he could tell how angry I was; I barely said a word, and every time he flashed his trademark smile—sly and snakelike, as if he was in on some joke the rest of us couldn't hear—I had to look down at my plate to keep from blowing up. Once the dishes were cleared, when he asked me to walk him out, I knew something was going down. One of us was going to strike. I just didn't who would be first.

"So I heard about what happened at your school," he said once we were out in the hallway, laying a hand on my shoulder, watching my face for a reaction.

"Yup," I said stoically to the linoleum floor.

We weaved around the corner and into the stairwell, which was when he pushed me up against the wall, hooking his elbow under my chin. Without thinking I shoved him back—he might have been older, but he was smaller than me, and years of lifting hundred-plus-pound bodies over my head had given me powerhouse shoulders—and he stumbled back, laughing in a way that made it clear he didn't find anything about the situation funny.

"Relax, cuz, I'm just playing," he said, giving me a hard, unfriendly stare. "I just want to talk to you."

"So talk," I said, crossing my arms. "Don't touch me."

"Liv thinks you narc'd on her," Dante said. "But I told her my little cousin would never do that. I just need to hear it from you."

"It wasn't me."

Dante looked genuinely relieved. "Well, OK then. Good. Any idea who it *was*?"

"No." I focused on keeping my face still so he wouldn't know I was lying.

Everything that had happened in the *Boroughed Trouble* cue-to-cue had trickled down from Faiqa Bashara, and there was no doubt it had been Ethan who'd turned Liv in. But I couldn't sic Dante on him. I couldn't even blame him, really. In his own twisted, dramatic way, he'd basically done the right thing. I should have done it myself. I realized that much once I saw how devastated you were when you found out. If it had been you, puking on your knees in some stranger's bathroom, and someone else had known . . . I didn't even want to think about it. Liv didn't mean as much to me, but that didn't excuse how I'd covered for her. I mean, everyone is somebody else's "you," right?

"Well, listen," Dante said, "if you'd do a little reconnaissance, that would really help me out."

"Why should I help you?"

"Come on." The snake smile again. "Because we're family."

"I'll do it if you stop selling to her." I tightened my arms around my chest, jutted out my jaw, did anything I could to look bigger, or more frightening. *Men don't have to be tough.* That's what my mom had told me, that day when I came home with the slur on my bag. *They can be soft and vulnerable, too.* I remember how she kissed my head, stroked her thin fingers under my chin. *All the good ones are.*

Dante gave me a funny look and then burst out laughing. "Sell to her? Man, she sells for me now. Girl's got that whole school on lock." He shook his head. "She's a natural, too, unloads a six-hundred-dollar bottle in a day."

I lunged at him. It wasn't planned, just animal instinct, fear and rage and shame. I'd worked hard to get where I was, to carve out a space in the world that was just mine, far away from the big-talking, wannabe-hustler letdowns who haunted me, past and present, in our apartment complex. Dante could have his little corner of the world, but I'd die before I let him take over mine. I hooked him by the neck and swung him back against the stairwell wall, this time holding *him* with *my* elbow.

"Shit, I thought you knew!" Dante cried, his eyes wide with shock and a touch of amusement. He tried to push my arm down and I let him; I didn't really want a fight. "Look, I get it," he said, "but some people don't have some fancy scholarship, you know? Some of us just gotta survive."

"I don't care what you do. Just leave her out of it."

"It's not that easy," Dante said, stepping back. "She's a valuable asset."

I swallowed bitter, coppery saliva. "But we're family," I said.

He shrugged. "Family is family, money is money."

"And which one's worth more?"

"It's not like that," he said. "Liv's a big girl, she can make her own decisions. I'm not some gangster keeping her in line. Every weekend when the new stuff comes in she just shows up. I don't know if she doesn't have anywhere else to be or if she just gets off on being a tourist in the projects, or what. But no one's got her on a leash. She can leave if she wants to." His face softened, and for a second, under the carefully manicured facial hair and studied Clint Eastwood squint, I saw the boy I used to look up to. "I could have let her OD or let her fall off the roof at that party, but what did I do? I called you, right? Doesn't that count for something?"

"Not much," I said.

"Whatever, man," he said, sneering and starting down the stairs two at a time with his hands shoved in the pockets of his hoodie. "Relax. It's not life or death."

Chapter Twenty-Nine

May 13
14 hours left

"ARE YOU READY?"

I woke up with a start, sweating and panting, reaching for you. In the dream, we'd been onstage, doing the pas de deux, in front of hundreds of people—a packed house (everyone had been dressed in suits, even my mom, which was strange, but otherwise everything was normal). Right before the press lift, you'd whispered, "Are you ready?" and I'd nodded, but when I lifted you into the final position, the muscles in my arm gave out—just crumbled to dust—and I dropped you from seven feet up. The look in your eyes as you fell was so real. I heard your neck snap. I could still hear it.

I flopped back on my bed and hugged a pillow to my chest. Above me, through the crack in the curtains, I could see a triangle of dark gray sky slowly giving way to sunrise. It was the morning of Showcase, the morning that was supposed to be the first day of the rest of my life, or something cheesy like that. And I was dreading it.

It's not life or death. That's what Dante had said, and probably why I had the dream in the first place. But I couldn't shake the uneasy feeling it left me with. It seemed like a bad omen, some kind of message I couldn't decode.

today's the day! I texted you, not sure what to do with myself.

AAAAAAAAAHHHHHHHHHHHHHHH!!!!!!! you wrote back, within seconds.

I smiled, then. That scream wasn't real yet.

"How you feelin', man?" I asked Dave as we met center court, in the playground on the corner of 77th and Amsterdam a few blocks from his house. It was almost noon but he looked like he'd just rolled out of bed, and his hair must have been in a special state, because it was stuffed under a knit cap even in the breezy 65-degree weather.

"OK, actually," he said, yawning and dribbling sloppily until the ball hit his sneaker and shot off down the pavement. I jogged after it, already feeling a little bit better with the spring air filling my lungs.

"You skip school yesterday?" I asked, taking an easy lay-up.

"Yeah." Dave yawned again. "Ethan sent us this incredibly long, pretentious e-mail Thursday night saying that the play was canceled and we were traitors and terrible people and bad actors, so I decided I didn't feel like dealing with that in person." I tossed him the ball, and he just held it, staring at it like he wasn't sure what it was for. "Then, when I found out the, um . . . other stuff," he said, "I guess I was glad I wasn't there."

"I missed it, too." I nodded at him, encouraging him to take a shot, and he hurled it half-heartedly, missing the hoop.

"I'm off my game today," he said.

"Yeah. *Today*," I joked. I ran after the ball again, since Dave didn't seem ready to move. "You talk to her yet?" I asked casually.

He shook his head. "I don't know what to say. I feel like I should have known."

"Nobody knew," I said, feeling a stab of guilt.

"Yeah, but I'm her—" He winced. "I've been with her every day, man. I knew something was going on. I just didn't . . . want to know. You know?"

"Yup." I held the ball in my hands, turning it slowly, working myself into a quiet panic. I'd known Liv was in trouble and I'd all but ignored it. What if my dream wasn't just anxiety, but a real warning? I'd known for months about your injury, and all I'd done was help you hide it. I couldn't afford to make the same mistake twice. Not with you.

Dave looked at me wearily, expectantly, and it took a few seconds to realize he was just waiting for me to throw. I took a jump shot and banked it. "You should call her," I said.

"Did *you* talk to her?" There was a weird edge to his voice; at least he was waking up.

"Yeah. I ran into her yesterday. She seemed pretty upset." Not entirely a lie. "But Joy says she won't pick up the phone, and I don't think her parents are exactly keeping her under lock and key, you know?"

I walked over to get the ball, turning my back on Dave's tortured expression.

"She texted me," he said softly when I got back in earshot. "Yesterday. A couple of times."

"What did she say?"

"That she was sorry."

"So tell her you forgive her."

Dave looked at the ground.

"*Do* you forgive her?" I asked.

"Yeah," he said quickly. "I mean, what's to forgive? I should be apologizing to her." He squinted into the sun. "I should have said something."

"Yeah." I paused, thought about telling him everything I knew, but didn't. That's another on a long list of regrets. "It's not too late to say you're sorry," I said.

He looked at me, confused. "What, like right now?"

"Tomorrow's not promised." (Another one of Mom's calendar quotes. I was just saying it to sound deep. I didn't know I was predicting the future.) I threw the ball at Dave's chest and he reflexively caught it. "No day but today."

"Are you quoting *Rent* at me?" he asked, cracking a half-smile. "I know you dance, man, but I wouldn't have pegged you for a—"

"Just shut up and call her," I said.

I watched him while he did it. It went straight to voicemail. But then I walked him to the downtown train. If anyone could

---

---

get Liv to stay still, it would be Dave. And if he could manage to find her, hold on to her, for just a little while, well—that would be a start, at least.

"Are you ready?"

A chill ran through me. I blinked, just to check, but nope—this time, when you asked, it was real. It was 7:45 P.M., we were standing out of sight in the stage-left wings, and I'd been relieved to note, courtesy of a packed-house snapshot my mom sent when she arrived, that almost no one in the audience was in a suit, aside from Mr. Dyshlenko, who looked like Arnold Schwarzenegger, his arms practically busting the seams of his jacket. I was in black tights and a black leotard, in my wide-shouldered bolero and enough hairspray for all of New Jersey ("It'll keep that hair out of your eyes, at least," you'd teased), and you were nervously swishing back and forth in your ruffled red dress, practicing the fingerwork on your fan, opening and closing the paper accordion folds while you marked your solo and gingerly warmed up your ankle.

It was happening, I realized. I hadn't stopped it. You'd shut me down with one sentence when I'd called you from Broadway, pacing back and forth in front of a newsstand full of tragic tabloid headlines.

"I didn't come this far to quit now," you'd said. But still, I couldn't shake the feeling that something was off.

"Are *you* ready?" I asked. Onstage, the second group piece was approaching its finale. In about two minutes, we'd enter on cue. We were the last act, the closers. It all came down to us.

"It's fine," you said, not looking up.

"Don't lie to me now," I said.

"Fine, it's worse today." You exhaled slowly, bouncing a little. Before a performance, we usually did jumping jacks to limber up, but I felt like if I jumped right then I might puke, and from the tears in your eyes I could tell you could barely tolerate any warm-up at all. "It'll have to do," you said with a grimace.

We'd already been at school for hours. The Drama Showcase performance had been that afternoon, so out of curiosity we'd gone to check out Ethan's one-man revenge special (we'd looked around for Liv, hoping that she'd show up in protest, but no luck). It had been . . . talky and self-important but thankfully short, just like its author. You'd been too angry to go see Ethan afterward, but I caught him just as he was leaving to go celebrate at P.J. Clarke's with his fifty Russian relatives. I asked him if he'd heard from Liv, but he told me "there weren't enough rice grains in the Goya factory" to ever make her talk to him again. I didn't get it.

Then we'd convened in Studio 1 with the other dancers and Ms. Adair had led us in a warm-up while casually dropping the news that reps from City Ballet, ABT, Joffrey, Alvin Ailey, Atlanta, San Francisco, Miami, and Boston had been confirmed for the show. "So, please, don't dance like no one's watching," she'd warned. "Dance like *everyone* is."

I clenched and unclenched my fists. Everyone would be watching, you were dancing on a foot that could give at any second, and I was more nervous than I'd ever been before a performance. My head was all over the place. When you and I had rehearsed alone, it had felt like we were in a bubble; all I could see was you. But then, I couldn't focus. I could barely breathe. So much was riding on what I was about to do—one minute to curtain and counting—and I couldn't pretend that I had no control. I had to pull it together.

"Relax your face," you whispered, elbowing me in the side. "Make it look *joy*ful." But then you must have seen the fear in my eyes because you grabbed my hand and said, "Oh, no. Oh, shit. You're really freaking, aren't you?"

"I'll be OK," I said, closing my eyes, shaking out my legs, trying to clear my head.

There was a swell of applause as the ensemble struck their final pose, and the curtain swished down from the fly loft. Our classmates filed quickly offstage, but I couldn't look at them. I couldn't lose what little focus I had left.

"Places," the stage manager whispered from behind us, and you stepped in front of me without letting go.

"You got this," you said under your breath.

"I know," I said. "I just can't stop thinking about what happens out there." Out there onstage, out there in the world. So many trains and so many tracks. No way to know which ones might derail. "I need to make sure I hold you up so—"

"Stop right there," you said. "Don't you worry about me for another second. I know this choreography inside and out. I could do it on one foot. I could do it on no feet. I could probably do it on my hands if I had to." You smiled, a beam of light in the dark. "You don't have to be my crutch anymore," you continued, "because you *already* hold me up. As good as we are by ourselves, we've always been better together. It just took me too damn long to notice." You pulled me into you and kissed me just as the orchestra started playing our intro music.

"Ten seconds," the stage manager said.

"You and me," I whispered, with our noses still touching.

"Blowin' up like spotlights," you finished. The curtain rustled to life, racing away from the stage floor faster than I was ready for. Two feet, then six, then ten. There was nothing standing between us and what we were about to do together. Except one thing.

"I love you," I said. "You know that, right?"

"I do now," you said, with a grin that lit my world on fire.

And then we were on.

Chapter Thirty

May 13
Two hours left

ONCE YOU'RE UP ON STAGE, there's no way to tell what the audience sees. All you have to go by is how it feels. There's an energy, a rhythm, that takes over when everything lines up right. We were always being reminded that the human body was our instrument, but mine never felt like one when I was performing. Calling it an instrument reminded me of something delicate or breakable, but on that stage that night we were a force of nature, like a fire spreading, alive and unstoppable. We ate up space.

Watching you made the rest of the world fall away. We flew, and time stopped. I watched your calves carve arrowheads in your legs as you nailed your manège of piqué pirouettes, smiling softly like it was the easiest thing in the world even though my heart paused for those thirty seconds. After that, though, it was on. Every step felt spontaneous, like the first time we'd ever danced it. You were right: As good as we were on our own, it was no contest. Together we were like two currents converging. A perfect storm.

Still, I couldn't stop a creeping feeling of déjà vu as we approached the press lift. Even with your hops en pointe and my jumps, the lift was the most dangerous moment because so many things could go wrong. It was a show-off move to thrill the crowd before our aerobic dash to the fish dive, and we had to stick it. More importantly, *I* had to stick it. You trusted me. And I swore I'd never let you down.

You stepped gracefully in front of me, into the arabesque that I'd lift you in, and I clenched my jaw, drawing every shred of strength I had, trying to prepare myself. I had one hand on your hip and was about to brace the other under your thigh when you turned your head slightly, breaking the perfect, paper doll profile that the girl dancers had always been taught to hold. My heart nearly stopped. We were nailing it, and you were breaking form.

Your lips barely moved. You kept your eyes focused straight ahead. But I heard the words clearly. "I love you back."

I lifted you then, just like Mr. D had taught me. I held on, and then—before I could think about it—I let go. The orchestra punctuated the moment with a dramatic crescendo, and when I dipped you into the fish dive, the applause started rolling like thunder. I spun you into me and we locked eyes, both breathless but beaming; we had *destroyed* the performance and we both knew it. It was glorious. The clapping didn't stop until after five curtain calls.

It was the best moment of my life.

We got swarmed backstage—Mom and Miggy and Emilio, your parents, Mr. D, who looked like he'd actually been crying, and even Ms. Adair, who kissed us both on the cheeks, double-French-style, and called us "exquisite."

"You know, you might be onto something with this dance thing," your dad said, handing you a bouquet of roses.

"Say what now?" you asked, laughing and hugging him. I'd never seen you look so proud.

"That jump when you slid on the floor was badass," Miggy said. "Can you teach me to do that?"

"If you're anything like your brother, I'll teach you myself," Mr. D laughed.

It was a crazy whirlwind of congratulations and thank-yous and high-fiving. Everywhere I looked, someone was clamoring for someone's attention, holding up their phones and cameras, balancing flowers and balloons, pushing through the packed crowd. So when a skinny older dude in a blazer stopped in front of me, I figured he was trying to get past, and moved aside.

"Diego, right?" he asked, holding out his hand.

"Um, yeah." I shifted the teddy bear with the CONGRATULA-TIONS! heart that Mom had forced on me into my left arm and shook.

"My name is Jefferson Bloom. I represent the Miami City Ballet, and I was just blown away by your performance."

"Um." I elbowed Mom away, who had straight-up turned her back on a conversation she was having with your mom to eavesdrop. "Thank you."

"Listen," he said, "we're always looking for strong male dancers, and I think you'd be an incredible fit for our company. We take a couple of apprentices every fall, and we'd like you to be one of them." He handed me a sleek business card. His name was printed in silver letters, raised up off the shiny surface. "I hope you reach out once you've had the chance to think it over."

"Wow," I said, instinctively searching the room for my constant. I found you about ten feet away, standing next to a tall, willowy woman with glasses and a waterfall of braids. While she looked for something in her bag, you turned to me and excitedly mouthed, "*Alvin Ailey!*"

"All travel expenses paid, of course," my guy said.

"Of course," I repeated, dumbstruck.

It happened twice more, with reps from Atlanta and San Francisco. They came over, told me they'd like to have me as an apprentice, handed me a card, congratulated Mom, and talked a big game about how I was gonna go far. I wish I could say I enjoyed it, but after the initial euphoria of the actual performance, I'd gone kind of numb. The words floated over my head, hanging there like sky writing. The Atlanta rep had wanted you, too, so at least for that one, we were together. You broke away from your own fan club and hobbled over, your expression hovering between a grimace of pain and a grin of relief.

"I landed kind of hard out there," you whispered apologetically. "I didn't even feel it till I got offstage."

"Well I hope you can rest it now," the Atlanta rep said. "I have a feeling you'll be dancing on that foot for a good long time."

You grabbed my hand and I squeezed it.

We were so close to our happy ending. We got so close.

After the Atlanta rep said goodbye, we just stood holding hands, looking at each other like, *What just happened?* while our parents loudly debated in the background about combining parties and changing dinner reservations. That was when Dave Roth made his untimely entrance through the backstage curtain.

"Hey," he said, walking up to us with a tight smile. "You guys were great."

"Did Liv come with you?" you asked hopefully.

"No," Dave said. "Actually that's kind of why I came in the first place—no offense."

"You didn't find her?" I asked.

He shook his head.

"What's going on?" You dropped my hand and turned to Dave. "You don't know where she is, either?"

"Her parents say she didn't come home last night," Dave said.

"Oh no," you whispered, your hands flying to your face. Real guilt hit me then, like a baseball bat to the stomach. I'd been the last one to see her, and all I'd managed to do was make her run.

"Could we have all non-dance department guests wait in the lobby?" Ms. Adair called out over the din. "We're getting ready for a group photo."

"I'll wait, I guess," Dave said, looking miserable. "I'll keep trying her."

Every weekend when the new stuff comes in she just shows up. It was Saturday. That meant if she was anywhere, she'd be looking for Dante.

It took forever to get all of the families to file out the narrow opening, but when they were finally gone I pulled you aside.

"I might know where she is," I said, keeping my voice low. Mr. D was starting to pull people into lines. Excited chatter was still bubbling all around us. Everyone was comparing notes about who talked to them after the show.

"What?" You drew back, confused; anger flashed in your eyes. "But, how—"

"Dante," I said quickly. "There's a party tonight."

"Diego! Joy!" Mr. D boomed. "I want you two front and center." We reluctantly took our places, standing stiffly as the photographer fiddled with his equipment.

"If you keep the parents busy," I whispered, "I'll make some excuse that I have to leave to run an errand, and I'll go check it out." You stared at me, incredulous, and I couldn't blame you. Even I didn't really believe me.

"No," you said. "I'm not letting you go alone."

"Well, I'm not letting *you* go," I said.

"Offstage drama?" Lolly muttered from the row behind us. There were muffled giggles.

"SMILE!" the photographer yelled. We looked out and did our best imitations.

"I didn't ask permission," you said once we unfroze, ignoring the others. "Look, you really think she'll go with you? I *know* her, I've known her since I was six years old. It should be me."

"I don't like the idea of you being there," I said, as we made our way toward the dressing rooms. "It's not exactly the crowd you're used to."

You stopped cold. "I don't care."

"OK," I sighed. "But you have to change."

"No shit, so do you. You look like Bruno Mars at a bull-fight right now." Your tone was still pissed but your eyes were softer. "What about Dave?" you asked.

I felt shitty for ditching him, but Dante and his friends would not be kind to Dave's brand of privileged pretty boy. "No," I said. "We definitely cannot take him."

"What do we tell him?" you asked, pausing by the entrance to the girls' locker room.

"Nothing," I said. "It's better if he doesn't know."

I was trying to act so brave, like some big man getting ready to take care of business. It felt like my mess, and I wanted to show you I could fix it, make you feel safe. I pictured us ending the night in some sweaty embrace, all dirty and hyped-up like the end of an action movie.

"*I love you,*" you would say, flashing a low sunrise of a smile.

"*I love you back,*" I'd respond, before kissing you passionately.

Yup, I was a regular Ethan, with my dialogue and action sequences all ready to go.

I just didn't know the ending yet.

Chapter Thirty-One

May 13
One hour left

THERE WAS A MAN playing djembe drums in the 66th Street station, his hands flying so fast you couldn't even see them. The beats ricocheted off the tile walls as we booked it for the approaching uptown train, a supercharged heartbeat layered under the metallic scream. We'd told our families we had to talk to Dave about something, and that they should go ahead without us. Then we went and told Dave we had to go to dinner with our families. We promised each other that we'd run, literally *run*, to the party, go in, grab Liv, if she was even there, and leave.

It was supposed to be easy.

The train was packed with the Saturday night crowd, a mix of families with young kids heading home and singles with no kids heading out. You and I squeezed in silently between the high-heeled girls with heavy makeup and tiny bags and the tired-looking moms clutching sleeping kids. We white-knuckled the pole on opposite sides, catching each other's eyes every so often, nodding along with the lurch of the train, trying to pretend it was all okay.

The party wasn't at Smoke Dog's that time but at a building across the street, the apartment of someone Dante would only identify as "T." It was a narrow, peeling walk-up on 104th, sandwiched between a Baptist church and an empty lot. There was a deli downstairs, and one of Dante's "associates" was leaning against a dented ice machine outside, one leg up on the building, his eyes half-lidded but watchful. I could feel them on us from a block away.

"I think you got the wrong address," he said as we stepped up to the door and peered at the row of unmarked bells. His face was fleshy, like an overgrown baby with a patchy mustache. A scar cut through his left eyebrow like a lightning bolt. From somewhere up above, a heavy bass thumped against the crumbling concrete.

"I'm Dante's cousin," I said, and he laughed, a quick, sharp exhale through his nose. He dialed his phone while we waited. I wanted desperately to hold on to you but knew it would make me look bad. Your face was calm, expressionless. If you were nervous, you didn't show it.

"Yo, D," he said, "You invited some kids?" He smiled and looked us up and down. "Yeah . . . a girl, too." His face darkened then, and he turned away. "Nah, nothing," he said. "I called him twice already. You called your guy?" There were a few more tense exchanges before he hung up and acknowledged us again. "Fourth floor," he said, opening the door, which apparently hadn't been locked. There was a tiny hole in the glass, right in the center, surrounded by a sunburst of shallow grooves.

The hallway inside stank of mildew and weed. We climbed carefully up the stairs—I realized, too late, that you could barely put weight on your ankle and were clinging to the bannister; I should never have let you come—past three other doors that were scary quiet. One had a big BEWARE OF DOG! sign but no sign of any dog, one was piled high with garbage, and the third didn't even have a doorknob, just a hole covered with flaking duct tape. Dante was waiting for us on the fourth floor landing, which vibrated with the hip-hop pumping inside the apartment. His face was tense, his eyes even shiftier than usual.

"Sorry about Tino," he said. "He's a little on edge because the delivery's late."

"We're just here for Liv," I said, keeping myself firmly in between you and Dante. "She in there?"

"Unfortunately." He rolled his eyes and pushed the door open into a huge, teeming mass of people. The living room was a crush of bodies, moving in and out of sync with the bouncing backbeat of the music. The air was thick with smoke, and lighters flicked in the dark like fireflies. Dante nodded us in, saying, "I don't even know what she's on tonight. It's nothing I gave her. She's actually being a real fucking downer, so you're doing me a favor."

I felt you stiffen behind me, but somehow we both managed to squeeze past Dante without punching him in the face. I instinctively reached back for you, but you didn't take my hand.

We found her sunken into the corner of a stained, ratty couch on the far side of the room, with her legs folded up under her, bobbing her head and moving her jaw in jerky circles. The street lamps shining through the dusty window shades threw shadows into the hollows of her cheeks. Her hair was plastered to her head with sweat.

"Oh my God," you whispered when you saw her. She didn't look as bad as when I'd seen her in the park—she looked much, much worse.

The other people at the party didn't seem to notice. One girl was on the edge of the couch, basically sitting on Liv's shoulder, like she wasn't even there. A burly guy with bright, restless eyes was sitting next to her, looking pissed and mumbling to himself. When we came over, he sprang up.

"I'm done babysitting this tweaked-out bitch!" he yelled, and the circle of people standing around the table laughed and nodded.

"This 'tweaked-out bitch' is my *friend*," you yelled even louder, and my heart sped up in the long seconds of silence before the angry guy finally just mumbled some curses at you and stalked away.

"Hi, baby girl," you cooed, kneeling in front of Liv. Her eyes floated down to your face and then immediately crinkled shut. Her lower lip trembled as you took her hand and stroked it, whispering, "It's OK, it's OK." I stepped back against the wall, not sure of my place. All I knew was that you belonged in yours. Liv didn't need a babysitter, or some wannabe white knight. She needed someone who loved her. She needed you.

"I'm sorry," Liv sobbed into your shoulder.

"No apologies," you said, starting to cry, too.

"*These* bitches," sighed the girl on the edge of the couch.

The music changed. The floor seemed to slant. I felt uneasy. Suddenly I really didn't want to be at T's apartment anymore.

We should have left right then. If we had left right then—

But I didn't want to scare you for no reason. I leaned over the couch and peered out the window. Below, on the street, everything looked normal. A bus droned by. A kid dribbled a ball. Just then, my phone chimed loudly in my pocket and I could feel everyone's eyes on my back like I was wearing a target.

"Sorry," I mumbled, and I heard a deep voice ask, "*Who the fuck is that?*"

It was a text from Mom: **Are you on your way?**

"We should go," I said to you, but you were still deep in whispers with Liv and couldn't hear me. I reached down and grabbed your arm.

"We should go," I started to say again, but I'd only gotten out the first two words when the bleep of a police siren drowned me out.

Murmurs like tremors cracked through the room. Someone turned the music down. I got shoved out of the way as a few guys rushed to the window. They moved in unison, like some ungainly corps de ballet.

"Oh *shit*!" one of them yelled. Then: chaos. People pushing and shouting, tossing full cups and lit cigarettes on the floor in their rush to get out.

My heart thudded helplessly against my ribs as I pulled you to standing. Someone kicked the coffee table into us and you screamed out in pain.

"Let's go, let's *go*!" I yelled. Liv was still curled on the couch.

"Help me get her up?" you asked. Outside, I heard the sound of tires skidding to a stop. The room was emptying out. There was weed piled on the coffee table just a few feet from us. I wasn't great at math but it looked like enough to get someone in trouble. I didn't even want to think about what else was in the apartment.

"Can she walk?" I asked, my voice far away, drowned out by the thick hum of blood in my ears.

"She'll have to!" you cried.

There was no yelling downstairs, no *"Freeze!"* or *"Come out with your hands up!"* The lookout by the ice machine had probably been long gone by the time the cop car turned the corner. I whipped my head around, looking for Dante to tell me what to do, but he was gone, too. *Everybody* was gone—everybody except us.

Don't run. That's another thing mom had always told me. *If the police stop you, don't run. No matter what.* But my body was screaming at me to GET OUT, every muscle fiber straining to move. And we hadn't even done anything. There was no way I was going to ruin everything I'd worked for when life was finally starting to line up for me, not with all those shiny business cards in my back pocket, lined up like wishes just waiting to be granted.

"We gotta go. *NOW!*" I yelled, finally loud enough to get Liv's attention. I grabbed her around the waist and dragged her onto her feet as you bolted for the open door, Liv stumbled forward a few steps before starting to move more assuredly.

"There's a back exit," she slurred.

In seconds, we were running.

Chapter Thirty-Two

May 13
15 minutes left

WE RACED DOWN to the third floor, me, you, and Liv, in that order, as another siren sounded outside. Luckily the urgency of the situation had finally sunk in halfway down the stairs and flipped Liv's switch, so even if she wasn't moving fast she could talk. No one lived in the second-floor apartment, she told us. It was empty, sometimes used as a meeting spot. There was a window in the back that opened onto a ladder. We could drop to the ground in between the buildings, to an alley that fed onto First Avenue.

I pushed past the stack of rancid garbage bags and got the door open just as the cops banged past the mailboxes in the lobby, their walkies hissing with dispatchers radioing in other nearby threats. I pulled you in behind me, hearing you suck your teeth as your ankle banged against the door frame, but there wasn't any time to look back and check on you. Hesitation was not an option.

"I think my heart's exploding," Liv croaked.

"Just breathe," you said, although I could tell by your voice that you weren't following that advice.

"We've got runners!" I heard a cop shout, the cry clanging off the stairwell, and for a split second I thought he meant us before I heard all hell break loose outside, shouting and scuffling, and then, in the distance, the unmistakable popcorn pop of a bullet that flooded me with terror. I'd seen police break up parties in our building before, watching the flashing lights turning our kitchen windows red, then white, then blue. People would scatter, some getting chased and thrown in cuffs, still mouthing off even bent over the back of the cruiser, but I'd never seen a serious bust. I'd never seen live fire. As we reached the promised window at the back of a dark, dusty bedroom, I felt more like I was in a video game than real life. What was that crazy one Ethan always talked about? *Destiny?* Mine seemed to be slipping through my fingers. I would have given anything to disintegrate into pixels.

The window was already cracked open, but it was stuck like that, so I had to wedge my shoulder under it to shove it up the rest of the way. Searing pain shot through my neck and I grunted as the glass crashed loudly against the top of the frame.

"Oh, no," you whispered. No noise was good noise.

"*Out*," I directed, helping you first, then Liv.

"My legs feel funny," she said, looking up at me with wild, glassy eyes. The drop was at least twenty feet, onto concrete. If she fell and didn't die, she probably wouldn't walk.

"I'll carry you," I promised. "Just make it to the ground." I said it like it was easy. As I swung myself out, feeling for the rusty metal bars with my worn-out Converse, I could hear foot-falls on the stairway, getting louder. Closing in.

I should have gone first; Liv was barely moving, and I kept stepping on her knuckles by accident, making her cry. You helped as much as you could, guiding her slippery wedge boots from one rung to the next, but there were a few times when her feet shot out, or she lost her grip, and one of us had to grab her to keep her from falling. The ladder didn't go all the way to the ground, either—it was a fire escape, and stopped about seven feet short. You made the jump first and landed hard—I could hear the smack, which sounded so much like the neck snap from my dream that I looked to make sure you were still alive. Somehow, though, you were already back up and reach-ing out for Liv, who dropped down onto you like a rag doll. As I navigated the last few steps, cursing myself for ruining the tread on my piece-of-shit shoes, I heard the telltale spit of the walkie up above.

I let go of the bar—*hands up, don't shoot*—and fell just as a cop peered out of the window above us.

"Stop right—!" he yelled, but we had disappeared around the corner.

"*I've got three on the ground in the back*!" I heard him radio to someone else.

I didn't need to remind you to run that time.

We bolted across the street, toward the dark labyrinth of build-ings of the East River Houses. I'd played there so often as a kid, I knew the layout cold. If we cut to the left there was a path, a straight shot past the basketball courts to 105th Street. If we cut right we could turn south, coming around the pavilion onto 102th. It was dark enough that once we got past the line of street lamps, we could fade into the background. We could disappear.

I looked over my shoulder once, just long enough to check we weren't about to get shot in the back, and almost tripped when I saw the scene on 104th. There were four police cruisers, parked nose to nose, blocking off the whole street. Outside T's building, at least two people were on their knees on the sidewalk; one was lying on the asphalt, facedown, with a cop straddling him.

Are you on your way?

I thought of Mom, sitting there in the restaurant, trying to keeping my brothers from spilling their sodas on the checkered tablecloth, wearing the pearl earrings she wore every time there was a special occasion. Whatever she was picturing me doing, it wasn't this. Another siren blared as a fifth cruiser sped around the corner two blocks down.

I grabbed your arm and started sprinting, instinctively heading north, toward home, even though I didn't know what I'd do once we got there. I could tell I was dragging you—you could barely walk, let alone run—and Liv was slowing us both down, and my lungs were burning, but I couldn't stop. Nothing mattered except getting out. We passed by a court where a couple of guys were playing a late-night pickup game, and they laughed, shouting after me that I'd better get you home quick before you changed your minds.

We were cutting through a courtyard when I felt our chain break. One second you were right behind me and the next I was flying forward, stumbling, looking back to see Liv sitting on the ground, you kneeling next to her, holding her by the shoulders.

"Something's wrong!" you cried. "She can't walk!"

"I c-c-can't m-m-ove them," Liv said, pausing between each word for a big, hitching gasp.

"Come on, I got you." I crouched down to pick Liv up when her feet started kicking, shaking violently. She let out a guttural moan. Her skin was cold and clammy, slick with sweat.

"What are you doing?" you asked as I lifted her. "Where are we going?"

"*Yo, Five-O, Five-O!*" Someone yelled. The basketball court. They were right behind us.

I looked down at Liv—her eyes were rolling back in their sockets. She didn't need to go home, she needed help.

"There's a medical center on 99th Street," I said quickly, my brain reeling. We'd been there with Abuela a couple times, when she had chest pains. But it would mean an abrupt change of course. It would mean doubling back across three blocks. I didn't know if we had time, but there was no room for hesitation. "Come on," I said, shifting Liv up onto my shoulder and reaching out for your hand. That time, you took it. We took a step. And then—

"GET YOUR HANDS OFF THAT GIRL!"

The voice pierced through the night, silencing the rest of the city like a hand clamped over a screaming mouth. No shouts, no horns, no sirens. No dogs barking, no kids laughing. Even the subway, which sometimes shook the ground when it passed, seemed to stall on the tracks underneath us. All I could feel was my heart, and your hand. A flashlight shined in my eyes, forcing me to squint. I couldn't see the cop's face, just that he was standing twenty feet away, and that he was pointing something else at us, too. He clicked the safety off and yelled at me again.

"PUT YOUR HANDS IN THE AIR!"

"*Diego*," you said. It sounded like a question, a warning, a prayer. I felt your fingers tighten around mine and I squeezed back.

"Unnnnnghhhhhhh," Liv groaned. What did the officer expect me to do, throw her on the pavement? I carefully shifted my weight, balancing Liv between my neck and the crook of my elbow so I could show him my palms without dropping her. It meant letting go of you. I didn't want to, but I had to.

"This is my friend!" I shouted. "She's sick! She can't walk!"

"SHUT UP AND PUT HER ON THE GROUND!"

"She's having an overdose!" you screamed.

"GET ON THE GROUND!" The flashlight darted over to you, then back to me. The beam shook, and I caught a glimpse of his face in the dark. All I could tell was he was scared, young, and white. I tried to swallow, but there was nothing in my throat.

"We didn't do anything! She needs to go to the hospital!" Your voice was even louder, full of rage, so hoarse it cracked.

"*Joy*," I said as calmly as I could manage. We'd never talked about it, but I figured you knew the rules. If a cop stopped, you didn't run, you didn't talk back, and you didn't ever, *ever* get angry. White people could do that—hell, they could shoot up a church and then ask for Burger King—but not us. We got killed at traffic stops for speeding, for having broken taillights, for knowing our rights. We were running from a drug bust. True, we hadn't done anything, but the cops didn't know that. To them, we were runners. We were criminals. We had no chance. It was already over.

"Everybody on the ground, *NOW!*" the cop shouted. I knelt down slowly and put Liv, still shaking, on the cool cement. Then I lay on my stomach and folded my hands behind my head.

"She could *die!*"

I turned my head, scraping my nose against the jagged sidewalk, to see your sneakers still upright. You were standing your ground like always, only this time you were looking down the barrel of a gun.

"*Joy!*" I hissed.

"Don't worry about her," the office yelled. "I told you to get DOWN!" He fumbled for his walkie-talkie and dropped his flashlight; it crashed to the ground and rolled toward my head. "Requesting backup!" he barked. Then, to you: "I'm not asking again. *DOWN ON THE GROUND WITH YOUR HANDS BEHIND YOUR HEAD.*"

"She's not armed, man!" I cried. "Joy, show him your hands!"

"Shut up!" he screamed. "I wasn't talking to you."

I heard retching sounds. Liv had rolled over onto her side and was throwing up.

Don't move, I thought.

"DON'T MOVE!" the cop shouted. But I knew you well enough to know they were wasted words. You took a step and crouched next to Liv, reaching for her face, and the next thing I knew the cop was on top of you, grabbing your hair as you cried out in fear, barrel rolling you into a ditch.

I bared my teeth and squeezed my eyes shut, a silent scream down into the earth. How had I ended up in this place? How had I let it happen? I hadn't dropped you onstage, but I didn't know then there was a worse way to fall.

"You're hurting me!" you sobbed.

"I'm not hurting you," the officer snapped. My limbs started to twitch.

Don't run.

"My *ankle!*" you screamed.

I tensed the muscles in my upper back and lifted my head with my hands still cupping my skull, twisting enough to see the cop—who must have been six feet, two hundred pounds—sitting on your legs, pulling your wrists back as he grabbed at his belt for handcuffs. Your face was a mask of pain.

"Looks like you were running just fine to me," he said, and then, with one wide palm, took the back of your head and shoved your face roughly into the dirt.

"GET OFF HER!"

My body moved before my brain could tell it to stop. My fingers found pavement and pushed, the muscles in my legs, conditioned by years of training to leap, sprung into action. I was on my feet, reaching for you. I didn't touch him, I swear.

I didn't touch him.

I heard it before I saw it.

Pop.

It felt like getting knocked down by someone sprinting, like a punch to the gut with a stick on fire.

"*DIEGO!*" That scream ripped through my bones. How had I gotten here? What had I done?

I saw you in flashes, a fouetté turn that wouldn't end, my eyes focusing for a split second, grounding me in between spins: your smile, your laugh, the way you looked so mad when you got nervous. The curve of your waist in your leotard. Your silhouette on the train that night, looking out the window with the whole city stretched out behind you like some crazy constellation. The weight of you in my arms. The weight of you.

You.

You.

It's always been you.

You know that, right?

Finale

Joy

THEY CLOSED SCHOOL for a week in your memory. The whole city felt like it shut down. There was a protest march in Union Square, people handing out fliers with your picture on them, carrying signs—or so I heard, anyway; I couldn't go. I was still in the hospital then. Officer Lorenz—that was his name, by the way, in case you feel like haunting him or something, 23rd Precinct—tore my anterior talofibular ligament, and even though my parents thought I should wait to have the surgery, I wanted it right away. I needed for someone to cut into my skin so the pain would be outside as well as in. Lying in recovery felt better than walking down the street because that way, everyone could see that I was suffering. I didn't have to pretend.

Liv is OK. I know you'd want to know that before anything else. She ended up at Lenox Hill with me, but the doctors stabilized her quickly. It turned out she'd been taking three times the recommended dosage of some prescription pills she got from Dante, plus a bunch of other stuff. He's alive, too. He got caught and charged and sentenced to a year in jail, but at least he cleared your name. The first *New York Post* headline after the news broke—thankfully I was still on heavy painkillers, and no one showed me, because I would have lost it—was TWINKLE TOE UP, and it was all about how you were some drug-dealing dancer who lunged savagely at a cop; within a week, after Dante went on record with why you'd been there, and I publicly challenged Officer Lorenz's account of you tackling him, it became HERO HOOFER: WRONG PLACE WRONG TIME. I mean, seriously, fuck the *New York Post*, but at least they printed a retraction.

Someone made a donation page to cover your funeral costs, and it raised over $200,000. Your mom set up college funds for Miggy and Emilio. Janus held a benefit concert, too, at the end of the year right before graduation. It was basically just a repeat of Showcase, but I wasn't a part of it. For one thing, I was still in physical therapy, and besides, they didn't include our pas de deux. It wouldn't have felt right. Not that anything feels right anymore, without you. Not that anything ever will.

I learned to walk again over that summer, and Liv went to rehab, some fancy place out in California. Dave went out to visit her a few times. They're still together and seem pretty happy. I try not to hate them for it, and usually I do a pretty good job. Both of them are still hustling, taking graduate acting classes, living at home, waiting tables to make money. We meet up whenever I'm back in New York. Ethan, too—after what happened, all of the other stuff seemed so incredibly petty that we all just forgave one another, without having to say it. I know this will shock you, but E takes his NYU workshops *extremely* seriously. He's always sending invitations to his staged readings, but luckily I'm 880 miles away, so I have an excuse.

Yup, I'm an Atlantan now. It took me a year to get back in the kind of shape where I could really dance again, but I worked harder at it than I've ever worked at anything. And when it was time, I walked into that first company class ready to drop a mic. I did it for you. Everything I do is for you. And not in some creepy shrine way, although I do have our photobooth strip in my wallet. It's just that, after you died, and after a few really rocky months I spent wishing it had been me, I finally decided I'd rather live for you than die with you. I wanted to live a life you would be proud of. And that meant getting back onstage. Now I'm in the corps de ballet, and I'm thankful for it every day.

When I'm not dancing, I'm actually working on starting an organization to help spotlight and promote community stories of police brutality from all around the country, a hub where people can connect and band together for support and social justice networking. I guess underneath all this tulle I am my father's daughter, after all. I'm calling it the Followspot Project, but only because every variation on "Spotlight" was already taken. I hope you can forgive me, even though you're the only one who would ever even know it was an inside joke. I like to think we can still have inside jokes, right? I mean, obviously I seem to believe you can still get letters wherever you are, too. Not that I'm sending this. I just like to keep it, to come back to every once and awhile so I can tell you things. Writing them down makes me miss you a little less. It only takes away one tiny drop from the ocean of missing you, but some days it's enough to keep from drowning.

There's a lot of comfort in the routine that comes with dancing in a company, but it's grueling, too. I take company class every morning, rehearse for up to seven hours a day, and then it's time to prepare for the performance. After the show I hobble home, exhausted and sore, but I never feel more alive. (The thing about the corps de ballet I never realized is that we're in almost every single performance—we may not be alone on stage, but we're always there.) I sometimes have dinner with friends, but mostly I head home to watch TV while I sew shoes and ice before bed. My parents were right—it's not an easy path. Something new seems to hurts every day. But it's an incredible life. We tour every summer and I get to work with some amazing choreographers. It's a lot harder than I expected, but it's worth it. It's what I love, and what I've chosen. I know it's what you would have chosen, if you'd had the chance.

So I'll dance for both of us.

I'll go on stage every night and dance like I'm trying to blow the doors off the hinges.

I'll dance like we're still out on the boardwalk in Coney Island, our hair blowing in the ocean breeze, grazing hands accidentally on purpose while music fills the darkening sky.

I'll dance like you just told me you loved me for the first time.

I'll be up there showing you I love you back.

Acknowledgments

EFFUSIVE THANKS, scribbled love notes, and poorly executed high-fives (my fault, not yours—I have terrible spatial skills) are due to the following people and things, in no particular order:

The incredible team at Razorbill/PRH: Have I used incredible in any of my previous acknowledgments? I'm too lazy to check. If so, please accept any and all of the following adjectives as potential substitutions: exceptional, fantastic, wonderful, top-notch, boffo, socko, gangbusters, crackerjack, dynamite. Special shout-outs to my editor, Jessica Almon, for her cool head, keen eye, excellent fashion sense, and for helping me to order and focus the five voices all talking to one another at once (in the book, not my head—although, that too); to my associate publisher and occasional publicist, Casey McIntyre, for her tireless support and for sending me to conferences all over the country in the fall of 2015 so that I could panic-write alone in nice hotel rooms; and to my publisher and publishing Yoda, Ben Schrank, for his unflappable leadership—and for occasionally liking my Instagram photos.

My beloved agent, Brettne Bloom, for her wit, wisdom, and Texas-sized belief in me. I will plot world domination over long lunches with you any day, lady.

Chris Silas Neal, for the breathtaking cover art. It makes my heart leap every time I see it.

Sophie Flack, my most favorite bunhead, for her friendship, gentle and nonpatronizing fact-checking (even when I got things completely ass-backwards), and early enthusiasm for this book. I owe you a Moscow Mule or seven.

My sister Zoe, for sharing her memories of LaGuardia High School and then letting me fictionalize them beyond all recognition (apart from location, Janus Academy has almost nothing in common with the *Fame* school, I swear).

Sarah Levithan, for generously providing background about the ballet world and its inner workings—and for the restorative walks through Fort Tryon Park!

All the performing arts students who told me their stories and who kindly suppressed their laughter even when I asked stuff like, "Do people still throw parties? Is that still a thing?"

The real, unbelievably talented dancers both professional and amateur who inspired the characters of Joy and Diego—I am in awe of you.

My parents, Ellen and Gara, who brought me up to love the arts and to dream of one day becoming a performer—which, okay, fine, I never did, but which I sort of experienced vicariously through writing this book.

My husband, Jeff, who let me work out of his office for half the summer of 2015 while he took care of our son—and who kept a jar stocked with Tootsie Pops, a.k.a. over-the-counter Xanax, in said office.

My friends, for being wonderful and tolerant and wise and lovely, and for giving me much-needed breaks from the anxiety-ridden isolation of my apartment.

My son, Sam, for being a wonder, a light, and a welcome distraction from my work—always.

My internet-blocking app, without which I would never write anything for the rest of eternity.

My phone, through which I was still able to complain about writing on Twitter when I had the internet blocked on my computer.